To Grandmother's House

This Large Print Book carries the
Seal of Approval of N.A.V.H.

TO GRANDMOTHER'S HOUSE

GLEN EBISCH

THORNDIKE PRESS
A part of Gale, Cengage Learning

GALE
CENGAGE Learning™

Detroit • New York • San Francisco • New Haven, Conn • Waterville, Maine • London

GALE
CENGAGE Learning™

LIBRARY OF CONGRESS CATALOGING-IN-PUBLICATION DATA

Ebisch, Glen Albert, 1946–
    To grandmother's house / by Glen Ebisch.
      p. cm. — (Thorndike Press large print clean read)
    ISBN-13: 978-1-4104-2385-6 (alk. paper)
    ISBN-10: 1-4104-2385-9 (alk. paper)
    1. Advice columnists—Fiction. 2. College teachers—Crimes against—Fiction. 3. Murder—Investigation—Fiction. 4. Large type books. I. Title.
PS3605.B57T64 2010
813'.6—dc22   2009044817

Published in 2010 by arrangement with Tekno Books and Ed Gorman.

Printed in the United States of America
1 2 3 4 5 6 7 14 13 12 11 10

TO GRANDMOTHER'S HOUSE

CHAPTER 1

I stuck my hand in the Super Shop More bag that sat on the floor next to my desk. It was filled with folded pieces of paper of various shapes, sizes, and colors. I moved my arm clockwise, creating a paper whirlpool. Occasionally, just for variety, I went in the other direction. This time, in a moment of impetuosity, I dug down deeper, almost touching the bottom. Closing my eyes and crossing the fingers on my free hand, I seized a piece of paper and pulled it out. Slowly I unfolded it, knowing that the next ten to twenty minutes of my life would be determined by what I read. Before the words came into focus, I could see that they had been laboriously printed with a dull pencil by someone whose hands were more accustomed to holding a larger tool: a hammer, a chisel, a pneumatic drill?

Dear Auntie Mabel,

When I go out to eat at my friend Duke's house, I often have a problem with getting pieces of meat stuck between my teeth. Can I ask Duke's lovely wife, Loretta, for a toothpick at the end of the meal? And is it okay to pick my teeth at the table as long as I do it neatly?

Very truly,
Jimmie Harding, Jr.

I sighed, then took a deep breath and sighed again. I wasn't sure which I disliked more, dealing with people's problems about life, love, and good manners or being addressed as Auntie Mabel. But for better or worse that was the name of the column: *Ask Auntie Mabel.*

Until last month, there had been a real Auntie Mabel who for thirty-one years had quite amply filled the chair in which I now sat. Amazingly, no one outside of the newsroom had known that Mabel Ann Rickdorf had written the column. She had gone by the name Ann in civilian life and had also handled many of the layout chores, so her authorship of the *Ask Auntie Mabel* column was a deep secret that both the author and the paper's owner had fiercely protected from anyone not on the staff.

Her sudden death by choking at the Big Bun on their all-you-can-eat shrimp and lobster night had signaled the end of an era. Since the column was one of the most popular features of the *Ravensford Chronicle,* it was quickly decided by Roger St. Claire, owner and editor-in-chief of the paper, that Auntie Mabel must be replaced. He figured that due to Mabel's anonymity this could be done with the public being none the wiser, and at exactly that moment the gods of journalism had provided me, Laura Magee, newest resident of Ravensford and one-time writer from the big city of Boston. How that happened is a story for another time.

I sighed one last time and wondered how Auntie Mabel had managed to put up with the job for thirty years. Over the last month I had often found my mind struggling to picture the woman who could happily provide this kind of advice day in and day out without suffering a nervous breakdown. There were no known photos of Auntie in the office, which was really surprising when you considered that Marty Gould, the resident photographer, seemed more than willing during slow news times, which were pretty frequent, to repeatedly snap pictures of every person and object in the office. Dorie, our part-time secretary, had whispered to me in confidence that Auntie was shy about her weight, and that she had once given Marty advice about a "personal problem" on the condition that he destroy all pictures of her and never photograph her again.

Whatever Auntie Mabel had looked like, I was determined that I wasn't going to end up like her. There was no way, I loudly pledged to the bathroom mirror every morning as I stood there evaluating my appearance, that I was going to be doing this job long enough to gain even one pound.

I typed Jimmie's letter into my computer, substituting initials for the writer's name. Then I composed my answer:

Dear J.H.,
   At the end of the meal you should excuse yourself and go into the bathroom. Having brought along your own toothpick or dental floss, it would then be appropriate to clean the meat from between your teeth.

I paused. As seemed to be happening more and more lately, I thought I could hear Auntie's voice clearly speaking to me. *"Leave nothing to chance, Dearie. If you don't spell it out, they won't get the message."* So I continued:

Dispose of the toothpick after use. It is not proper to return to the table with the toothpick in your mouth. And do not place it behind your ear in case you need it after dessert.

I smiled and pushed the key that would send this letter to the managing editor down the hall and hopefully into next week's column, then leaned back in my desk chair, being careful to maintain my balance. Years of trying to support Auntie Mabel's bulk had dangerously weakened the springs and, as I had already learned, a gentle tilt could easily turn into an impressive backward somersault onto the institutional green tile floor.

I closed my eyes and relaxed. It was half past twelve and my day to cover the office alone during lunchtime. I would take out my bag lunch in a few minutes, but right now I wanted to savor the rare quiet of the newsroom. Even the presses in the Quonset hut attached to the rear of the main building were silent. The two-man printing crew was probably sitting on the loading dock, taking an outdoor lunch break on this beautiful late September day. My mind slowly began to drift toward a state somewhere between sleep and meditation. A gentle place where there were no distractions and all of my many problems seemed to float . . .

"Can I get some help here?"

It was a man's voice. Impatient? No, more than that. Angry. It reminded me of Owen when his painting wasn't going well and he decided that I wasn't sharing enough in his pain. I opened my eyes with intentional, impudent slowness. I stretched my arms over my head languorously, then turned slowly in my chair to see who this irritating man was at the front counter. I'd really had it with guys who thought I had to jump at their command. But what I saw made me sit bolt upright.

It was indeed a man, but what a man. He was a paragon of the breed. If men were like horses, as some of my more rural friends have leeringly suggested, then Secretariat had just cantered into my life. He had dark, wavy hair, was tall with broad shoulders, and his face would have been ruggedly handsome if it weren't currently a bit red with emotion. The irritated twitch of his mouth told me that overwhelming passion at the sight of me wasn't the emotion du jour. I quickly climbed out of the defective chair, desperately smoothing down my linen slacks and hoping they weren't a hopeless mass of wrinkles. But as I walked over to the counter, I reminded myself to be cautious. After all, Owen had been both handsome and famous, and look where that had gotten me.

"Sorry to disturb your beauty sleep, but I want to see Auntie Mabel. Is she around?" He leaned over the counter to get a better view of the entire newsroom, as if expecting to see Auntie cowering in a distant corner.

I stared at him, knowing that I must seem to be slow-witted not to be able to answer such a simple question, but he had placed me on the horns of a dilemma. If I admitted to being the new and improved version of Auntie Mabel, there would be a good reason to prolong our conversation. Maybe that would lead to lunch and perhaps a lifetime of happiness. However, if the expression on his face was any indication, he wasn't here to compliment Auntie Mabel on her profound insights into human nature or her ability to apply a healing balm to troubled relationships.

I decided that caution might be the wisest course. "She's not here right now."

"When *will* she be here?" The question snapped like a whip.

When the final trumpet has sounded and the dead rise from their graves seemed a bit too obscure to be a responsive answer, and since I was to all intents and purposes the new Auntie Mabel, it was also not precisely true.

"I don't know. Her hours are . . . hmm . . . a bit erratic."

The man gave me a lupine smile. His mouth, that under different circumstances I would have loved to have nuzzling my neck, at the moment looked capable of doing serious damage.

"I wouldn't admit to ever being in the office either, if I ruined people's lives in the casual way that old biddy does. It's irresponsible of the owner of this paper to let someone who is clearly senile continue to write what purports to be an advice column."

Senile! That seemed to be going a bit far.

"Did you have a problem with something that Auntie Mabel wrote a while ago?" If the column in question had been out over a month, I could admit my role and be both honest and sympathetic.

"Not unless you consider yesterday to be a long time ago," the man shot back.

Oops! I took a deep breath, desperately seeking inspiration. I cast my mind over my answers of the previous five days. None jumped out at me as being particularly insensitive, although I had to admit to myself that they all began to blur together a bit after twenty-four hours. Actually, make that twenty-four minutes. Maybe senility wasn't so far off the mark, I thought uncomfortably.

"If you could tell me about the letter you wrote, I'll convey the information to Auntie Mabel. She can check her files, and if she thinks that her original reply was in error, I'm sure that she'd be more than happy to print a retraction."

I smiled helpfully at the man, trying to exude kindness and understanding. He rubbed his hand briefly over his face. Sadness suddenly replaced the anger.

"I doubt that it would make much of a difference now. You can't repair a shattered crystal vase."

"And you can't put the toothpaste back in the tube," I replied automatically. I hadn't been around handsome men in way too long.

The man raised a quizzical eyebrow, which just made him look more seductive.

"Sorry," I said. "But even if it won't make any difference in the present, I'm sure Auntie Mabel would still like to know for future reference which letter it was. You never know when someone else might write in about something similar. The letters can be pretty repetitive, you know." I caught

15

my breath at almost revealing the truth. "Or so I've heard. What did you write to her about?"

"I didn't write to her. Do you think I'd write to a newspaper for advice?" he said, getting riled up all over again. He took a deep breath and made an obvious effort to control his temper. "My girlfriend — I guess I should call her my *former* girlfriend — sent the letter."

"And your *former* girlfriend's name?"

"Heidi Lipton. But she signed it 'Pottery Princess.' She's a potter. She teaches in the art department up at Ravensford College."

"And you are?"

"Keith Campbell. I'm chief of security at the college."

"I'm Laura Magee." I stuck my hand across the counter. After a moment's hesitation the man took it in his own.

Chief of security, not my type at all, I thought. All that macho, *let's play cops* sort of thing. But as his large hand encompassed mine, I felt as if my fingers were directly connected to every erogenous zone in my body. I must have let out some small squeak like that of a squirrel racing on estrogen.

"Did you say something?" Keith asked.

"I'm pleased to meet you," I said, sounding out each word as if I were learning a foreign language.

He nodded curtly.

"What did Heidi want to know?" I asked, when my heart rate returned to fast normal.

He ran his hand through his dark, wavy hair, and I found myself wondering what that sensation would feel like.

"It's kind of embarrassing to talk about."

"Maybe you could just summarize," I suggested with my ever-helpful smile.

Keith took a deep breath like someone about to go under water. "Heidi wants us to get married, and I've been . . . well . . . reluctant to make a commitment."

"I see," I said encouragingly.

"Heidi keeps accusing me of not being willing to give up my freedom. Of being like Peter Pan." He paused and scowled, as if there was nothing worse than being accused of resembling a fictional character.

"Are you?"

I could hear a growing sharpness in my tone. The letter was coming back to me now. The Pottery Princess had wanted to know how long she should wait for a man to make up his mind. Her boyfriend seemed to enjoy going out with her, but she was beginning to wonder if he was a Peter Pan type, not willing to take on adult responsibilities. She wanted to know whether she should pressure him to make a commitment.

"If Peter wants to fly, then cut his strings and let him fall," Auntie Mabel, a.k.a. me, had tersely replied. "Find a man who needs a wife, not a mother."

A brutal response, but the question had hit a nerve after my dismal relationship with Owen.

Keith was now looking at me doubtfully, as if unsure whether he was going to get a sympathetic hearing or a poke with a cattle prod.

"I don't think that's the problem here," he explained. "Sure, I may be reluctant to rush into things, but I don't think Heidi is really taking the idea of marriage all that seriously."

"Are you sure that's fair to Heidi?" I gave him a smug smile.

"Well, she has been married twice before."

"Oh." Pottery Princess had failed to mention that in her letter.

"Her first marriage lasted a year and the second one six months."

Six months, I thought. *I've had leftovers around longer than that.*

"Why do you think Heidi had this problem prolonging her marriages?"

Keith shook his head. "She says that she's

an independent woman and her previous husbands wanted to curtail her freedom."

"In what way?"

"They wanted her to take an interest in their jobs and hobbies."

"That doesn't seem unreasonable."

"Exactly what I said. But Heidi claims that to be a real artist you have to be committed to your work twenty-four hours a day."

"She works that many hours?"

"No, not really. But Heidi says that you have to be free to work when the muse strikes. You can't be off in Buffalo on a business trip with your husband or down in Orlando sightseeing with the kids when a creative inspiration strikes. You have to be near your welding torch."

I thought that I'd been traveling along the conversational road just fine with Keith, but this unexpected speed bump caused my mind to lose traction.

"Did you say welding torch? I thought you said she was a potter?"

Keith nodded. "Heidi's also a sculptor. She works with metal, usually stuff that you'd get from a salvage yard. I guess in the art world they call it 'Junk Art.'"

I nodded. I'd heard Owen go on often enough about avant-garde trends in art, his voice dripping with scorn, his contempt almost palpable. Of course, as a Super-realist who considered even the Impression-ists suspect, most art done in the last hundred years was cutting edge enough to draw a nasty response from Owen. But I thought that even a less reactionary person might draw the line at welding hubcaps together.

"Forgive me for prying, but how did you and Heidi get involved in the first place?"

"You mean why would a sensitive, creative artist type want to have anything to do with a security guard?"

"I didn't say that."

He nodded and gave me a shy, sweet smile. "Sorry, I guess I'm a little sensitive on that point. I suppose Heidi and I are an odd couple, but I thought that maybe I could provide some stability in her life. You know, give her someone to lean on when the creative juices weren't flowing. Plus, we had a lot of good times."

"But she wanted to make it something more permanent, and you didn't. Hence the letter to Auntie Mabel."

"That's not true. It's just that I don't think we're ready yet. We've only been dat-ing for about three months."

The Pottery Princess had made it sound

like years. I'd have to keep in mind that the letters I received were only presenting one side of the problem.

"Then this Auntie Mabel advised her to break it off with me. So last night Heidi informs me it's all over because of what some half-baked advice columnist told her. She even read me the answer in the paper word for word."

Wow! Somebody really followed my advice. That was truly frightening to think about. I could see it all now: engagements ending, marriages breaking up, children leaving home, people quitting their jobs. All of this based on the recommendations of a dead woman reincarnated as a twenty-seven-year-old. I shook my head. I'd have to forget that anyone actually read my column or else I'd be paralyzed with fear at the consequences of my advice, like the centipede that couldn't walk once it began to think about how it was done.

"Are you okay?" Keith asked, looking at me curiously. "You seemed to be out of it for a moment."

"I'm fine. I was just upset at the way your relationship with Heidi ended." Not completely true, but I couldn't very well tell him the truth.

Keith looked at me appraisingly for a moment then gave me another of his dynamite smiles.

"I apologize. I really shouldn't be laying all this on you. After all, it's not like you're to blame for the things Auntie Mabel wrote. Right?"

I nodded, tempted for the first time since childhood to cross my fingers behind my back.

"I'm sure that once I explain what happened to Auntie Mabel, she'll send Pottery Princess a new answer that will straighten things out." And straighten out the Princess as well, I thought. P.P.'s letter had positively distorted the facts, attempting to put all the blame on this nice, handsome . . .

"I doubt that will matter to Heidi. Once she gets an idea in her head, she just keeps running with it until a new and stronger one takes over. I guess that's part of the artistic temperament."

When Keith said "artistic temperament," a sort of dreamy look came into his eyes. I knew what that meant. Owen had sold me the same bill of goods; the idea that any stupid, unreasonable, childish form of behavior was acceptable if done by an artist because it was all part of the "creative process." I had believed it for a while — a long while — and I could see that Pottery

Princess had done the same number on Keith. It had taken me ages to see through Owen, and I could tell that Keith was still hung up on Heidi-the-artist. If only there were some way I could do him a favor, show him that he was wasting his time on this self-centered, serial-marrying welder. Somehow it would strike a blow for all of us who had been exploited in the name of art.

An idea began to form in the back of my mind. It was the sort of idea that would have the *front* of my mind — the sane part of my mind — crying out in protest. But it was an idea.

"Would you say that Heidi is a jealous woman?" I asked, trying not to sound too wily.

He paused for a moment. I thought I even saw him shiver a bit in fear, but that may have been my imagination.

"I think she could be, but I've never given her any reason to feel that way."

"Then why don't we?"

"*We?*" Keith asked, clearly startled.

"Sure. If Heidi thought *we* were going out together, don't you think that might give her some second thoughts about dumping you? Wouldn't she quickly come to appreciate what she had lost?"

Keith rubbed his chin. "It seems a little

crude to me."

"Some of the best ideas are. Let's give it a shot."

"But are you sure that you want to get involved?"

"It's the least I can do after what . . . um . . . Auntie Mabel did to your relationship. I'll run it by her, but I'm certain she'll approve."

"That doesn't give me much confidence," he said.

I reached over and patted the back of his hand.

"Have faith. Everything will turn out fine. Now, how are we going to plan this? Heidi has to see us together."

Keith snapped his fingers and I watched his sensual lips form into a delightful grin.

"There's a beginning-of-the-year dinner at Ravensford College tonight. A lot of the faculty and upper administration will be there. I can bring a date." His smile disappeared. "I was going to go with Heidi, but now . . ."

"Are you sure she'll show up?"

Keith nodded. "She doesn't have tenure and the president of the college puts a black mark against any junior faculty member who doesn't attend. She wouldn't chance missing it. I know it's short notice, but are you free tonight?"

"Yes, I happen to be." *Like almost every other night since moving to this town.*

"And you think that once Heidi sees us together —"

"She'll realize that she's made the mistake of a lifetime and come running back to you."

Keith put his hand across the counter. "It's a date, then."

"A date," I said, putting my hand in his and once again feeling all warm and gooey inside. When he followed this up with another fabulous smile, it was all I could do to stay on my side of the counter.

"Where should I pick you up?"

I gave him the address of my grandmother's house. The thought of explaining all this to Gran almost made me suggest that he pick me up here at the newspaper, but I'd still have to tell her where I was going. Better to have Gran actually see I wasn't going out on a date with an ax murderer.

"I hope this works," Keith said.

I smiled and gave him a confident thumbs up.

When the door closed behind him, I returned to my defective chair. If this did work, I was pretty confident that Heidi would be out of Keith's life forever. And maybe, just maybe, I'd be in. After all, once Keith realized what it was like to be with a nice, attentive, mature woman such as myself, he'd understand that his infatuation with Heidi could only be the result of temporary insanity.

"Don't you feel the least bit guilty about deceiving a nice young man like that?" Auntie Mabel asked in the back of my mind.

"I'm doing it for his own good," I said to the figment of my imagination. "I wish some sweet, handsome man had rescued me from Owen before he had the chance to break my heart."

Although I said that bravely, I had to admit that I really wasn't comfortable tricking someone into going out with me. But I was feeling desperate, and I sincerely believed that Keith needed help.

"Oh what a tangled web we weave," Auntie Mabel began.

"Yeah, yeah," I muttered. "Save it for the column."

CHAPTER 2

"Was that who I thought it was out in the parking lot?" Dorie Lamont asked as she burst through the doorway.

"Who did you think it was?"

I wasn't paying attention because I was lost in a daydream about Keith. I had reached the part where he told me how lucky he was to have met me at just the right time in his life and his lips were about to meet mine.

"Keith Campbell. Only the most eligible bachelor on campus," Dorie bellowed.

I snapped back to reality. "I thought about half the student body was made up of single men?"

"I'm not talking about *kids*. A mature woman like myself isn't interested in *them*. I have my eyes set on faculty or staff."

"You should have your eyes set on graduation."

"Now you sound like my mother," she

27

said, giving me a sulky look.

"Sorry," I replied, relieved to see Dorie's expression immediately change into a forgiving smile.

At twenty-three, Dorie's only four years younger than I am, but I keep thinking of her as a younger sister and regularly give her unwanted advice. Not that she wouldn't benefit from listening to some. She's been going to college for the past five years. Her mother works in the registrar's office at Ravensford, so Dorie had free tuition for the first four years. By then she had managed to pass enough courses to be a sophomore, and her mother declared in disgust that she was on her own.

Now Dorie lived at home with her family and took two courses a semester at her own expense, paid for by her part-time job on the newspaper and teaching yoga at the Ravensford Meditation Center. She said that she was determined to have a degree by the time she hit thirty. The smart money was betting against her.

"So what do you know about this Keith Campbell?" I asked with feigned indifference.

Dorie came over and leaned on my desk. She wore a sweater that left her midriff bare, and a pair of low-slung jeans, so I was eye level with the ring that went through her navel. I twisted my head away. Call me old fashioned, but even the thought of having a hole pierced in such a sensitive spot made my abdominal muscles tighten.

"Do you have a death wish?" she asked, seeing right through my pretended indifference and smiling as if she knew something that would ruin my whole day.

"What are you saying?"

"Forget about him, he's already spoken for. Heidi Lipton, the Mistress of Auto Parts, has her hooks firmly into him."

I shrugged, privy to a higher wisdom. "He mentioned her, but I hear they're breaking up."

"Don't believe it. When Heidi gets a man, he stays got. At least until she decides to take him to divorce court."

"You seem to know a lot about her."

Dorie patted her spiky hair, which was dyed an improbable shade of red.

"My mom tells me things. She usually knows the latest campus gossip."

"Apparently not always." I repeated my conversation with Keith.

Her eyes turned saucer-like as I explained my plan to free Keith from Heidi's domination.

"Jeez. It was nice knowing you, Laura. I

thought we were at the beginning of a wonderful friendship. But if you try to steal Keith away from Heidi, she'll snap your spine like a dry twig."

"But she doesn't want him anymore," I said, sounding lame even to myself.

"Yeah, right now maybe. But just like in your phony plan, as soon as she sees him with you, suddenly he'll be mister super-desirable. And if she can't win him back, she's gonna blame you and not him. Especially when she finds out that you're Auntie Mabel. Then she'll be sure that in some diabolical way you fed her a line just to get your hands on her man."

"And how is she going to find out about that?" I gave Dorie a sharp glance.

"Hey! My lips are sealed, like with glue, but this is a small town and people talk. Maybe your Gran says something about your job to someone on her seniors' bowling team, who then mentions it to her daughter who works in the cafeteria at the college. Before long — bingo! — Heidi's coming after you with a blow torch."

I frowned. As much as I wanted to deny it, Dorie's little scenario had the ugly ring of truth.

"So what are you telling me to do, forget about Keith?"

She shrugged. "He's definitely a major looker. Plus, his story is so sad."

"His story?"

"Sure. Did you notice that he sometimes walks with a slight limp?"

I shook my head, not willing to admit I'd been so focused on his face that I hadn't even noticed if he had legs.

"What story?"

Dorie leaned further over my desk with the blissful expression she got when imparting a particularly juicy piece of gossip.

"Well, the story is that he was a cop in Boston, a detective or something. And he got shot when he happened to walk in on a bank robbery and tried to stop it."

"And that's why he came out here and took a job at Ravensford?"

"There's more," Dorie said, wiggling around on the desk with delight at having a good piece of gossip. "A few days after he got shot, when he's still in the hospital recuperating, his fiancée tells him that she's dumping him because she can't put up with the stress of worrying about him all the time."

"That's terrible."

"Yeah. Talk about your lousy timing. And it gets even worse. Because the bullet messed up his leg, the Boston PD told him he could either take a desk job or go on permanent disability. From what I've heard, Keith figured he'd rather get another job where he would be out doing something rather than sitting behind a desk all day. He started at the college about four months ago. Heidi showed up a month later and the rest is history."

"She's a fast worker."

"She's had practice. Becky, the art department secretary, told me that she was married to the head of her department at the last college she worked. Part of the divorce settlement was that she'd go somewhere else and leave the poor guy alone once they split up. I'll bet he paid plenty for that. So I figure her first order of business was to see what the pickings were like at Ravensford. She'd latched onto Keith by the beginning of July."

"Can't he see what she's like?"

"Probably all he sees is that she's a great-looking blonde who has this way of making any man she's with feel like he's a star. Plus, she could win an Academy Award for playing the poor, sensitive artist who needs a big, strong man to lean on. Any guy who's got any juice in his stem is going to fall for that." Dorie winked. "Of course, underneath it all she's about as soft as one of her metal sculptures."

I frowned. Although my first inclination was usually to side with the woman when hearing about relationship problems, Dorie certainly seemed to have a lot of evidence to indicate that Heidi was a man-eater of the first order. Just as I had suspected, poor Keith sounded like he was definitely in need of help.

"What I don't understand," I said, "is why Heidi would dump him."

"I figure it's because Keith has proved to be a little tougher than she expected. From what I've heard, she's been after him to tie the knot for almost a month now. Hitting him with all that stuff about love at first sight and not wasting the rosebuds. But he's been stubbornly refusing to take the plunge. Maybe his cop instincts are telling him that he's walking into an ambush."

"So you think this was her way of saying either you marry me or you're going to lose me?"

"Loud and clear."

"Why would she want to get married again so soon?"

"She was hired on a one-year contract that could possibly become a full-time position. But I hear that the chances of that happening are pretty slim."

"So she decided to find security by getting a permanent contract with Keith?"

"You've got it."

"She must be pretty confident he'll cave or she wouldn't have given him an ultimatum like that."

"Confidence is one thing she's got plenty of, in addition to conceit, nerve, sneakiness and good looks. So that's why if you foul up her project 'Land-Keith,' she is definitely going to want to hurt you."

"So I'd better give this some thought before I get involved. That's what you're telling me."

"Give it plenty of thought. And if you do decide to go ahead, buy lots of life insurance. You might even consider naming me beneficiary. After all, it's only right that every cloud should have a silver lining for someone. And it may as well be me. Maybe that way I can graduate by the time I'm twenty-eight."

I laughed a little nervously and shoved Dorie off my desk. But by the time she had reached her own small desk by the counter, I was already giving it thought — plenty of thought. After ten minutes I had decided that all the artists I'd met had been bigger on using words than their fists. The cutting insult and the snide put-down were their weapons of choice, not the switchblade or the automatic. I asked myself: How dangerous could Heidi really be?

Not getting an answer, I decided that faint heart never won fair knight, so this was one time I should get on my steed and ride. After all, I was twenty-seven, coming out of a wretched relationship, living with my grandmother, and pretending to be an elderly know-it-all for a living. I was virtually the poster child for pathetic.

And why am I in such a sorry state? Ever since college I've been attracted to two kinds of guys: the exciting ones and the reliable ones. And I swing like a pendulum between the two types. Owen had been one of the exciting ones, and, like all of his predecessors so far in that category, he had proven unreliable. What I really wanted was someone who combined both — a guy who was a lot of fun but also faithful and stable. Was Keith that kind of man? Would he provide the steadying hand that could support without stifling? Could he be fascinating without spinning out of control? Decent without becoming dreary? I had no idea, but what did I have to lose?

After such an incredible pep talk, I decided I deserved a reward. I opened my brown bag and began to eat my tuna on rye.

CHAPTER 3

"How's it going, Gran?" I asked.

My grandmother was sitting at the kitchen table looking a decade younger than her seventy-five years. Her gray hair was cut short but nicely layered, and although she was thin, there was nothing frail about her. The Formica table was covered with a thick layer of brown leaves. She was picking them up one at a time, examining each against the late afternoon sunlight streaming in the kitchen window, then carefully attaching those that passed her mysterious inspection standards to a plastic wreath. She glanced up at me and smiled.

"In early times intelligent people had an intuitive grasp of things that could not be stated in words."

"Right you are," I said, giving her a peck on the cheek.

I should explain. According to my mother, for the last year or more, ever since she took a course at Ravensford College on Eastern religions, my grandmother has started to frequently quote the *Tao Te Ching,* the ancient Taoist religious text. I had thought that these bits of Eastern wisdom might come to an end when my grandfather died shortly before I moved to Ravensford. However, my grandmother continued to lace her conversation quite liberally with selections from the venerable wisdom of Lao Tzu, which occasionally made our communications rather mysterious.

"What are you up to there, Gran?"

"I am arranging leaves," she replied, not afraid to state the obvious, as she slid another dung-colored leaf into position.

I wondered why, at the height of the foliage season in New England, when vividly colored leaves were in abundance, she was using only those that were the color of old parchment. I debated whether it was worth asking when all I could expect to receive was an obscure reply. I decided to take a shot.

"Nature is already as good as it can be," Gran said, then gave me a benign smile as if nothing more needed to be stated.

"I see," I replied, deciding that I'd think about her answer later.

"That man came around again today," my

grandmother continued, searching carefully through the pile of leaves as if one shade of faded brown was clearly superior to the other.

"What man?"

"Oh, that rather annoying fellow. What's his name? Jim? John? Jason?"

"You mean Jack Proctor?"

Jack Proctor had been a student of my grandfather's many years ago. My grandfather had taught art at Ravensford College for forty years, and Jack had returned to teach at Ravensford himself after leaving to get an advanced degree. He had taken over as chairman of the art department when my grandfather had retired over a decade ago.

Gran nodded. "That's the guy," she said, and pounced on a dingy brown leaf that she had, for some reason, decided was head and shoulders above the others. She carefully poked it into the form, then leaned back to examine its placement.

"Was he going on about the same thing?" I asked.

"Yes. He still wants me to donate Victor's paintings to the college art museum."

Starting on the day of the funeral, which I thought was more than a little tacky, Procter had been trying to convince my grandmother that my grandfather should have his paintings become "part of the Ravensford College artistic tradition," as Proctor put it. And this could only be done by giving them to the college art museum.

I slid into the chair at my grandmother's left. "I can see why that would upset you. After all, it's only been a little over six weeks since Grandfather's death. That's way too soon to begin parting with such important things."

My grandmother's china blue eyes focused on me with an expression I couldn't decipher.

"I don't like Jack Proctor," she said. "He is all yang. A large mouth ever seeking to be filled."

I grinned. "Did you tell him that?"

"No. I merely nodded and said that I would think about it. The female always overcomes the male by means of passivity."

I wondered if that had worked with my grandfather. He had been a garrulous, expansive man who had charmed me as a child by teaching me to paint during my many visits. But I wasn't sure that female passivity would have made much of a dent in my grandfather's tendency to do things his own way. Nor was I sure it would discourage Jack Proctor.

"He'll be back," I warned.

"Yes. He is like a force of nature. Driven by his needs. He wanted to go up into the attic to look at Victor's work. I told him the time was not yet right."

I nodded. When I had visited regularly as a child, Granddad had always kept the walls of the house covered with his various works, rotating them with curator-like care every month. I had been surprised to find when I came out for the funeral that all of his paintings had disappeared and not been replaced. The only picture left was on my bedroom wall. An imitation of a Mondrian by someone named Torvic, who must have been one of granddad's students.

In answer to my question as to where granddad's paintings had gone, Gran had said that she'd taken them all down and stored them in the attic. I could understand how Gran might not like to have the paintings around reminding her daily of the death of her husband of fifty years, but the bare walls, with their shadowy outlines of where the paintings had once hung, gave the house a ghostly, forlorn air. When I pointed this out, my grandmother had only smiled and said something typically enigmatic about what is not there being as real as what is.

"I'm going out tonight, to a dinner at Ravensford College," I said.

My grandmother looked off into the distance.

"I met your grandfather at a Ravensford dinner."

I leaned forward eagerly because Gran rarely offered any personal details about her past. "I didn't know that was where you went on your first date with Granddad."

"I didn't go with him. I went with Roger St. Claire."

"My boss? The guy who owns the *Chronicle*?"

As usual Gran was full of surprises. I was aware of her friendship with St. Claire, since she had recommended me for the job, but I hadn't realized how personal it must have been.

She nodded. "He was a lovely boy. His father owned the paper then, and Roger was right out of college, just starting to learn the ropes. All blonde hair and bright-eyed enthusiasm. I was quite enchanted with him. Then I met your grandfather. He had recently returned from studying in Europe and had just begun teaching at the college. He had this marvelous beard and a way about him that made all the other men seem like boys. I'm afraid that once I met him, poor Roger never had a chance."

"How romantic," I said.

My grandmother's eyes took on a more cautious expression. "Who are you going with to the dinner?"

"Keith Campbell. He's the chief of security at the college. I just met him at the newspaper office today."

"You must have made quite an impression on him if he's invited you out after such a brief acquaintance."

"Oh, he was probably just looking for a date, and there I was." I wasn't about to reveal the matter of Heidi's letter to my grandmother. I rushed on as I always do when I'm trying to avoid telling the truth. "I know it doesn't sound as if we'd have much in common. Most of my work has been for art journals, not the crime page."

"The tension of opposites is the source of growth," Gran said.

"It can also be the source of conflict."

My grandmother smiled and put her hand on top of mine.

"In nature all conflicts are resolved because the opposites need each other," she said.

Did that mean that Keith, my opposite, needed me? I almost asked Gran, but guessed the answer probably wouldn't be very enlightening.

"Well, I hope you're right," I said, standing.

She shrugged. "Years confer only age, not wisdom."

On impulse I bent down and kissed her on the top of her head.

"Not in your case, Gran. Not in your case."

I changed clothes four times before the doorbell rang, announcing Keith's arrival. I started with a sequined black blouse and a long black skirt, but decided that it might be too elegant for a dinner with staid academics. I switched to a conservative dark blue suit that I had last worn on my last job interview in Boston — the one at the Life Enhancement Fertility Clinic when I'd wanted to make it clear that I was applying to write brochures, not donate eggs. But the suit was rather severe and seemed to be going too far in the other direction.

Finally, I settled on my white poet's blouse with the long black skirt and a black bolero jacket. I was studying myself in the mirror, wondering if I would be mistaken for a waitress, when I heard the bell. That outfit would have to do, I decided, because I wasn't about to leave Keith alone very long with my Grandmother and her buddy Lao Tsu.

"The man who controls others is powerful, but the man who controls himself is more powerful," Grandma was pointing out as I came down the stairs.

Oh, God, I thought, is this Gran's Taoist way of warning a man not to make any moves on me on the first date? If it was, it didn't seem to be bothering Keith any. He was seated on what had once been an overstuffed sofa, but was now a sagging relic with a mind of its own as to how you could sit. Still, he managed to appear astonishingly relaxed and was nodding with interest, and — even more amazingly — comprehension, at Gran's words.

"You're right, Mrs. Hallowell. Self-discipline is the first thing a person learns when he or she becomes a police officer. If you don't have that, then you're just another guy with a gun."

"And one should only use weapons with reluctance and restraint."

Keith smiled. "You should be teaching at the police academy."

Deciding that the Tao of policing had gone on long enough, I entered the room and greeted Keith.

"You look lovely," he said.

The hint of surprise in his voice made me wonder what he had expected and that I'd been dressing down a bit too much since I started working on the *Chronicle*. I'd have to watch that, or soon I'd be a junior version of Auntie Mabel. Short, dumpy, and unloved.

Honestly, I'm not *that* bad. True, I'm only five-five and would never make it as a high fashion model, but my hair is pretty close to a nice chestnut brown and naturally curly. With my rather round face, I do look sort of like one of those cute Greek boys you see on old vases, especially when my hair is cut way too short the way it is now. Fortunately, below the neck I have all the normal female curves.

I cut my hair short for a reason. Owen, the unfaithful bastard who was my previous boyfriend, had always liked my shoulder-length hair, so my first act after leaving him was to make a visit to the nearest salon. I wasn't sure whether I liked the look myself — I always seem to do stupid things either because I love a man or hate him — but the style was easy to care for and when I studied myself in the mirror I was pleasantly surprised to see a rather together-looking woman staring back at me. Although I will admit that my face did seem a shade too plump.

Anyway, I may not be a raving beauty, but I don't exactly think of myself as a major dog. All of this goes to explain why I got a little ticked at Keith's surprise and snapped, "You don't look so bad yourself."

"You both look very nice," my grandmother said, perhaps afraid that we'd be squabbling before we ever made it to the door. She then gave Keith a look that bordered on the simpering.

I was certain that particular expression was prohibited somewhere in the *Tao Te Ching.* But I had to admit that in all honesty Keith did look very fine. The dark blue suit he wore would have made most men look like stodgy investment bankers, but on Keith's tall, lanky body it looked rather rakish. The thought of Keith's body made me suddenly feel warm.

"Are you okay, dear? You look a little flushed. Not coming down with a cold, are you?" asked my grandmother.

Since Gran normally never fussed over me and there was a mischievous twinkle in her eye, I figured that she had sensed the general cause of my discomfort and I was being teased.

"It's working on that newspaper," my grandmother continued, warming to her little charade. "You come in contact with all sorts of people there. And then there's touching all those letters, imagine the germs you pick up just by contact."

"Letters?" Keith asked.

"I open Auntie Mabel's mail," I said quickly, seizing Keith by the arm and half-dragging him toward the front door, hoping that I could get him out of the house before Gran spilled the beans.

"We'd better go now. We wouldn't want to keep the president of Ravensford College waiting, would we?" I said.

"I guess not," Keith replied, resisting my tenacious pulling on his arm in order to turn back to my grandmother. "It was nice meeting you, Mrs. Hallowell."

"Hope to see you again, Keith," she called back, "if nature so provides."

"Right," Keith responded doubtfully.

"Don't mind Gran," I said, as Keith and I went down the front walk to his car. "She just likes to sound like a Chinese fortune cookie every once in a while."

"I see," Keith replied in a tone that suggested he didn't see at all. "But she's really charming."

"Yes. I guess she is," I said, suddenly aware that it was true. Although I thought of my grandmother as *Gran,* I had to admit

47

that the woman had an off-beat sense of humor and was pretty good at intuiting what was on a person's mind.

As we pulled down the driveway and out into the road, Dorie's comment about Heidi's homicidal proclivities made me ask, "Do I have reason to be concerned about meeting Heidi tonight?"

"In what way?"

I hemmed and hawed. Finally, I said, "You know, some women get violent when they're jealous."

Keith smiled. "If you're asking whether I think Heidi will pull your hair or punch you in the nose, I'd have to say that I don't think so. In fact, she'll probably be angrier with me than with you."

Unless she discovers that I'm Auntie Mabel, I thought; *then I'll have to run like the wind.*

"I know I asked you this before, Keith, but how did you and Heidi become a couple in the first place?"

"She was beautiful, intelligent and interested in me. I'm not sure any man could have resisted," he said, like a guy overcome by a force of nature.

"Doesn't she have any negative characteristics?" I tried hard not to sound catty.

"Well . . . she can be a bit assertive," Keith suggested mildly.

"Aggressive," I suggested to up the ante.

"That might be a little extreme, although she did knock Jack Proctor down the stairs once. But that was an accident."

"Jack Proctor, the art teacher?"

Keith raised a sexy eyebrow. "How do you know Jack?"

I noted a slight edge of cop-like suspicion in his tone. Probably suspected student vandals saw that raised eyebrow a lot and didn't find it to be the least bit sexy.

"My grandfather taught art at Ravensford for years. Jack was his student." I paused for a moment. "Heidi pushed Jack down the stairs?" Maybe she isn't all bad, I thought.

Keith chuckled. It was a low, rumbling sound that made me want to put my head against his chest to hear it more clearly.

"That's what Jack claimed, anyway. Heidi said that she just took a step toward him, and he panicked and fell backward."

"Why would he panic?"

"Apparently he'd asked Heidi if she would pose nude for him, and I guess she took it the wrong way. Jack claimed that it was a perfectly innocent request and all in the interest of art." Keith's tone suggested that he didn't believe that for an instant.

"But Heidi took exception."

"She called him a dirty old man and a few other choice things, then Jack claims that she gave him a good solid shove that sent him flying backward head over heels," Keith chuckled softly. "Fortunately it was a short stairway. He only fell three or four steps. Gave him a nice goose egg on the back of his head, though. He was lucky he didn't get a concussion."

This is really great, I thought. I'm trying to steal the boyfriend of a woman who thinks nothing of trying to kill a man who innocently asks her to take off her clothes. What will she try to do to me?

"I warned you, Dearie," Auntie Mabel said from the back of my mind. *"Stealing another woman's man is like taking a bone from a hungry dog. You're bound to get bit."*

I gave a low moan.

"Something wrong?" asked Keith.

"No. Just listening to an old friend."

"Is there something wrong with your friend?"

"She's dead."

"Oh."

Way to behave, Laura, I said to myself. That's a tried and true way to keep a conversation going on a first date. Act like a demented lunatic who hears the voices of dead people.

"Did you grow up in Ravensford?" Keith asked, obviously making an effort to get the conversation back on a less paranormal track.

"No, but my mother is from here. She went to college in Boston. That's where she met my father. After they got married they stayed near Boston. I grew up in Milton."

"Did you go to college in Boston?"

"Yes. Boston University."

"Why did you decide to go into journalism?"

"I didn't, not at first. I majored in art. When I discovered that I didn't have enough talent to make a living as an artist, I decided to double-major and added journalism. I figured if I couldn't do art, at least I could write about it."

"And did you?"

"For almost six years. I worked in the publicity department of the Boston Museum of Fine Arts and did some freelance writing on the side for magazines."

"Such as?"

"*Picture This!*"

Keith waited expectantly.

"No, that was the name of the magazine: *Picture This!* It's a magazine about new trends in contemporary art."

"I'm afraid I've never heard of it. Sorry."

I shrugged. "That's okay. It only sold about a hundred copies a month, and almost all of those were to artists in the Boston area, hoping to read something about themselves."

"Do you still write for them now that you live out here?"

"Nope. You really can't do that stuff unless you're right on the scene and getting to know the artists personally."

The way I had gotten to know Owen Reynolds, master of Super-realism in art, but a lying, no-good in real life.

"Do you miss it?" Keith asked.

At first I'd thought that Keith had gotten into my head and was asking whether I missed Owen. A very good question. Did you miss a wart when it finally disappeared? Did you miss athletes' foot when the itching stopped? Did you miss a toothache after you finally kept your appointment with the dentist? Of course you did! Because, for a certain period of time, it had taken up most of your attention. That's the way it had been with Owen. Now that he was gone, I had nothing to focus on. My mind skittered from here to there like a little kid's eyes in a candy store.

"Laura?" Keith asked, a trace of worry evident in his voice.

"Hmm."

"I asked whether you missed writing for *Picture This!*"

"Oh, sorry. Sure I do, sometimes. But writing for the *Ravensford Chronicle* is challenging in its own way."

"What sorts of stories do you write?"

Red lights went off and buzzers sounded. Not a question to be answered! We were getting into Auntie Mabel territory.

"Oh, look! There's the college!" I shouted in the tone probably used by Columbus's lookout when he first spotted land. Fortunately, through the darkness, the gates of the college miraculously did appear. I was saved. At least for now.

Keith pulled between the gates and drove around a dark, looming building. Attached to the back was a wooden structure built in the style of a Swiss chalet. It was brightly lit, and through the large front windows I could see people bustling around and rows of tables set up for dinner. Keith parked in a small lot labeled "Faculty and Staff Only." As we walked toward the front door I made a point of noticing that he did have a slight limp. The kind the hero in the movies casually dismisses as the result of a little scratch that he got in the war while saving his regiment from annihilation.

"Is there any information I should have before entering the lion's den?" I asked.

Keith smiled. "It won't be that bad. Most of these lions lost their teeth years ago. The worst that can happen is that they'll gum you into boredom. The president's name, in case you didn't know, is Winthrop Vanhouten. He likes to be called Winnie. He thinks it makes him Churchillian, and he's big into giving rousing speeches. The vice-president is Ben Mather. He's the guy in charge of finance who has to come up with the money to pay for all the stuff Winnie promises. Other than those two, I'll make the introductions as we go along."

"You can skip Heidi," I said, clutching my jacket nervously around me. "I have a feeling she won't need any introduction."

CHAPTER 4

There were about fifty people in the room, divided into small groups. They were milling around in an open area near the bar like a herd of antelope that were afraid to drift too far from the watering hole. Once Keith had secured a white wine for me and a beer for himself, he led me over to a bald, pudgy man who was listening with barely concealed impatience to a thin woman who gesticulated nervously as she proclaimed the urgent need for better chalk at the blackboards. When she finally paused for breath, the man quickly turned away from her and toward Keith.

"Laura, I'd like you to meet Winthrop Vanhouten," Keith said.

"Call me Winnie," the man announced with shaking jowls as he seized my hand in a moist, meaty paw.

His resemblance to the former prime minister was rather striking, I had to admit, but then so was his resemblance to a bulldog if the way he was holding onto my hand was any indication.

"Very nice to meet you," I said, politely managing to extricate my hand.

"Laura works on the *Ravensford Chronicle*," Keith said.

"Always pleased to have members of the fourth estate present for our college festivities," Winnie said, reaching out to grab an elbow this time. I managed to move out of range at the last moment.

After a few polite words to the president, Keith quickly guided me away.

"Some female faculty have suggested that Winnie engages in 'inappropriate touching,' but so far no charges have been filed. I think that's because he's just as touchy with men," said Keith.

"Probably he's insecure and wants to make sure that his listener is paying attention when he makes his pronouncements."

"Can I have a word with you, Keith?" A thin man with a protruding nose edged his way between us.

"Laura, this is Ben Mather, our vice-president. Ben, this is Laura Magee."

Mather spared me a quick nod.

"I need to talk to you for a few minutes, Keith, if Ms. Magee will excuse us."

Before I could even smile my willingness to be left all alone in a crowd of strangers, Mather had grabbed Keith by the arm and moved away. Keith gave a small shrug of regret that I optimistically took as a promise that he'd return as soon as possible. I wondered if Ben was part of the Mather family that went back to the Puritans. Maybe a distant relative of Cotton Mather. From the look of his suit, he might be Polyester Mather, I thought with a smile.

"I never expected to find you here."

A hand grasped my arm, and for an instant I thought that the highly improbable had happened and Winnie had managed to sneak up on me unawares with his pincer-like hands at the ready. A quick glance to my left told me that I was wrong. Wrong, but no better off. It was Jack Proctor whose florid, sweating face was pushed forward close to my own. I took a step back.

"Hello, Dr. Proctor."

I hadn't seen him since my grandfather's funeral, but his insistent approach to my grandmother over the matter of my grandfather's paintings didn't put him at the top of my list of favorite people.

He opened his hands wide in a gesture of supplication.

"Please, call me Jack. Dr. Proctor makes

me feel so old."

He followed this up with a wheedling smile that tried to suggest he and I were separated by only a few insignificant years rather than three decades.

When Proctor realized I wasn't going to parrot back his first name just to make him smile, his expression soured. "So what are you doing here, Laura? Is this event being covered by the *Chronicle*?" Proctor paused and snapped his fingers. "But I forgot, you don't actually do *news* stories for the *Chronicle,* do you? You write that lonely-hearts column. Isn't that correct?"

I glanced in Keith's direction and was relieved to see he was far enough away and so engrossed in his conversation with Mather that he couldn't have heard Proctor's remark.

"How do you know I'm Auntie Mabel?"

He smiled maliciously. "Your grandmother let it slip."

"Well, this is a purely social occasion."

"Oh? Are you here with someone who works at the college?" Proctor pretended to glance around the room with great interest. "Now who could be the lucky man who gets to date Auntie Mabel?"

A tall, young woman with a tray of pigs in a blanket suddenly thrust the hors d'oeuvres between us as if hoping that someone would take the entire tray and perhaps the whole lousy job off her hands.

"Keep quiet about the Auntie Mabel thing, will you?" I said, grabbing one of the little franks on a toothpick and thrusting the point at Proctor's face.

The woman gaped for a moment, then moved off when I glared at her.

"Your secret is safe with me — for now. So who is your fortunate escort?"

"Keith Campbell," I said, hoping to bring the charade to a quick conclusion.

"The head of our campus constabulary. But I thought he was already involved." Proctor paused and a smile of anticipation slowly grew on his face.

"I know. He's been going out with Heidi Lipton," I said in what I hoped could pass for a bored, oh-so-worldly drawl.

"Heidi will be here, you know."

"So I've heard."

"And she won't be happy."

"She's broken up with Keith."

Jack Proctor chuckled the way one might when a child has just said something cute but incredibly naive. It made my skin crawl.

"The fact that she's ended her relationship with Keith is irrelevant, my dear. She has not yet seen Keith fully experience the

59

pain and suffering of losing his position as her pet paramour. If she even suspects that you are a more than adequate substitute in Keith's eyes . . . well . . . let's just say that I wouldn't want to be in your little black pumps."

"They're navy," I said.

I tried to paste a brave smile on my face, but my teeth were so dry that my upper lip stuck to them. I was sure that I bore a striking resemblance to a corpse with rictus. I hoped that didn't constitute prophecy.

"But on to more important things," Proctor said, as if my imminent death by violence would be a passing inconvenience. "As you know, I've been attempting to get your dear grandmother to donate Victor's paintings to the college, but she continues to resist my pleadings. It's not as though the college or I have anything to gain by this. Lord knows, however technically skillful Victor may have been as a painter, his works were never exactly valuable."

That much I knew to be true. My grandfather had often angrily complained that frauds such as Warhol and Lichtenstein were much admired and sold in major six figures, while his own more skilled, impressionistic works never got any further than his dining room wall. I had sympathized and shared

60

his anger when I was a girl because he was my grandfather. Since I had been to college and learned about art, I hadn't been back to the house to examine his works more closely. Maybe he was right about being underappreciated. I'd like to think so since he was my grandfather. But this was the same tiresome tune sung by all the starving artists who'd tried to hit me up for loans in Boston bars, and most of the time their work was receiving exactly the amount of attention it deserved.

"If they have little or no value, why do you want them?" I asked.

Proctor seemed a bit startled by the question.

"Well, Victor was one of the most productive members of the fine arts faculty we've ever had."

"Considering he was the only full-time faculty member in art until you came on board, that isn't saying much."

A defensive expression passed over Proctor's face. "And I've never fancied myself to be more than a teacher."

My grandfather had once told me that Jack had spent a number of years trying to paint, but his skills were never more than average and his level of inspiration even less than average. I didn't see any point in mentioning it right now.

"Of course, Heidi Lipton is an active artist," I said, just to annoy Proctor.

"I suppose some might say that."

"I wonder what my grandfather would have thought about adding someone to the faculty who welds hubcaps together?"

"The point is," Jack continued with a sigh, as if I were constantly distracting him, which, of course I was. "I think the college has a responsibility to show the proper respect for the work of one of its long-time faculty members. It would also be an ideal way to encourage our art students. We would kick the whole thing off with a large-scale exhibit. Maybe we could combine it with a memorial ceremony of sorts. Have some of the faculty and several of Victor's former students talk about his influence on their lives."

"What does my grandmother think of all that?"

"Who knows? She answers me with some Chinese obscurity like 'a man's reputation is not made by wallowing in the mud like a turtle.' Then she tells me that she'll think about it. She won't even let me up into the attic to do a rough cataloging of what's there." Jack spread his hands in front of him and gave me a smile that I'm sure he thought was charming. "Can't you talk some sense into her?"

The suggestion that my grandmother was lacking in sense made me furious, and I was about to open my mouth to say something that I would probably end up regretting when the entire room suddenly grew quiet. Psychologists tell us that even in the largest groups there are certain times during an hour when a natural lull falls over even the most chatty group. For a moment I thought that was what had happened. At least that was what I thought until I heard Jack's malicious little chuckle in my ear.

"Maybe I'd better move away from you," he whispered. "I wouldn't want to end up as one of those innocent bystander casualties you always hear about."

I followed his gaze to the doorway.

Several years ago a friend had taken me to a small neighborhood theater in Boston called The Mute Met, a sort of karaoke opera house. Performers, usually young actor wannabes chosen for their physical resemblance to characters in famous operas, would lip sync to the music. Whereas in the real opera you often had singers who couldn't act, here you had actors who couldn't sing: a toss-up, in my opinion. Anyway, I was crazy in love at the time with the guy who invited me, so I agreed to go with him to The Mute Met. They were having what was advertised as the Boston Bayreuth, after the place in Germany where a complete performance of Wagner's Ring cycle is held over several days. Since these singers weren't straining their vocal cords, the Boston version was a marathon. Something like forty-eight hours of solid Wagner. You see, I wasn't joking about being crazy in love.

Our relationship never got past the third intermission. Nine hours of Wagner, whether sung live or on tape, would bring most couples to the brink of homicide. In this case we simply agreed to go our separate ways, his being back into the theater for more aural torture while I hit the street. What reminded me of this low point in my music-listening history was that the woman who played Brünnhilde had been a tall, blonde warrior princess type who looked very much like the person now standing in the doorway.

Keith chose this moment to slip up next to me and put his arm around my waist. With laser-like intensity the blonde's eyes zeroed in on Keith and myself. Suddenly I knew the loneliness of the goat that's been staked out to attract the Bengal tiger.

As quickly as it had begun, the silence in the room disappeared as people returned to talking with renewed intensity, but I suspected that everyone was keeping at least one eye on Keith, Heidi and myself. After all, who drives past the scene of an accident without doing a little inconspicuous rubbernecking?

Heidi's shoes, more a high-heeled boot really, rang out like gunshots as she strode across the hardwood floor toward Keith and me. She was wearing black velvet pants and a blood-red blouse that covered a chest any man would want to get a better look at. As she drew nearer I saw that even though her boots added a couple of inches to her height, without them she would still be almost as tall as Keith. They must have made a dramatic couple, as if they were made for each other. The founding parents of a biological master race.

Maybe you should excuse yourself and leave, suggested a frightened little voice in my head that I recognized as my own.

Keith's arm tightened around my waist as if he could read my thoughts. If he could, he was seeing c-o-w-a-r-d, spelled out in ten-foot letters.

"Don't worry," he whispered, "she won't bite."

An athletic build, probably from tossing around all that scrap metal, suggested that she wouldn't have to resort to her teeth to make me regret my choice of a date for the evening. A series of thick silver bracelets covered her right arm from wrist to elbow. I wondered if she wore them as examples of her work, or to protect her arm during sword fights.

"Good evening, Heidi," Keith said, once she was standing in front of us. His voice managed to sound friendly but firm.

"Keith," she replied grimly, as if logging his name into her online revenge site. She peered down at me from her seven-inch height advantage, regarding me like a Chihuahua who might attempt to bite her ankle and have to be kicked to death.

"Heidi, I'd like you to meet Laura McGee. Laura, this is Heidi Lipton."

"Hi," I said in what sounded, even to me, like a mousy squeak.

I was relieved when she didn't offer me her hand. I had no intention of letting her get a good grip on any of my body parts.

"How did you meet Keith?" she asked me, skipping right over the friendly chit-chat. Clearly she was wondering how her prize stud had so quickly gotten involved with the neighborhood mongrel.

"I went to the *Chronicle* to have a talk with that idiot, Auntie Mabel. Laura works there and she was very sympathetic."

"I'll bet," Heidi said, managing to twist her pretty face into a truly ugly and terrifying sneer. She redirected her gaze to Keith. "And don't start criticizing Auntie Mabel. At least she told me the truth about you."

"That old crone wouldn't know the truth if it bit her on her frigid old butt."

I was having a little trouble taking sides on this one. It seemed unfair that the president of my fan club would probably kill me if she knew my true identity, but I wasn't crazy about having my hopefully future boyfriend saying unkind things, even unknowingly, about my anatomy.

"She certainly had the straight dope on you, Peter Pan," Heidi said, managing to spray spittle in my face with the double p's.

"Look this way, folks," I heard a familiar voice call out. Marty Gould, the *Chronicle's* photographer, was standing to one side and looking the same as always, like a face with a large camera in front of it.

We all paused in our squabble and dutifully plastered blinding smiles on our faces. Have you ever noticed how people do that? Someone could be in the midst of projectile vomiting and if a camera got poked in her face with the order to smile, she'd somehow manage to hold back the next heave and give a sickly grin. A picture may be worth a thousand words, as the saying goes, but every one of them could be a lie.

As soon as the photo op was over, Heidi turned with military precision and strode off across the room, where she inserted herself into a group that timidly made way for her.

"That went well," I said to Keith.

"Do you really think so?" His eyes were filled with doubt.

Of course not, you idiot, I wanted to say. But I was afraid that if I admitted that things were not going according to plan, he would be across the room groveling to the Hubcap Queen before I could tell him about Plan B. Since there wasn't actually a Plan B just yet, I didn't want him deep-sixing Plan A before I'd had a chance to think.

"Sure. Let's give Heidi a while to absorb what's happened," I suggested, trying to sound like I had a clue to the workings of the giantess's mind. "Once she really thinks about the fact that you've found someone new, she'll probably soften like butter on a summer day."

"Really?"

I nodded. Even I couldn't quite get out the words to support that big a whopper. Heidi would probably soften like a stone in the arctic. Still, I had to find a way to keep Keith by my side until he lost interest in Heidi.

"Her pride is keeping her from admitting it to herself," I said like a perfect talk show psychologist. "If you stay away from her for a while, she'll soon come crawling back to you on her knees." Which would still make her a couple of inches taller than me, I figured.

By now people had begun to seat themselves, and the meal was ready to start. Two long tables faced each other, capped by a head table that had places for Winnie and several others who appeared to be administrative types. Between the long tables was a space about fifteen feet wide. It was just as well that we had the little buffer zone because Heidi was sitting almost directly across from me, and I figured that fifteen feet barely put me out of arm's reach.

Winnie gave a brief opening speech in which he declared that this was going to be the greatest year ever for Ravensford College, where, as he concluded in ringing tones, "Every student counts!"

I wasn't sure whether that was supposed

to mean that all the students had basic math skills or that the registrar kept accurate enrollment figures. But I didn't really care once the signal was given to start eating.

Keith was on my right, but his attention was in demand by the heavy-set woman on the other side of him. She taught in the criminal justice department and wanted to discuss her findings with him on the morphology of the urban criminal class. Keith's eyes glazed over almost instantly, but every time he turned away from her, the woman would seize his arm and keep tugging until she regained her audience.

When it seemed that Ms. Criminal Morphology wasn't going to run out of energy, I directed my attention to my meal, which was a thick piece of meat that at least had the appearance of prime rib. I'm a good eater and I began to dig in with gusto. But the steak knife, although it had a very sharp point on the end, had a dull blade that seemed to do nothing more than make shallow furrows in the meat. When I switched to using my butter knife, I actually had better luck. If I kept the pieces small, I figured I could probably finish the meal before my wrist went into spasms.

Tired of my aerobic meat eating, I turned to my left, where the nervous woman who had been discussing chalk with Winnie when I'd first arrived was seated. I wondered if she was a custodian. Who else would be concerned about the quality of chalk? Since I wanted to make a good impression on Keith, I decided to give polite conversation a shot.

"I heard you talking to the president about chalk earlier," I said, not sure where to go with that particular conversational gambit, hoping that she'd pick up the ball and carry it for a few more yards.

She put down her knife and fork and twisted her hands together into a nervous knot. I noticed she was wearing a pearl choker that actually seemed tight enough to live up to its name. If it was cutting off the flow of blood to her brain, that might account for her odd behavior.

"It's not dustless."

"Oh?"

"The chalk we use here isn't dustless. Do you know what that means?"

"That you shouldn't wear a black cashmere sweater?"

She pursed her lips disapprovingly as if I were making light of a life and death issue.

"It's like writing with a stick of asbestos."

"Really? I didn't know you could write with asbestos."

She sighed. "I mean the chalk particles fly into the air and get into your lungs where they do who-knows-what."

"Who knows what?" I asked.

She looked at me as if I were a lunatic intent on echoing her words, so I decided to rephrase. "I mean, does it do anything if it gets into your lungs?"

"How should I know?" She waved her hands within an inch of my nose. "I teach English literature. I despise science."

I was sure the feeling was mutual.

"But I know that anything outside our bodies should stay there."

Does that include food? I wanted to ask, but decided to let the conversation languish from lack of fuel. I nodded politely and returned to chiseling my meat.

Between bites, I glanced across at Heidi. She had started off by making a great fuss over the wizened man next to her, who seemed to alternate between being flattered and frightened by her animated attention. She would frequently glance across at Keith to see if he noticed that she was having a simply fabulous time with her wrinkled friend and had no need of a handsome hunk in order to have a perfectly delightful evening. But Keith's morphologist, who was preventing him from talking to me, was also keeping him from noticing Heidi.

This must have been very frustrating for Heidi because she got up while most people were still eating and flounced out of the room. The twitch of her shapely rear end seemed to convey contempt, anger and a desire to see me gutted like a small trout. But perhaps I was reading too much into it.

"Do you know what the wave of the future is?" the nervous woman to my left suddenly asked.

I wondered if this was a trick question and the right answer was going to turn out to be dustless chalk.

"What's the wave of the future?" I asked, bracing myself for the worst.

"Home dec."

"Home dec?"

"That's right. Being able to decorate your home so that it becomes your own personal nest. A place to cocoon."

"Oh, you mean learning how to make crafty little baubles, discovering new wall painting techniques, figuring out how to arrange the furniture in your postage-stamp-sized room so it looks like the hall of mirrors in the Palace of Versailles. That kind of thing?"

She nodded vigorously. "Most women learn soon enough that, even more than good sex, what men want is comfort. They want a nice, cozy home where they can relax after a day at work. Most men don't just marry their mothers, they also want to live in their mother's house or in the house they wish their mothers had provided for them. The woman who can come up with that gets to keep the man."

"But aren't most women putting in a hard day at work, too, these days?"

"Of course. That's why there's a need for books teaching simple home decorating techniques that can be done quickly and with little experience. I don't know much about such things myself, of course, being an academic."

I nodded sympathetically, hoping she didn't take my gesture to mean academics didn't know anything.

"But I work on the side as an editor for a publishing house that puts out such books." A dreamy expression came over her face as she looked across the room, perhaps picturing row upon row of helpful home decorating books marching toward us in lock step.

"What publisher is that?" I asked.

She leaned toward me until I could feel her breath in my ear. "Subservient Press," she whispered.

"Ah," I said, trying to sound properly

impressed.

Apparently I failed because she said in a challenging tone, "It's an important job. The editing must be meticulous. This isn't James Joyce, you know, every word really counts when you're writing a book about crafts. If the directions aren't exactly right, the publisher is hounded by hordes of dissatisfied customers with blotched walls and misshapen afghans."

"Yes, I can see where accuracy would be vital," I said, trying to soothe her.

It didn't work. Her eyes narrowed as if she were assessing me anew. She took another gulp of wine from a glass that had been refilled twice.

"This is a secret."

"What is?"

"My work for Subservient Press. If my colleagues in the English Department ever found out, they would destroy me with ridicule. They'd say I was worse than a hack writer. They'd say I was a hack editor."

"Don't worry, I won't tell anyone."

She reached over and seized my wrist, digging my watch into my arm until I was certain "Timex" would be permanently imprinted on my flesh.

"Promise."

"I promise," I said. I moved my hand to

the other side of my body as soon as she released it, and pulled hard on Keith's arm, dragging him away from Ms. Morphology.

"Where are the restrooms?" I snapped.

"Out that way and down the hall," he said, pointing toward the doorway that Heidi had left through.

I was faced with a dilemma. Should I leave and risk the possibility of facing Heidi in a room composed of porcelain and other hard surfaces? Or should I remain seated and hope the human time bomb next to me didn't explode until after dinner? Since Heidi had already been gone for at least ten minutes, I thought she might have left the restroom by now, whereas my table companion was already giving me a slit-eyed stare, as if wondering whether she would have to kill me now that I knew her secret.

As I stood up, she glanced at me and made what appeared to be a throat-cutting gesture. On the other hand, she could have been adjusting her pearls. Hard to tell.

I dodged around the wait staff, who were bringing in dessert, chocolate cake with vanilla ice cream, and walked down the hallway, searching for the ladies' room.

Perhaps in keeping with Winnie's wartime British approach to things, the bathrooms were purposely unmarked so they wouldn't be discovered by the invading Hun. Whatever the reason, I reached the end of the hall and went through the fire doors to the stairwell without spotting a door with any of the normal words or symbols for my gender written on it — not even one of those ambiguous little stick figures wearing a triangle for a skirt. I decided to give the stairway a pass. It was poorly lit and seemed to lead down into subterranean depths. Determined to return to the dining room and demand that Keith give me more precise directions, I had just turned around. And heard a groan.

It must be something with the pipes, I told myself. Or the building settling. Or the wind in the willows, I continued more desperately. But there had been a definite human quality to what I had heard, and it was coming from the bottom of the dark stairway in front of me.

A human being in serious distress.

Now let's be honest. Everybody who has ever seen a grade B horror movie knows that the one thing you don't do in a situation like this is slowly descend the stairs to discover the source of the sound. By Hollywood law, it's bound to be a blood-sucking monster putting on a pity act to entice its next victim. The smart money would say run back to the dining room and find a red-blooded male willing to make the ultimate sacrifice. What that scenario didn't take into account was how foolish I would feel if this heroic male discovered he was rescuing a leaky toilet or a loose storm window. I thought about all this as I slowly descended the stairs, trying to reassure myself that bad things never happened to alert people.

As I got closer to the bottom of the stairway, the sound seemed to die away. I had almost talked myself into turning around and going back up, when I stepped down onto a squishy-something that moved in a sickening way under my foot. I lost my balance. I grabbed at the banister to break my fall but my hand slid off, and I pitched forward. Instead of bouncing down the remaining couple of metal stairs and sustaining broken kneecaps or a memory-impairing concussion, I landed on something soft.

What good luck! I thought. But then, by the red light glowing from the nearby exit sign, I saw that I was lying on top of some guy who was spread out on his back over the last three steps. I frantically pushed myself partly off of my human cushion and turned my face to the right, just in time to see Jack Proctor's eyes pop open. We couldn't have been closer if our heads had been lying on the same pillow together, a position even less likely than this one.

"Jack, are you all right?" I said. Not my brightest question ever, I'll admit, but ask yourself, what you would have said under the same circumstances?

For an instant his eyes seemed to gain focus. His lips parted.

"Heidi?" he said.

"No, it's me. Laura."

A puzzled expression came over his face, then his eyes closed and his features went slack. Just like a man. He's lying next to you, he forgets your name, then he goes to sleep.

"Jack," I said, prodding his shoulder.

His eyes popped open, but this time I could tell they would never close again without help from my thumb and forefinger. And that wasn't going to happen. I knew I had just witnessed the awesomeness of death. I didn't have time to dwell for long on what this meant because a beam of light came down from the top of the stairwell. For one crazy moment I thought that I was seeing the proverbial light at the end of the tunnel, and half expected to spot Jack's soul float out of his body and begin its ascent to some heavenly realm. For Jack, heaven would doubtlessly be a place in which he was a half-decent painter.

"What's going on down there?" a woman demanded. The distinctive voice left no doubt: it was Heidi.

"Get help, Heidi," I shouted, rolling the rest of the way off of Jack.

The flashlight found me and illuminated the little tableau for a long moment. Then, proving her resemblance to Brünnhilde was more than just a matter of size, she immediately broke into a scream that was truly operatic in its dimensions.

I'll bet they even heard it in Bayreuth.

CHAPTER 5

"She was having sex with Jack," Heidi was announcing for at least the fifth time to the crowd that had gathered at the top of the stairs. "I looked down and she was on top of him and now he's dead."

The men seemed to draw back in fear at this announcement of my succubus-like qualities, while several of the women came closer, perhaps hoping for pointers.

"I heard a moan and went to check it out," I repeated, trying to work in a healthy chuckle of derision at Heidi's story. "I slipped and fell on top of Jack. He had already been injured, then he died."

By now, my version of events was sounding improbable even to me. I could see why the crowd preferred Heidi's.

Instead of valiantly standing at my side and holding back the angry villagers with torches who were intent on lynching me for killing one of their own, my date had rushed down the stairs to examine the body. He had then whipped out his cell phone, notified his own security people, and called the police. I decided that if Sir Galahad wouldn't come to me, I'd go to him. So I edged away from the mob, not taking my gaze off them, and backed down the stairs. A low rumble went up from the crowd, as if to warn him of my approach.

"This is a crime scene, don't contaminate it," he warned me as I got closer.

"Like I haven't already wallowed all over the corpse," I replied irritably.

Keith ignored me. He had a flashlight out and was running it over the body. A flash of something shiny sticking halfway out of one of Jack's sport coat pockets caught my eye.

"What's that?" I said.

As Keith bent closer, I edged down a few steps until I was right next to him. He took a pencil and gently lifted the object a little further out of the pocket.

"It's one of Heidi's bracelets," I said.

Now, I have to admit that it would have been in my self-interest, given the charges of sexual homicide that were being leveled against me by Heidi, to have bellowed out this particular revelation, thus shifting the blame from myself to her. However, I did not intentionally do that. The loudness of my comment was due solely to my surprise at recognizing the object as one of her bracelets and the fact that I was standing in a stairwell with acoustics that would be the envy of any concert hall.

At any rate, everyone in the crowd standing at the top of the stairs who was not stone deaf immediately knew that one of Heidi's bracelets had been found on Jack's rapidly stiffening body. The group intake of breath above me, followed by a low murmuring, made that clear. As I climbed back up the stairs at Keith's insistence, I could see that, just like in a close tennis game, the audience's gaze had shifted from me to the other side of the net. Heidi stood there, looking like a larger than life–sized piñata. Somehow, she managed to appear more vulnerable than any giantess has a right to.

"Smile," Marty Gould called out and snapped her picture.

No sooner had she been bleached white by the flash than Heidi turned and marched back toward the dining room.

I'd forgotten the *Chronicle* was on the job.

"Surprised to see you here, lil' darlin'," Marty Gould said, taking the camera away from his eye and sidling up to me.

Photographer and sometime sports writer, he wore his usual blue denim shirt, faded jeans, and a pair of boots made out of some kind of reptile skin. Those clothes on a hundred and thirty pounds, spread out over a six-one frame, gave him the look of a newsroom cowboy, which wasn't so strange considering that his last job had been on a paper in Tempe, Arizona. In his mid-thirties and still unmarried, he had a reputation as a slow talkin' ladies' man. But he wasn't my type. So after a little back and forth when I'd started at the paper, we'd sort of mutually agreed to be friends, nothing more, nothing less.

"I didn't know the *Chronicle* covered events like a dinner at the college," I said.

"St. Claire wants us to do more community stories, so I'm here on my own time. I take the picture and do a little write-up. That means a touch more in the paycheck at the end of the week. Lucky for us we're both here. This is your big chance." He gave me a long, level stare as if he was a gunslinger who had just challenged me to reach for leather.

"What do you mean?"

Marty glanced over his shoulder down the stairwell. "There's a dead body at the bottom of those steps. Somebody's going to have to pay."

I sighed. Marty had seen so many Sergio

Leone westerns, he couldn't actually come right out and say anything without going through a lot of stylized conversation.

"So what's your point?"

"You aren't getting any younger."

"Thanks. The point, Marty."

"Do you want to be Auntie Mabel for the rest of your life?"

"Of course not," I said, motioning with my hand for him to keep his voice down.

"Well, lil' darlin', we've got what looks like a murder here. I'm a photographer and you're a reporter, right?"

I nodded. I wasn't sure that doing publicity for the Museum of Fine Arts or my articles for *Picture This!* exactly constituted reporting. But Marty did have a point. If I was going to stay on the *Chronicle* and not remain Auntie Mabel until the day I succumbed to a rogue shrimp, I had to branch out. This could be my big chance.

"What should I do, Marty?"

"Talk to the perp. Get blondie to spill the beans," he said, shifting from Zane Grey to Raymond Chandler.

"Why would Heidi talk to me?"

Marty grinned. "If she doesn't take the fall, you're next in line. You've got something in common. You're both sisters in need."

I figured he had a point. Maybe Heidi

would confess her guilt in my sympathetic ear, and I'd get a scoop. So I followed the crowd that had already grown bored and slowly begun drifting back to the dining room to finish their desserts. After all, death was forever, but cake and ice cream have a limited shelf life. Heidi was sitting by herself at a table near the front door. She stared out the window. I noticed the two college security officers, standing on either side of the door to prevent anyone from leaving.

Ignoring the fifty sets of beady eyes that followed me, I walked over to her table.

"Mind if I join you?"

She gave me a long look, more sad than hostile. Then she shrugged. I took that as a "yes" and settled in across from her.

"Tough evening," I said as a conversation opener. With a start I realized it really had been. It was just sinking in. I had very likely been in close proximity to a murderer and had certainly been face to face with the victim. My hands started to shake, and I struggled to suck in a deep breath. After hyperventilating for a few seconds, I saw my hands settle down into the subtle tremor of old age.

"It's tough when someone accuses you of murder," Heidi said, arching an eyebrow.

"You accused me first."

She smiled slightly and extended her hand across the table. "Truce?"

I shook her hand, which was large enough to engulf two of mine.

"So how *did* Jack end up with one of your bracelets in his pocket?" I said. "And in the interest of honesty, I have to tell you that I'm covering this story for the *Chronicle,*" I added, dimly recalling the one class I'd had on journalistic ethics.

"I've got nothing to say for the record."

"Okay, let's talk off the record." I could be flexible, and, after all, my involvement wasn't purely professional.

She fingered the remaining bracelets; there were enough left to start a small jewelry store.

"When I left the dining room," she said, "I went to the ladies' room."

I made a mental note to get directions.

"When I came out," she continued, "Jack was standing across the hall, waiting for me."

"What did he want?"

"The usual." She grimaced. "Jack was supposed to write an evaluation of my first semester's work, and he'd made it clear the evaluation wasn't going to be based primarily on my performance in the classroom."

"Was he coming on to you the first time

you pushed him down the stairs?"

"I never pushed him. He pretended he wanted me to be his model, but given that the guy hadn't picked up a brush or pencil in a decade, we both knew what the word 'model' meant. We got into an argument. I stepped toward him and the miserable little coward got frightened and fell."

"So what happened tonight?"

"He made the same pitch. I tried to reason with him. I told him I'd like us to be colleagues because I wanted this job to turn into something permanent. He just laughed and said the only way I'd be back next year was if he gave me a good evaluation, and it wasn't going to be based on my welding skills. I told him to get lost and walked away from him. He grabbed me by the arm, and I guess one of my bracelets came off. I didn't even notice it at the time because I was so anxious to get away from him."

I looked at Heidi with new eyes. Even though she was big and strong enough to have bench-pressed Jack Proctor, maybe she wasn't as physically confrontational as she appeared to be. Her first instinct had been to run. Maybe this hidden vulnerable side had been what first attracted Keith, in addition to her enticing measurements.

"What did Proctor do?"

"I don't know. I went back into the ladies' room. I thought that he might actually follow me in there, so I locked myself in a stall."

"Did he come in?"

"Someone did, but I don't think it was him. I guess even he wasn't willing to take a chance that he might get caught coercing me in the ladies' bathroom."

"How long did you stay?"

"Ten minutes, maybe more. I really didn't want to see Jack again tonight."

"What did you do after you came out?"

"I was going to head back into the dining room, when I heard this noise at the end of the hall. I always carry a small flashlight in my pocket for walking across the parking lot. That's when I saw you . . . and Jack. I screamed. I know that was silly, but seeing Jack down there was a wish come true. I guess I just didn't want anyone to think that I was the one who had done it."

"So that's why you accused me?"

"I didn't know you hadn't done it."

"C'mon. You don't push a guy down the stairs, then go and lie on top of him."

"Okay, okay. I guess I wanted people to blame you, so they wouldn't think about me. Sorry."

I nodded. Heck, I might have done the

same thing.

A man and a woman wearing EMT garb rushed into the room and were quickly directed toward the stairwell by several helpful members of the crowd. A man in a suit arrived right behind them, trailed by a tall, strapping young man in uniform. The man in the suit spoke to the college security people by the door, then said he wanted everyone to remain in the room until officially released.

Heidi and I stayed at our table, not saying much. Whispered comments were followed by oblique glances from our fellow diners. Popular opinion still had it that one or both of us had done in poor Jack. Keith found us a few moments later, sitting there like the two unpopular girls at a school dance. I could see it was difficult for him to decide which potential murderess to talk to first: his date for the evening or his former girlfriend.

"How are the two of you doing?" he asked, coming up with a noncommittal compromise.

We both stared at him incredulously. How did he think we were doing? We'd just found a dead man. That metallic clang I heard in the distance was the prison door slamming shut.

"Right," he said when neither one of us bothered to respond. "Well, it won't be long now. The police are here. They'll have an officer take the names and contact information on everyone else, but the chief of detectives will want to interview each of you."

"Couldn't it have been an accident?" Heidi suggested.

"Yeah," I chimed in. "After all, Jack had fallen once before. He could have had some kind of balance problem, maybe an inner ear infection."

Keith nodded doubtfully. "Tell the chief exactly what you know and I'm sure everything will work out fine."

I wondered how many folks on death row have heard that one.

As if on cue, the man in a suit walked across the room directly toward us, accompanied by the tall young man in uniform. This caused a collective intake of breath among the audience, as if they were anticipating that Heidi or I, singly or together, might make a desperate break for freedom and be gunned down in the process.

The men introduced themselves. The tall fellow, who appeared younger than me, was Sergeant Kelly. The shorter, painfully thin man in the suit, who looked like Al Pacino after a year or so on a near starvation diet, said he was Captain Farantello, chief of detectives. I liked the way they were so careful to let us know their names. My mother had always taught me politeness was a virtue, and I knew they would also politely have me duck my head before I entered the patrol car. Nothing makes an arrest go more smoothly than following the amenities.

"I'll talk to you first, Ms. Magee," the chief said, looking at me. "Sergeant Kelly will speak with Professor Lipton."

I immediately wished I had a title other than Ms., which seemed rather pale and inadequate by comparison. I also wished that I was wearing my blue power suit. If only I'd known I was going to be a murder suspect.

Sergeant Kelly led Heidi off to another table, while Chief Farantello sat down across from me. He asked me to tell him in my own words what I had seen. When I had recounted the entire story, he made me repeat it all again from the beginning. I wondered if the next step would be to have me say it backward like a bizarre Alzheimer's test. Then he and Sergeant Kelly changed places, and we went through the entire routine again.

Finally, the two policemen stood in a

corner by themselves and conferred. After a moment, they called Keith over. Whatever they said to him, he became rather animated and appeared to be objecting to their proposed course of action. I was desperately trying to decide who I would contact with my one phone call. My grandmother would probably know a lawyer in town, but upon hearing I had been arrested, she might respond with something like "the wise man suffers his adversities calmly." I decided a better choice would be to call Roger St. Claire. As the newspaper's owner, he would probably have a lawyer on retainer. It would also alert the police to the fact that they were imprisoning a working journalist — sort of.

But instead of approaching my table, the two men walked over to where Heidi was seated. They stood over her and said something. She slowly got to her feet, putting her hand on the table for support. Sergeant Kelly delicately took her elbow and directed her toward the door. Before she reached it, Heidi turned and looked at me. The expression on her face said here-but-for-the-grace-of-God-go-you. As the sergeant urged her out the door, I rushed forward and grabbed Chief Farantello by the arm. I was surprised at how easily I was able to turn the guy around to face me. He really needed to eat more.

"You can't arrest her," I said.

Farantello sighed, as if this was a foolish remark. I noticed he had soulful brown eyes and a face that looked as if it had seen everything at least twice.

"We aren't arresting her. We're just taking her down to headquarters for more questioning."

I put my hands on my hips. I only had to look up slightly to be staring into those soft puppy eyes. "Why are you so sure a crime has even been committed here? Maybe Jack Proctor fell backward down those stairs. Why are you assuming this is murder?"

The chief gazed off to one side, as if considering whether to arrest us both and make his final decision down at the station, eenie-meanie-minie-mo style.

"I'm *assuming* Mr. Proctor was murdered because he wasn't killed by his fall down the stairs. He died as a result of a knife wound."

"Oh," I said, deflated.

Since I couldn't think of a snappy comeback, I politely stepped out of Farantello's way and let him leave. Then a thought occurred to me.

"Why wasn't he covered with blood,

then?" I called out to the chief's back. "I would have noticed that."

He turned slowly and walked back to me, his expression combining infinite patience with his usual sadness.

"Because the wound was to his heart. Most of the bleeding was internal."

"Oh."

Then the chief left, no doubt relieved that I hadn't shouted out any more questions to his retreating back.

Keith walked up to me. "I'll drop you off at home, then I'm going down to the station to be with Heidi."

Great. I may have avoided life in prison, but now I was going to lose the guy. Heidi had really outfoxed me in the sympathy department. Nothing like getting arrested for murder to get back an old boyfriend.

Clever girl.

"Did they find the weapon?" I asked, as I hurried along next to Keith, who was making a beeline for the exit, as if they were already strapping Heidi into the electric chair and turning on the juice.

He nodded.

"And was it Heidi's?"

"Hard to tell."

"What do you mean?"

"It was one of the steak knives from the

table. Until we check it for prints, we won't know who it belonged to."

I stopped and pointed toward the table. "One of *those* steak knives?" I said, and heard the disbelief in my voice.

Keith nodded.

"You couldn't even cut meat with them."

"Jack wasn't cut. He was punctured," Keith said, making an abrupt forward motion with his hand. "Those knives have sharp points and a strong blade."

The thought of having one shoved into my heart made me shudder, and Keith took my arm.

"Are you okay?"

"Yeah." I shuddered again. "But I think I'd like to go home now."

He nodded and continued to hold my arm all the way to the car.

CHAPTER 6

Early the next morning I sat at my desk and stared at the blank computer screen as I thought about the ride home with Keith. When he pulled up into my driveway, there had been a moment of awkward silence. After all, the usual remarks like "I had a wonderful time" or "We should do this again next week" didn't seem appropriate. This was an evening that no sane person would want to repeat. But there was a deeper problem lurking under the surface. Just when I thought I'd have to be the one to bring it up, Keith did.

"Look, Laura," he said, using the kind of voice some men have when they're getting ready to dump you, "our plan to make Heidi jealous doesn't really apply any more."

I nodded. Making a woman jealous when she was probably going to end up in the slammer for murder did seem to fall into the category of kicking someone when she was down.

"I know you were trying to help me and I do appreciate it," Keith continued. "I'm certain our plan would have worked, eventually, but under the circumstances I think my place is at Heidi's side, if she'll have me. She's going to need all my help until she's proven innocent."

If she *is* innocent, I wanted to add, but thought that might sound rude.

"Once this whole thing is settled, maybe we can return to making Heidi jealous, if she hasn't changed her mind and gotten back together with me by then," he said.

I was so focused on his wonderful smile, I hardly noticed how close he was until his lips gave me a brotherly peck on the cheek.

"Uh, I'd like that," I said, wittily.

After a couple of incoherent "goodnights," I scrambled out of the car and back to the tranquility of my grandmother's kitchen, where I settled wearily into a chair. Fortunately, Gran had already gone up to bed, so I could sit there without answering questions or hearing what the wisdom of the East had to contribute on the subject of murder.

"He seems like a nice man," Auntie Mabel said in the back of my mind. *"A man who's*

loyal to his old girlfriend will be the same way to his new one."

"I'm not his new girlfriend," I pointed out with regret. "And as long as Heidi is a murder suspect, I never will be."

"Well, if you want my advice . . ."

I frowned. "I'm going to get it anyhow, right?"

She ignored me. *"I'd say that the answer to your problem is obvious. You have to find out who killed Jack Proctor. Once Heidi is off the hook, you'll be able to resume your plan to steal her boyfriend."*

I ignored the disapproval in her tone. "What if the killer turns out to be homicidal Heidi?"

"If conclusive evidence of her guilt can be found, I think Keith will feel justified in severing any connection to her. He was a police officer, after all. The problem right now is that I don't think he's sure whether she's guilty or innocent."

"Let's say you're right," I said. "I don't know anything about solving crimes. I'm not even an investigative reporter. All I've ever done was track down the artists I interviewed for *Picture This!* Some had really weird day jobs."

"Just approach it in a logical fashion," Auntie Mabel said in a clipped tone that

didn't allow for any whining. *"You have to consider motive and opportunity."*

"Everybody at the dinner had opportunity, along with anyone else who might have been able to get access to the building and knew Jack would be there."

"Not quite. It had to be someone at the dinner. A person who slipped into the building and lurked in the shadows wouldn't have had access to a steak knife."

"Unless an intruder swiped one. But even if true, it only narrows the field down to the fifty or so guests, plus the wait staff," I said. "Still not a very manageable number."

"We will have to concentrate more on motive."

"Heidi certainly had one. And she had opportunity," I pointed out. I still felt that Heidi the convicted would be less of a problem for my future plans with Keith than would Heidi the exonerated. I'm all in favor of the search for truth, but isn't it nice when the truth turns out to be in our own interest?

"But we must consider whether some of the other people at the gathering also had motives, and any number of them could have gone down that hall to use the restrooms."

"So how do I find out about the motives

of the faculty?"

"Well, forgive me for reminding you of a journalistic term," Auntie Mabel said in a tone that suggested she didn't care two figs about my forgiveness, *"but what you need is a source. Someone who knows the college community, and who will give you accurate information. I believe you know just the person."*

"You mean Dorie Lamont?"

"That young woman is a terrible gossip, but even somewhat tainted information might be useful in a situation such as this."

I'd nodded and gone to bed with a renewed sense of purpose. I would come up with an alternative suspect, get Heidi off the hook and return to my original plan of stealing her former boyfriend.

Whereupon, I slept with all the soundness that only a clear conscience and a well-formulated scheme can produce.

"Laura, may I speak with you for a moment?" said Roger St. Claire.

The owner and general manager of the *Ravensford Chronicle* stood over my desk and looked down on me. His tall, thin body, ramrod straight and dressed in dark gray, made the newsroom seem very shabby. I wondered how long he had been standing there while I'd been lost in my own reveries.

"I was thinking about an answer to a letter," I said, hoping my expression had appeared thoughtful rather than clueless.

He gave a thin smile. I didn't know whether that was a good sign or a bad one. Aside from a brief interview when he hired me, we'd never spoken. The word on him was that he had a paternalistic view of the paper and wasn't keen on having his people engage in yellow journalism, which he defined rather broadly to include any kind of undignified or disruptive reporting. Funny how he had let Auntie Mabel slip past. Anyway, I had decided a low profile was the best way to keep my job.

I followed him down the short hall to his office. He sat behind his desk and indicated a chair directly in front of it. The straight wooden back hit me across the shoulder blades, making me feel like I'd been called into the principal's office.

Roger placed a single sheet of paper in front of him on the desktop. I recognized the copy I had written on Jack Proctor's murder. I'd come in early to get it done and placed it in Stan Aaronson's box. Stan was the managing editor and had a tiny office next to St. Claire's. He usually edited my

Auntie Mabel replies directly online to save time, but I figured he'd want to see hard news like a murder in paper copy. I'd expected Stan to question me on why I was poaching on the news division's turf, but I hadn't expected him to take the matter right to the top.

St. Claire said, "How are you enjoying the Auntie Mabel column, Laura?"

Perhaps he had read somewhere that you should begin conversations with employees by making a pleasant inquiry.

"It's interesting to read the questions people send in." I needed the job too much to volunteer the actual truth.

"I realize that it may not be quite up to the level of your talents and experience."

I remained silent because even I know quicksand when I see it. The boss talks down the job, then when you say that golly-gee, sure you should be working at a much higher level, you suddenly find yourself out on the street, fired for being a dissatisfied worker.

When I just sat there smiling politely, he said, "But, of course, you have to earn the right to move up the ladder."

"Of course," I replied.

He cleared his throat, indicating the end of the amenities.

"I read the piece that you submitted on the murder last night at the college."

He glanced up at me as if I might not recall the incident, so I nodded.

"It's a good article. You present all the facts clearly and don't draw any conclusions."

I nodded again. I was starting to feel like one of those dashboard dogs.

"However, I received a call from Chief Farantello this morning. He would like us to report the death was due to unknown causes for the time being. He feels it will give him more time to investigate the murder without having the big Boston papers pick up on it."

"An *unknown* steak knife through the heart?" I asked dryly.

St. Claire granted me a small smile and said, "It's just a delaying tactic."

"Why would the chief want a delay? I thought he already had a suspect in custody."

"Professor Lipton, you mean. Yes, she's their prime suspect, but she hasn't actually been arrested yet. The chief wants to see if there are any prints on the knife and would like to get the preliminary medical examiner's report before making an arrest."

"So what *can* we say right now?"

St. Claire looked into the distance. "We can say Jack Proctor is dead. We can say he fell backward down the stairs during the dinner. And we can say the police are examining the facts surrounding the case."

He reached across the desk, handing me back my copy.

"You want me to make the changes?"

"It's your story."

"But Bill and Joy usually do the real reporting."

"Unless you don't want to do it," he said, starting to withdraw his hand.

I snatched the paper from between his fingers. "I'll take care of it right away."

It was his turn to nod.

I pushed myself forward in the chair, ready to make my exit while I was ahead.

"How's your grandmother doing?" he asked suddenly, then looked away as if slightly embarrassed.

I remembered my grandmother's description of him as having "blonde hair and bright-eyed enthusiasm." The blonde hair had faded to gray, but there still seemed to be a lot of life in those blue eyes, especially for a man who was in his seventies.

"She's doing pretty well."

"I'm sure she misses your grandfather greatly."

"Of course," I said automatically.

I really couldn't say with honesty how Gran felt. She had handled the funeral arrangements with a quiet, businesslike efficiency, and she had shown her appreciation to all of Grandfather's many friends who had come to express their condolences. But I had to admit that at no time had she demonstrated what I would call open grief. Even though I had been living with her ever since the funeral, there had been no long, tearful conversations about my grandfather, no remembering things he had said or fondly recalling his rather numerous eccentricities. And my few attempts to discuss the past had been turned aside with simple factual answers or Taoist sayings about the inevitability of change. It was almost as though my grandfather's death, which had been the result of an unexpected heart attack, had instead been the wished-for release from a long illness.

St. Claire cleared his throat as though preparing for a painful speech.

"I was wondering whether Jessica — and I know it's rather soon after Victor's death — but I was wondering whether Jess . . . your grandmother might be ready to start going out into society again?"

"Out into society?" I felt as if I had fallen

into the middle of a regency romance. Gran had never stopped shopping, attending church, going to yoga class, and doing all of her normal weekly chores.

I was about to say this when I realized he was really asking whether Gran would be interested in going out with him. I knew his wife had died several years ago, but the job of fixing up my grandmother still came as a bit of a surprise. I didn't honestly know how she would feel about having another shot at the old dating game. But I wouldn't stand in the way of a man who wanted to rekindle an old romance. If Gran wasn't interested, she could come up with an appropriate Taoist saying to get her point across, sort of. And after all, only yesterday she had spoken about him as having been a lovely boy. Maybe she'd find the more mature version equally enchanting.

"I can't speak for my grandmother," I began.

"Of course, of course," St. Claire said.

"But I think she might enjoy hearing from you. She mentioned you only recently."

His face lit up with a boyish glow, and I could see that he was dying to ask what she had said. I wasn't going to give him the satisfaction of reporting Gran's remarks. Plus, it might only serve to remind him that he had lost out to my grandfather all those years ago.

"I'll get in touch with her, then," he said, standing up to show that our interview was over.

As I walked down the hall, I switched my thoughts back to my own plans. If Chief Farantello wanted more time to work on the case, then there had to be some doubt as to Heidi's guilt. Now if only I could find a suspect or two to take her place, she would be home free and I could once again try to steal her boyfriend. Life would be good.

"Wow, you go to dinner at the college and people die!" Dorie shouted when I entered the empty newsroom. She must have come in early to get the scoop.

No one else was around, and I breathed a sigh of relief. I remained a little skittish from last night when it came to accusations of guilt, no matter how well intentioned.

"Only one person died. And it had nothing to do with my being there," I said, just in case our conversation was being taped by the authorities.

Dorie gave a shrug that brought her shoulders up to meet her three-inch-long earrings. "It was only a matter of time."

"What was?"

"It was only a matter of time until someone did in Professor Proctor. But stabbing him with a steak knife is really gross."

So much for the idea of concealing the fact that it was murder. Take the fifty people who were there in the room, multiply it by six, and you'd have a rough estimate of how many people already knew more than would be in my expurgated story. It would grow by geometric progression. By the time the *Ravensford Chronicle* hit the stands at three o'clock, the whole town would be laughing at my timid effort at reporting.

"Why would someone want to kill him? Was he a tough grader?" I settled into my chair and smiled indulgently, the older woman who had graduated all of six years ago talking to the younger student.

Dorie came over and sat on my desk, leaning so close to me that I could see that her earrings were composed of vertical rows of tiny Buddhas. Gran would love them.

"He was the Ravensford Peeper," she whispered.

"The who?" I whispered back.

"Our very own campus Peeping Tom."

"He used to peek through dorm windows?"

Dorie nodded. "Well, actually he only peeped through one window. At the back of Thornberry Hall one of the windows in the girl's section is on ground level, and there are some bushes right under it. That was his usual hiding place."

"It sounds as though everybody knew about this."

"Well, sure, it's been going on for a couple of years."

"Didn't any of the girls report it to security?"

"Why? The Peeper was harmless. He was just a looker. The floor advisor warned the girls to pull down their shades. Sometimes, depending on who had the room, they would do a little striptease if they thought he was out there, then pull the shades at just the right moment. It was a lot of fun."

I shook my head. Maybe it came from living in Boston, but I never intentionally tempted the fates of weirdness. Some of the guys I'd dated had supplied enough of that. I didn't need to provoke strangers.

Dorie seemed to sense my disapproval.

"It wouldn't have mattered if they had called security. A boyfriend of one of the girls caught Professor Proctor right there under the window. Proctor claimed he was on his way to his car after a night class and had dropped his notes. He said he thought they had blown into the bushes under the window. Nobody reported him. How could campus security prove that he was lying?"

"Okay. But they could have kept a watch on the building, and if they caught Proctor there enough times, he'd have some serious explaining to do."

"Most students don't want to have security hanging around the dorms."

"So everybody knew about the Ravensford Peeper, and nobody cared?"

Dorie hesitated. Then she said, "Nobody cared until recently. A new student who lives on the first floor was freaked out by the whole idea. Other people in the dorm told her to pull the shades and forget it, but she said that even suspecting there was someone outside her window was driving her crazy. I heard she'd had a bad time being stalked by an ex-boyfriend when she was in high school."

"Couldn't she get her room changed?"

"She put in for it, but the dorms are overcrowded. She'd have to wait until next semester unless she gave the real reason for why she wanted to change, and I guess she didn't want to get involved with some kind of investigation."

"What's her name?"

Dorie hopped off my desk and wrapped her arms around her chest, suddenly looking very young.

"I don't want to get anyone in trouble," she said.

"Jack Proctor was murdered. Somebody is going to get into trouble. The point is to make sure it's the right person. And you said yourself that Keith Campbell is a good guy. He's not going to try to railroad some student for this, but he has to know about it."

"Okay, but you didn't hear it from me."

I nodded.

"Her name is Keri Tinsdale. But I don't think she could kill anyone." Dorie paused. "At least not with a steak knife."

CHAPTER 7

I was alone in the house since Gran had gone out to her chanting and meditation class. I perched on the sofa near the dimly glowing lamp on the end table and studied the front page of the *Chronicle*. Gran never purchased anything stronger than a sixty-watt bulb and many of the fixtures were outfitted with forties. This may have given the house a charming, romantic atmosphere, although someone less charitable might call it spooky, but it meant you risked having to hold your reading material close enough to the bulb to set it on fire when you tried to make out the words.

The absence of light was not a big problem tonight, because what I was reading for about the twentieth time was my article on the murder of Jack Proctor. By now I could have repeated it word-for-word, in the dark, with a bag over my head.

Even though it had been censored to the

point of untruthfulness, I still found myself taking a ridiculously high level of pride in actually seeing my name in the byline of a story. My writing for the Museum of Fine Arts had always been unsigned publicity material, although some of it, in my humble opinion, was pretty good stuff. I was also proud of the titles I had given to several of their exhibits. "Reubens to Rembrandt: The Long Road from Antwerp to Amsterdam" was one of my favorites, until someone who knew more about geography than I did pointed out that it really wasn't that long a road. And the harsh criticism I received for "I'll Keep an Ear Out for You: Van Gogh in Arles" was completely undeserved. I meant that as an interoffice joke. Really! How could I have known a humorless supervisor would forward it to the printer?

I never took much pride in my articles for *Picture This!* because I could never quite convince myself that it was a professional publication. The office atmosphere, not to mention the staff, always seemed to have the lingering reek of a punk high school paper. And since most of the subscribers received their issues for free, how professional could it be? Auntie Mabel's answers, of course, were written under an alias. So this small news article was the first time a piece of my own attributed writing had been professionally published.

My pleasure at seeing my name in print got me to thinking about something I'd been carefully trying to ignore recently — my future. You may be wondering why a woman who was living in Boston, one of the more interesting and pedestrian-friendly cities in the most dynamic nation on earth, would have given up her career, her very own apartment, and the joys of urban life, to relocate to her grandmother's house in Ravensford, Massachusetts, a town two hours from Boston and at least that far from anywhere else worth visiting.

Good question.

The reason, as you've probably already figured out, was a man. A man named Owen Reynolds. Owen, at the age of thirty-five, was one of the up and coming young painters in the Super-realist school. He'd already had highly acclaimed one-man shows in prestigious galleries in Boston and New York before I interviewed him for *Picture This!,* and during our eighteen months of being more or less together, he'd also received considerable attention in England and on the Continent.

Was his success part of why I had fallen head over heels in love with him the first time I saw him, to the point where I could barely phrase a coherent question at our interview? Oh, maybe a little. But there was something about him, about his essence, to use a fancy word, that really attracted me. Tall and razor thin, he looked like a man who suffered for his art. A sculpted gauntness to his face and a nervous energy to his every gesture suggested he was a conduit for some higher creative power.

Although his features were not exactly handsome — his nose being a bit too long and his eyes having a slightly hooded, reptilian quality — his thick, sensual lips and marvelously long, strong fingers gave an overall impression of pure masculinity. All of this was topped off with thick, black hair, which, even at the age of thirty-five, already had a distinguished sprinkling of gray.

The gray hair had only served to remind me that he was almost a decade older than me. Having recently gone through several fragile guys around my own age, I was ready for someone who had the personal and professional confidence and maturity to let me be myself, without feeling his ego was in jeopardy. When my interview concluded with our getting into a passionate discussion over the merits of representational art, and he had asked me out to dinner, I was ecstatic. Here was a man with whom I could truly be myself.

Just proves how wrong a person can be.

I turned off the lamp and lay back on the spavined sofa. In case you're wondering why I left Owen, I'll give you the answer I gave to most of my friends. He was a consummate egotist who had no respect for the work I did. When his painting was going well, nothing else existed for him. When he relaxed between periods of feverish creativity, he expected me to be constantly available.

Now for the real answer that I gave to only a few select friends, which comes down to, as Freud predicted everything would, sex. I had unexpectedly stopped by Owen's apartment during one of his creative vacations, willing to offer my company and my body for the afternoon. Although he tried to block my view of his apartment when he reluctantly answered the door, his ex-wife Philippa had been less concerned with appearances. In fact, she pranced proudly through the living room, clad only in a smile, with every intention of being seen. The revenge of the ex-wife on the new girlfriend. Particularly galling since she was at least fifteen years older than I am.

My accusation that he was an unfaithful

rat was greeted with a condescending smile by Owen. Everyone knows that sex with an ex-spouse is not really sex at all, he said. It was really nothing more, he claimed, than a brief nostalgic reliving of a dead relationship, more bittersweet than passionate. A sort of genital trip down memory lane. Finding this Auld Lang Syne approach to sleeping with his ex less than convincing, I had stormed off.

Owen made repeated attempts to heal the rift over the next few weeks, with variations on the twin themes that Philippa meant nothing to him and I really should be more sophisticated about such things. Although his efforts look anemic to me now, they had begun to work, and if he'd had a couple of more weeks, I probably would have gone running back to him, wagging my little rump. What can I say? Why are good women attracted to bad men? I guess it's like standing too close to a blazing fire. You know it's dangerous, but at the same time there's something damned warm and fascinating about flirting with the flames.

What saved me from returning to Owen was my second stroke of misfortune: unemployment. With a scant two weeks' notice, I was let go from the Museum in the midst of one of their periodic budget crises. Never having been able to save very much due to the generally high cost of living in Boston and my rather meager salary, I was left with few options. When the frantic search for another job that paid anything near the same as the Museum proved fruitless, my options narrowed even more. Living with Owen wasn't one of them. He'd always made it quite clear that he needed his creative freedom and living with a woman would definitely stifle it.

I could have returned to the parental home in Milton. My parents would certainly have welcomed me back, after delivering a stern lecture on the need to save for the future and go into a line of work that provided more security. After all, Dad was a banker and Mom was a school teacher. This would be followed by a strong urging that I return to school to get my certification as a teacher so "I'd always have something to fall back on," as Mom would say.

What saved me from this fate was my third stroke of misfortune: the death of Granddad. As soon as Gran called with a report of his heart attack, my mother was on the phone urging me to move out there to be with Gran. His death two days later made my mother's appeals even more urgent. I suspected my mother was afraid if I didn't look after Gran, the responsibility would fall to her. When I called my grandmother, she seemed very happy with the idea of my living with her for a time, but I never detected a burning need for my company, and she seemed far more independent than my mother's ominous warnings had indicated. Perhaps I needed Gran more than she needed me.

At any rate, here I was. Two weeks after I arrived, I answered an advertisement in the *Ravensford Chronicle* and became Auntie Mabel. Now, a month later and six weeks after losing my job in Boston, I had gotten something published under my own name and was finally starting to really think about my future. This was, as you already know, thanks to a fourth misfortune: the murder of Jack Proctor.

You'd think that all this benefiting from the misfortunes of others would make me feel guilty. It didn't, because I always figured someone out there is making out like a bandit from mine.

Since thinking about my professional future, even at the best of times, which these definitely were not, made me tired, I closed my eyes and nestled down into the long, plush sofa. Nothing like relaxing in an empty house to give the mind the freedom and leisure to come up with a viable plan for the future was my last thought before I began to doze.

I don't know how long I had been asleep when something awakened me.

"Gran?" I called.

I received no reply. Not surprising, since my illuminated watch dial said that it was only nine o'clock. Chanting and meditation went on until nine-thirty and was usually followed by herbal tea and Third World–acceptable refreshments like rice cakes and seaweed dip, or honey that had been voluntarily donated by the bees — don't ask!

I lay on the sofa with my eyes open, filled with the mental alertness you always seem to have when your vision is shut down to near zero. I listened. Could it have been the refrigerator recycling or the antique furnace switching on? Both seemed to be sending out constant noisy pleas for maintenance or replacement. But the more I thought about it, the more I felt certain I had heard a noise in the same room with me.

I slid off the cushions onto the floor and crawled on my hands and knees to the end of the sofa. Slowly, I reached up and turned on the table lamp. The living room looked exactly how I had left it, except I saw it from a new angle, sitting on my haunches on the floor. I stood up and stared into the large ormolu mirror on the wall to fluff my hair, which had gotten matted down by all my heavy thinking.

I stood there mesmerized, or maybe a better word would be entranced, because the mirror had become a painting. In the foreground I saw myself, small and vulnerable, clad in jeans and an old sweatshirt I've been promising myself for years to sacrifice to ragdom. Behind me stood a man wearing a black ski mask. A man who had obviously slid out from behind the sofa. For a moment I wondered how the painting should be interpreted. What was the mysterious allegorical intention of the painter? Innocence about to be attacked by evil, perhaps?

The man in the picture raised his hand, which held some kind of object, and brought it down toward my head. Something clicked. It occurred to me that what I was watching was happening in real time, as the computer wonks say. Even more importantly, it was happening to the real me. I quickly twisted to one side as the hand came down. A glancing blow hit the back of my head. Pain traveled down the side of my neck to my shoulder while I fell to one knee. The room dimmed for a moment, as if there had been a power outage. When I could see again, I caught a glimpse of a dark figure racing across the living room and into the kitchen. Then I heard the outside door open.

Leaning against furniture to keep my balance, I made my way into the kitchen. I closed and locked the door. I sat down at the kitchen table and carefully studied Gran's leaf arrangement for a few minutes, marveling at how it suddenly seemed to be such a thing of beauty.

Then, with a hand I am pleased to say shook only slightly, I reached for the phone.

CHAPTER 8

Chief Farantello wasn't really my kind of man.

I know that sounds ungrateful, given that he had come running over with Sergeant Kelly in tow right after I called the station to report an assault and attempted burglary. But the thing is, I've always preferred tall men. Of course most men, and lots of women too, tower over my five-five frame, but I've always felt a sense of comfort around men who topped out at six feet or more. The Chief was taller than me by only a few inches, not enough to give me the confidence I craved. Or maybe the lack of confidence came from the worried expression on his face as he sat across from me. His expression seemed to say I had battled death to a draw and the bell for the next round was about to ring and I might not be so lucky twice.

"Your door wasn't locked?"

I didn't bother to answer. I'd already told him about my door. The sergeant was searching the house from top to bottom, just in case I'd been mistaken about seeing a man in black run out through the kitchen, and, instead, he hid upstairs in my bedroom. Unlikely, but at the moment I didn't mind having a strapping guy checking under my bed.

The EMTs had also come and gone. In their professional opinion, I had managed to avoid a severe blow to the head and a possible concussion by twisting out of the way. They would have been happy to take me to the hospital for an overnight, just in case, but I told them I'd take my chances. I don't care for hospitals. Too many sick people are there, and you never know what you might catch.

So now I sat at the kitchen table and watched Chief Farantello, while my head pounded and a twenty-two-year-old was probably rifling through my underwear drawer. Life was sweet.

"Can I ask you a question?" I said.

His sad eyes didn't change and he didn't speak, but I thought I detected a slight nod of the head.

"Why are you here?"

"You reported a crime."

"Right. But does the chief of detectives show up every time a citizen reports a break-in?"

"I was on duty and recognized your name."

I wasn't sure whether his admission was an attempt at flattery, so I ignored it.

"Be honest with me," I said. "Do you think that what happened tonight has anything to do with Jack Proctor's death?"

"Do you?"

"No. How could it? But then, I'm not a detective. I may not have your special insights."

I managed to keep any hint of sarcasm out of my voice. I haven't reached the ripe old age of twenty-seven without learning something about how to flatter men. Even a man like Chief Farantello, who had to be in his mid-thirties and has as much salt among the pepper of his black hair as Owen does, likes to hear his skills mentioned. All the same, he gave me a rather fishy look. Maybe I hadn't laid the compliments on thickly enough.

"Jack Proctor was a friend of your grandfather's, right?"

I nodded.

"Have you seen much of him since the death of your grandfather?"

"I hadn't seen him since the funeral, until last night. But he's been around a few times to talk to my grandmother."

"Were they friends?"

I decided not to give him any direct quotes from Gran's frequently stated opinions of Jack, or she'd be right at the top of his list of suspects, next to Heidi.

"They weren't friends. Jack was after her to donate my grandfather's paintings to the college collection."

"How did your grandmother feel about that?"

"She was undecided."

"Why?"

I shrugged. "I guess she wasn't ready to part with them yet. We're not talking about a big business deal here. My grandfather wasn't a famous artist."

"How did you come to know Keith Campbell?"

The question took me by surprise. No one had bothered to ask it last night, so I didn't expect to be taken over that stretch of ground.

"We met at the *Chronicle*." I could tell that the chief was waiting for more, but I decided to make him ask.

"Why was he there?"

I wasn't about to reveal my Auntie Mabel

identity unless they brought out the rubber hoses, so I explained about Keith's problem with the Auntie Mabel column without admitting that I was her new incarnation.

"So you were aware that Professor Lipton had just ended a relationship with Campbell when you agreed to attend this dinner, knowing she'd be there, too?"

"Sure."

A quick smile slid over his lips. "I guess you're not afraid of trouble."

"If you must know, Keith and I were trying to make Heidi jealous so she'd make up with him."

"I see."

I couldn't detect any expression in those soulful brown eyes, but nonetheless I felt as if he had instantly seen through my little scheme to get Keith for myself.

The guilty mind needs no accuser," Auntie Mabel intoned. I quickly shut her up. I was having enough trouble with the external world.

"Is it true that Keith was shot while he was with the police in Boston?" I asked. It was time to go on the offensive.

A slow nod.

"And did his fiancée leave him as a result?"

"You'd better ask Keith about that,"

128

Farantello said.

Sergeant Kelly returned from rooting around in my belongings, and declared the house was free of invaders. Farantello made some imperceptible gesture. Kelly gave me a polite nod and scurried out the door.

The chief rose from the table.

"Is that all?" I asked.

"Keep your door locked from now on. Not even a small town is as safe as it used to be."

"Okay," I said, anxious for him to be gone so I could pop some aspirins for my headache.

He paused in the doorway and stared at my grandmother's leaf arrangement like it might make sense to him, too.

"It's not that uncommon, you know," he said.

It took me a moment to make a guess at what he was talking about.

"Attempted burglary? No, I guess it isn't."

He shook his head. "Having a woman change her mind when she gets a sense of what the job is all about."

I kept silent in order to pick up his train of thought. Then I said, "I guess it's better than having her wait until she's your wife to find out."

"Yes, it is," he replied with certainty.

CHAPTER 9

I sat in the back room of the cement block building that housed the Ravensford College police. It was located in a remote corner of the campus, hovering right on the edge of the college grounds where it wouldn't be noticed by parents and prospective students taking a tour. No sense disturbing the cozy academic atmosphere with any suggestion that the college community was anything less than one big happy family, the Ravensford Peeper notwithstanding.

I was there because, due to Aunt Mabel's prodding, I wanted to help get this case solved as quickly as possible so that Keith and I could get back on track, if at all possible. Which is why, when I called Keith to give him Keri Tinsdale's name as the Peeper's latest and last victim, I sort of made my presence at the interview a condition for sharing what I knew. Reluctantly, he had agreed.

Upon my arrival, the young officer at the front desk told me with a kind of nervous formality to take a seat in one of the interview rooms. He said the director of security would be with me shortly. As I sat on a hard plastic chair at a table made of synthetic material, and stared at the vanilla walls punctuated by a large mirror that looked suspiciously like it might be two-way, I decided "interview" was a euphemism for "interrogation." Since I had nothing to hide, at least nothing with regard to the Proctor case, and since I had not slept very well the night before, due to being bopped on the head, I found my mind wandering.

When Gran had come home last night and I reluctantly told her about the intruder, her instinctive reaction broke through her usual Taoist calm. She had jumped to her feet and insisted on examining my head wound. Once she had determined — by pressing hard enough to make me flinch — that it was a benign goose egg, she had slipped back into character.

"Violence injures the doer as much as the victim," she had intoned.

"Then I certainly hope whoever hit me has the same raging headache I do."

I had to admit she was taking all of this violence pretty well. When I told Gran at

131

breakfast about the death of Jack Proctor, and explained my physical involvement with the crime scene, leaving out the more gory details about my rolling around on top of the dying man, she had shown little reaction — aside from saying that he who confronts will be confronted. Since a burglar in the house didn't seem to throw her off her stride much, either, I decided to pick her brain.

"Do you think that there's any link between Jack Proctor's death and this burglar?" I asked.

"All things in the universe are interconnected."

"Right. But do you think that there might be a more specific connection between these two events?"

"I don't see how," she had said with a frown.

Neither did I, so I'd left it at that. But now, as I sat in my own little interrogation chamber, I wasn't so sure. Despite Chief Farantello's intimations that Ravensford was the leader of the pack for small-town crime, my grandmother had never been burgled before. Gran said she couldn't even recall one burglary happening in the neighborhood. At least not since the Andrews boy, who had lived on the next block and was a known drug fiend, had been sent away to prison ten years ago.

On the other hand, coincidences do happen, and anyone who thinks otherwise is probably deeply into their own paranoid world where every glance and gesture has some hostile significance.

The door to the interrogation room opened. Keith poked his head into the room and flashed me a quick wink. My heart fluttered disobediently. He gallantly held the door open for a tall, young woman who slowly entered the room and gave me a long, suspicious glance. I think we recognized each other simultaneously and with apprehension. If I had known who she was, I might not have given Keith the name I'd pried out of Dorie. She sat across from me and twisted her long hands together.

"This is Keri Tinsdale," Keith said. Then he introduced me. Guilt must have made us unconvincing strangers because Keith glanced at us with his police antennae waving in the air like a manic ant's. "Do you two know each other?"

I considered lying. However, the odds of being caught in a lie, if Keri turned state's evidence, so to speak, made honesty seem the better policy. "Keri was at the college dinner. She served hors d'oeuvres to Jack and me," I said, and immediately felt like a jailhouse snitch.

Keri Tinsdale was, indeed, the less than gracious young woman who had shoved a plate of appetizers at me at exactly the same moment Jack was revealing — to all who could hear at a minimally acceptable level — that I was Auntie Mabel. I hoped Keri wouldn't realize the significance of what she had heard and spill the beans to Keith.

Keith began thumbing through a sheaf of papers in front of him.

"I don't see your name on the list of people who were interviewed by the police," he said to Keri.

"I left by the service entrance. No one took my name."

"You should have waited for an officer to speak with you."

"I had an exam the next day, and I couldn't wait around."

"Did you know Professor Proctor?"

"No."

"But you knew of him."

All signs of nervousness left her as she leaned across the table, her face a mask of outrage. "I knew he was the disgusting little sleaze who tried to peek in my window."

"Did you know him by sight?" Keith said,

remaining remarkably calm. I was poised to jump out of the way in case she lunged across the table.

Keri nodded, suddenly somewhat subdued. "Another student pointed him out to me."

"You should have notified security. We would have handled the situation," Keith said in a gentle voice.

The girl shrugged, which could have been interpreted to mean she had no confidence in the authorities. Or the situation had already been solved via a steak knife, so why worry about it?

"So, you knew who Professor Proctor was when you saw him at the dinner," Keith said. "Did you try to talk to him alone?"

"No," Keri said.

Her lie was so unconvincing, even I could spot it.

"Are you sure?" Keith asked, managing to make it sound like one could easily forget talking to a man on the night he was murdered.

Keri caved. "When he left the dining room to go to the bathroom, I followed him."

"Were you right behind him?"

She shook her head. "I saw him leave, but I was busy and couldn't get away for another five minutes or so."

"What time did you return to the dining room?"

"When I came back, my supervisor yelled at me for being late to serve dessert, so it must have been around eight-thirty. I was gone less than ten minutes."

"Did you talk to Professor Proctor?"

"When he came out of the men's room, I told him who I was and warned him to stop looking in my window."

"What did he say?" I asked.

Keith gave me a sharp look, like I was horning in on his territory, but I figured if he didn't want me to say anything, he shouldn't have invited me to the interrogation.

"Proctor denied it. He said he would sue me for slander if I spread the story around. He said he was a professor, and if I tried to make trouble for him, he'd get me expelled."

"What did you do?"

"I ran down the hall and went into the ladies' room."

Damn! Everyone had been able to find that place except me.

"Was Professor Lipton in there?" I asked.

Keri gave me a puzzled look before she said, "I didn't see her."

"Were any of the doors to the stalls closed?"

"I think so."

I nodded to let Keith know he could take back his investigation again.

"Thank you for speaking with us, Keri." Keith gave her a dazzling grin that brought a faint smile to her face. "If we need to talk to you again," he added, "we'll be in touch."

Keri stood. "Am I going to get into trouble over this?" she asked, her face stiff with apprehension.

"Not if you've told us the truth," Keith said. "But I'll have to pass along what you've said to the police for them to check out. This is a criminal investigation and under their jurisdiction. However, unless there's something more to what happened between you and Professor Proctor, I think this will be the end of it."

Keri nodded and hurried from the room.

I smiled happily at Keith. My secret identity as Auntie Mabel remained safe. Life was good.

"So what do you think?" he asked me.

"I think Heidi is off the hook because Keri saw Jack after Heidi did."

"Unless Heidi went back out into the hall after Keri left and had it out with Jack," Keith said.

Obviously, he wasn't willing to compromise his professionalism to give his girlfriend an easy out. I stared at him, hoping my expression conveyed admiration.

"Only three people we know about saw Jack in the hallway: Keri, Heidi, and yourself," Keith continued.

The fact that he had added me to his list made me feel less happy about his professional approach. I decided it was time to sum up the evidence to date.

"Look, this is the way I see it. If everyone is telling the truth, Jack must have left the table ten minutes before the dessert was served, based on when he talked with Heidi. After his confrontation with her, he went to the men's room. When he came out, he ran into Keri. After they had their argument, she went into the ladies' room, which was empty except for the stall where Heidi was hiding. Keri must have come back to the dining room just before I left, because they had begun to serve the dessert when I left the room. That means there must have been almost ten minutes from when Keri talked to Jack until I found him at the bottom of the stairwell. Where was Jack all that time? Unless he had a serious bladder problem, he didn't go back into the men's room."

"He didn't. Three other men went to the restroom during that time, and none of them saw Jack. And they didn't think there was anyone in the stalls. However, they were together in the men's room, so they can alibi each other. They remember leaving the dining room before the cake came out. That must have been a few minutes before you left the room."

"Did any women other than Heidi and Keri go to the ladies' room?"

Keith shook his head. "Not at that time. Two women went together earlier, before Heidi left the room, but they came back before the dessert was served, just as Heidi was leaving.

Keith stared across the room as if working through the problem.

"Maybe the reason no one else saw Jack was because he was waiting for someone," Keith said. "Someone he had arranged to meet in private. So after he talked to Heidi and after Keri approached him, he made a point of staying out of sight until that person came along."

"Proving the killer doesn't *have* to be Keri, Heidi, or even me, right?"

He gave me a level stare. "All three of you were in the hall at the time of his murder, so you're all still possible suspects based on timing."

"But it could have been somebody else from the dinner," I said. "The somebody he was planning to meet."

Keith nodded. "Chief Farantello's people and mine have questioned everyone who was there, but it's possible someone left the dining area or kitchen without being seen. Keri apparently did."

"But where did Jack hide, so the three guys who went to the lavatory didn't see him standing around like he was waiting for a bus?"

"None of them wandered all the way down to the end of the hall like you did," Keith said, making me feel like I was some kind of freak who loved to hang out in dark hallways. "If the end of the hall was where Jack had arranged to meet somebody, no one would have seen him. As you know, there are double fire doors just before the stairwell, so you can't see to the end of the hall."

I remembered pushing open the doors and hearing the groan from the landing below. I felt a tightening in my throat at the memory. Terrible things can happen to you when you can't find the ladies' room.

"So we're no better off than when this whole thing started. In fact, we're worse off because we've added Keri and the mystery man to the list of suspects," I said. "What about the fancy forensics stuff you always see on television? I thought all you had to do was look at the body through a magnifying glass, and you'd know the perp's name, date of birth, and last book borrowed from the library."

Keith reddened and cleared his throat.

"So you do know something!" I pointed an accusatory finger at his broad chest. *Some almost-boyfriend you are,* I wanted to shout, but even I have some shred of dignity.

He studied his hands as if he hadn't noticed them for a long time. Then he glanced up. "Look, don't let Farantello know I told you, but you are definitely at the bottom of our suspect list."

"Why?" I felt relieved, but also a little bit insulted. After all, I was as capable of murdering someone as the next woman.

"Jack was stabbed in the back. Off to the side and right below his left shoulder blade, with an upward thrust. The knife pierced his heart from the rear. He was probably turning away from his killer to go back to the dinner. We surmise from the bruising that the killer put an arm around Jack's throat from behind, jammed the knife into his back, then twisted him around and shoved him forward down the stairs. He must have turned onto his back as he fell."

"So?"

"Jack was a six footer. You're not tall enough to grab him around the neck from behind."

He sounded slightly apologetic at mentioning my short stature. And he was right. Barring the use of a step stool, it wouldn't have been possible. Even if I had jumped on Jack's back, I couldn't have stabbed him and thrown him down the stairs. Although it made me feel ineffectual, I really didn't have the ability to pull it off.

"But Keri or Heidi could have done it because they're taller?"

Keith nodded. "Heidi is definitely strong enough, and Keri could have managed it if she caught Jack by surprise."

"But she said she talked to Jack right outside the men's room. She couldn't have killed him there and dragged his body all the way down the hall to the stairwell. Somebody would have noticed."

"What if she's lying? What if she had arranged to meet Jack down at the end of the hall? What if Jack suggested that, instead of peeping through her window, they do something more intimate? You saw how angry she was at Jack. It might have been enough of a spark to set her off."

I had to admit it was possible. Both Keri and Heidi had good reasons to do in good old Jack. Reasons that any red-blooded woman might even find justifiable. I could see one of them pushing him down the stairs. But sticking a steak knife in his back? That seemed a bit harder to imagine because it meant the killer had gone to meet Jack prepared to kill him. Of course, Heidi or Keri could have taken a knife from the table for protection. Still, stabbing Proctor in the back didn't make a good case for self-defense.

"I guess there were no fingerprints or you'd already have made an arrest," I said.

"Just smudges. Nothing we can use. From the angle of the wound, we know the person was right handed. But both Keri and Heidi are right handed."

"So am I," I added, just to keep in the running.

Keith coughed slightly to indicate a change of subject. "Chief Farantello told me about the break-in at your house last night. How's your head?"

"Pretty hard, fortunately."

Keith kept looking at me with a sympathetic smile, so I figured that I owed him more than a snappy tough-girl response. "I saw him coming at me and twisted away at the last minute. It was only a glancing blow. I had a headache last night, and this morning my neck is a little stiff. Otherwise, I'm fine. Thanks for asking."

"Farantello called me last night on my cell phone. I would have stopped by to see how you were, but I thought you might be resting." His gaze slid away from mine.

"Sure."

"And I was busy comforting Heidi. She's still pretty upset."

I nodded, thinking how naive or indifferent Keith was to share that with me. "Comforting" was a euphemism if I'd ever heard one. He had probably "comforted" her between silk sheets, several times, was my guess. But hey, why should I be surprised? He figured he owed it to her, and maybe he did. If I had a level playing field, I'd certainly give Heidi a run for her money. It would be David and Goliath all over again. First, however, I had to come up with who killed Jack Proctor, Satan's gift to women.

I stood and headed for the door. Keith started to get to his feet, but I put a hand on one of his muscular shoulders and gave it a hard squeeze.

"Stay in touch, Keith. And if *you* need any comforting, you know where I live."

He had the decency to look embarrassed.

CHAPTER 10

I took a deep breath and stared across the newsroom. I could see the dust motes floating in the rays of the afternoon sun. I didn't usually work afternoons, but since half my morning had been spent at the college, I had Auntie Mabel letters to catch up on. The office was more crowded than usual because both of our reporters, Joy Pleasant and Bill Lamb, were at their desks. We were rarely together at the same time because they wrote their stories in the afternoons for the next morning's edition, or at night in the case of late-breaking news or a town council meeting. Unlike Auntie Mabel, whose advice was for the ages, their articles were about current events and had to get into the paper the next day. The rather sexist division of labor gave Joy the human interest stories, social events, and any important personal events in the lives of local citizens. Bill Lamb was assigned politics and all the less happy incidents.

I've been a bit skeptical about people looking or acting like their names ever since I met Prince Charming. Yes, that was actually his name. Not the one given to him by his parents, although their last name really was Charming. I believe he had been named George.

Prince Charming wasn't. When I interviewed him for *Picture This!,* he was the surliest, dirtiest, most obscene man I'd ever met, which is saying quite a lot. With lank, greasy hair, his body odor would stun a buffalo and his teeth needed to be power blasted. Worse, he had a completely unfounded belief that I was only interviewing him as a way to get to know him personally. Pure olfactory revulsion forced me to give him a straight arm to the chest as he tried to put his arms around me while muttering what I'm sure he thought were highly arousing four letter words. I must have hit a pressure point because he began gasping for air and his face turned purple. I waited long enough to hear him begin to slowly breathe again before I made my exit. Whereupon, I wrote a semi-decent review of his work, which had a few interesting monochromatic aspects to it.

Because of Prince Charming, I doubted

people truly resembled their names. Joy and Bill, however, were exceptions. Joy Pleasant was a woman in her mid-forties. Her nest of blonde hair constantly seemed to be in the process of falling down around her ears, and she was always happy.

This probably helped her professionally, particularly when attending a wedding where the participants were beginning to have doubts about the wisdom of going through with it. Joy could personally attest to wedded bliss, based on twenty-five years of marriage to her gynecologist husband. Her presence at a wedding had probably led to a multitude of doomed marriages in Ravensford. But at least she was able to write a glowing article about the event in the short term, and divorce wasn't part of her beat. As our photographer Marty Gould once commented, Joy could cover an execution and have the prisoner go out smiling, convinced he was, indeed, heading toward a better place.

If Joy was joyful, then Bill Lamb was, as you might expect, meek. I'd like to tell you the color of his eyes, but he never raised his head high enough in my presence for me to see them. It was as if he had taken a monkish vow not to gaze upon a woman's face. And, in fact, to keep the religious terminology going, he was what people used to call a confirmed bachelor, never having expressed any romantic interest in a person of either gender.

Since Bill served as the political reporter, he covered the various town meetings and interviewed local politicos. Because he was so reserved as to be almost invisible, he managed to get some pretty good stories because people would talk in front of him, unaware he was even there. The hard part was getting Bill to write anything mildly controversial, or anything that could be even remotely construed as being offensive to anyone living or dead. He had the knack of making a juicy exposé sound like a weather report.

This morning it was Bill who had walked up to my desk. He stood there, shuffling his feet on the green institutional tile until I noticed him and glanced up from my keyboard.

"Hi, Bill, how are you?"

His answer was directed to his shirtfront and I only caught something that sounded like "okay."

For a moment he studied his shoes. Just as I was about to give up and return to my work, his gaze rose fractionally, reaching the surface of my desk.

"Good work," I thought I heard him say.

"Excuse me?"

"Good work on that article on the . . . um . . . death at the college."

"Thanks."

I waited for him to say more, but he continued shuffling, as if he were about to launch into some break dancing. Finally, he nodded and drifted back to his desk. I wasn't sure how I felt about his compliment. After all, Bill had lots of experience, and his comment might indicate my writing was adequate in that I had conveyed all the relevant details. On the other hand, he could have been admiring it based on the give-no-offense standard he applied to his own work. I had to admit that writing a story about a murder without once saying it was a murder was in the great tradition of pillow-hard reporting the *Chronicle* was known for. Chamber of Commerce press releases sounded like the howling of a bunch of radical dissidents, compared to the powder-puff stories we produced. So maybe Bill's compliment was a sign that I fit right in with the tapioca atmosphere of the place. I sighed deeply. Maybe I'd be better off sticking to the Auntie Mabel column. At least she could, occasionally, be hard hitting.

Roger St. Claire appeared in the doorway of the newsroom. He crooked a finger at me, and as I scrambled to my feet and headed across the room, I could feel two sets of envious eyes focused on my back. Joy and Bill might wish me well up to a point, but they couldn't be happy seeing me in a personal huddle with the big boss.

St. Claire settled into his chair behind his desk. He didn't motion for me to sit down, but I wasn't going to stand at attention like some raw recruit, so I slipped into the uncomfortable wooden-backed number that I'd tried on the day before. He stared at his desktop for so long, I was certain I was about to be fired. Well, it certainly wouldn't be for writing anything libelous in my first news story. Maybe I was being fired for blandness, I thought, which would certainly be a first at the *Chronicle.*

"I'm going out with your grandmother tonight," he said in the tone of a man announcing he has terminal cancer.

I wondered how he would have sounded if she'd refused.

"That's great," I enthused, trying to lighten the atmosphere.

Gran had already left for her dawn Tai Chi class when I got up this morning and last night she had probably been distracted by

150

my confrontation with the intruder. Otherwise, I was sure she would have told me about having a date. At least I thought she would. Maybe, like your average teenager, she was trying to hide things from her family. Who could tell?

"We're going to the Collins' Inn."

I nodded. Of course he'd take her there. It was distinguished to the point of stuffy. The inn was named after Captain Ashcroft Collins, a not particularly distinguished officer on the American side in the Revolutionary War. The story was that when Collins returned home from his sleepy posting along the Massachusetts–Vermont border, he was determined to avoid manual labor for the rest of his days. He did this by opening an inn to be run by his industrious wife and five daughters.

The local historian, whose recent lecture at the town library had provided me with all this information, claimed Collins became famous for sitting in the bar and recounting fictitious stories about his wartime heroics to passing travelers. All the while, the female members of the family slaved away, preparing food and the four upstairs guest rooms. As time went by — and Collins lived to be eighty-five — those who could convincingly contradict his tales of heroism died off, and as they did, his stories became more and more fantastic. By the time of his death in the 1840s, his family believed they were descended from a giant who stood only one rung below the Founding Fathers on the great ladder of American patriotism.

This must have been the explanation for why, as Dorie once told me in her own subtle way, Millicent Ashcroft Collins always acted like she had a broomstick stuck up her butt. The last and still unmarried member of the family, now in her sixties, she ran the inn with rigid formality, as though her own thin body was all that held the line between aristocratic quality and the deluge of democratic tastelessness. I knew, because I had eaten there once since my arrival on an unfortunate date with a guy I had met at the gym. But that's a story for another time.

"Don't you think your grandmother will like the inn?" St. Claire asked, studying my anxious expression. The concern on his face was obvious. "It's a very elegant place."

"I'm sure she'll like it fine," I said, forcing myself back to the present moment.

St. Claire gave a curt nod, as if locale was one concern he could cross off his checklist.

"I called yesterday," he said. "I planned to invite your grandmother out for Saturday night. I thought she would want at least five days' notice, but she was the one who said we should make it this Wednesday night. She said that she had something to do Saturday evening."

He looked at me expectantly, as though I was supposed to supply an itinerary of Gran's social life. Was he going to turn out to be a jealous boyfriend who would suspect my grandmother of cheating on him with every senior citizen in town? Of course, in a way, you could hardly blame him. He had lost her once when she dumped him for my grandfather. Maybe you never get over the romantic jolts you receive in your twenties.

I shook my head. "I don't know what her plans are for Saturday." Heck, I didn't even know what my own were, and Gran's were probably going to turn out to be more interesting.

He nodded again, even more curtly, as if slightly embarrassed at having attempted to pry into my grandmother's life. I started to stand, figuring the inquisition was over.

"Good job on the college story," he said.

"Thanks." The official seal of approval had been given, and I now knew my story was bland to the point of boring.

He cleared his throat, indicating considerable thought. Then he said, "I think that you can continue with a follow-up story on the . . . incident."

"You mean the murder?" I tried to look innocent, even though I was still angry about describing the so-called incident as an accident.

He ignored my question. "I'm not talking about anything that will take away much time from your column." He paused to give me a thin smile. "Auntie Mabel is pretty popular in this town. You can't disappoint your readers."

I returned his smile with an even thinner one of my own.

"You might have a chat with Chief Farantello and see if he has any new information that he'd be willing to give out to the public."

"Can I openly refer to it as a murder now?" *Now that everyone else in town, including the pre-school kids, are calling it that?* I wanted to say.

St. Claire steepled his fingers and gave my question due consideration. "Check it out with the chief," he finally said. "If Chief Farantello says it's okay, then do it."

I stifled my sigh of exasperation as I stood up and headed for the door. I turned in the doorway and glanced back at St. Claire, who was looking particularly pompous sitting there with a bemused expression on his face.

"Have a good time on your date tonight," I said, and smiled to myself when his face clouded over once again with anxiety.

CHAPTER 11

Since I had to work later in the day than usual to get my column finished, I skipped my normal afternoon visit to Big Billy's Gym and drove home. I circled the small green that made up the center of Ravensford. A Congregational Church, the Town Hall, and a few small stores dotted the outside perimeter of the circle. Gran told me that up until a few years ago, a shoe store, a small hardware store and a dress shop had been included in those storefronts. Since the new strip mall went up on the road heading out toward Springfield, they'd been replaced with an art gallery, a tanning salon and a cheese shop. Some of the locals thought this was the first sad step in the gentrification of a simple New England town; others thought it was the inevitable cycle of economic life and the locals should take advantage of it.

I was of two minds about the green.

"Cloyingly Norman Rockwell," my urban side would declare on one day. On the next, my developing rural self would appreciate a serene oasis in the center of town. It produced a feeling of safety in a world of conflict and pain. A feeling, I suspected, that went back to those first settlers who had clustered together in small settlements, surrounded by uncertainty and danger.

I mentioned this to Gran once. She laughed and said, "Gathering the huts or wagons in a circle and preparing for the worst is our common heritage. It's American *feng shui.*"

Upon arriving home, I walked into the kitchen, and immediately smelled something burning. I raced over to the stove and shut off the heat under a large kettle. It was giving off an odor that would have had them gagging in a glue factory.

As I was about to risk my life by lifting the lid and peering inside, Gran said, "What are you doing, Laura?"

"Something was burning on the stove."

Gran came over and looked inside the pot. "Seems perfectly fine to me," she said, turning the burner back on.

"Don't you think that the . . . ah . . . aroma is a little strong?" *Like on a busy day in the tannery,* I wanted to say but hesitated.

Perhaps the olfactory sense was the first to go in some elderly people. No point being insensitive.

"To the queen in her tower or to the dung beetle?" my grandmother asked.

To a normal person with five senses, I almost replied. *And enough of this Eastern relativity!*

Instead I said, "What are you making?"

"Squid stew. What you smell are probably the Japanese roots and herbs I used to season it. I had to mail-order them especially for the stew."

If that stuff could make it through the mail, we were hardly safe from a multitude of biohazards.

"But Roger St. Claire told me that you were going out with him tonight," I said, and had the pleasure of watching her blush.

"I plan to have a bowl of this soup in preparation."

"In preparation for what?" Was the soup something to line her stomach with in preparation for a night of heavy drinking? If so, it might be worth learning about.

She turned an even deeper shade of red. "It will strengthen my yin."

"Let's see. Yin is the female side, right?"
She nodded.

"So this stew will make you more feminine?"

Again, a somewhat reluctant nod.

"I don't think you need it."

A quick smile of delight passed over her face.

"Really?" she said.

I walked over and gave her a hug. "Really, Gran. Nature provides whatever is necessary. Haven't I heard you throw that quote at me?"

She nodded and returned my hug. "Sometimes the young must educate the old."

"And to be honest, even if you did want to add to your yin, I'm not sure your stew will do the trick."

Gran bent her head over the pot and took a long whiff. "Hmm," she said, turning pale. "Perhaps you're right."

That evening, after Gran left on her date, I walked downstairs. I'd stayed in my bedroom because I didn't want to be sitting on the sofa when Roger St. Claire arrived to pick her up, putting him under a microscope as if I were an overbearing parent. As pleasant as watching him squirm might have been, as my employer he could do worse to me.

I entered the kitchen, planning to rustle

159

up something to eat. The squid stew was no longer on the stove. A window had been opened to air out the kitchen. Thank goodness Gran had decided to go with her natural complement of yin. I figured that would be more than enough for St. Claire to handle.

Not feeling in the mood for anything too spicy after the squid stew experience, I made a cheese omelet. I had just finished washing up from my meal when I heard a noise outside the kitchen door. I waited for the bell to ring or a knock on the door, but there was silence. A tense silence. I waited, still certain someone stood on the other side of the door. I heard the boards of the old porch creak ever so slightly.

I debated with myself. Should I call the police? After the other night, they would probably come running. But could I keep calling them every time I thought I heard strange sounds in the night? The girl who cried intruder would quickly become old news. Eventually, a call to 9-1-1 — while I was being hacked to death — would be greeted with a bored ho-hum.

No. The best thing to do would be to open the door and confront my fears.

"Be prudent, Dearie," Auntie Mabel warned. *"Courage is no substitute for ad-*

equate preparation."

"Well, I've had some kick boxing," I told her. "And I did stick with that kung fu class for a couple of weeks. What's the tiger form again?"

"Cast iron," Auntie Mabel replied.

"Huh?"

"Use the cast iron skillet."

"Ah."

I pulled the heavy frying pan out of the closet and hefted it. If I put my shoulder into it, I could probably swing it around strongly enough to floor an elephant. I approached the door. Despite Farantello's warning, I knew that it would still be unlocked. Gran never locked the door. All I had to do was pull it open and confront whatever awaited me on the doorstep. Easy, right? No different than any other day in my life. My hand closed around the door handle, and I pulled.

A man stood on the porch, just out of range of the light from the kitchen. He didn't say anything, but took a menacing step toward me. I launched myself into my samurai frying pan swing. I brought the pan up, ready to wallop a serve right past my opponent for an ace. The frying pan reached the height of its arc, ready to come down on whatever part of the man's anatomy was closest, when he stepped forward into the light.

"Laura?"

I checked my swing and went toppling forward into his chest. The frying pan fell from my hand and thumped hard on the porch. I leaned on his chest for a moment while I caught my breath. Then I angrily pushed him away.

"Are you trying to scare me to death? What are you doing lurking around out here, Owen? And how did you find me?"

Yes, it was Owen, former boyfriend and Super-realist painter, looking more attractively boyish than any thirty-five-year-old lying cheat had a right to look. He picked up the frying pan and hefted it.

"You could hurt somebody with this," he said. "I know you're angry with me, but I never expected my behavior to make you homicidal."

I grabbed the frying pan from his hand. I figured I might still have some use for it. "Come inside, Owen. It's cold out here and there's no sense in disturbing the neighbors."

He waltzed into the kitchen, stood in the center of the room, and looked around. "Very Norman Rockwell," he said.

"I asked you some questions."

"And I will answer them in order. I was not exactly lurking, as you put it. I was indecisive. I reached your door with every intention of knocking. I came to the kitchen door because I saw the light, and I seemed to remember that out in the country families always congregate in the kitchen."

"Get to the point."

"Well, it suddenly occurred to me you might not be home and it might prove difficult explaining to your grandmother who I am. Then I thought that even if you were home, seeing me like this without warning might . . . disturb you."

"How about *annoy* me?"

"I was considering what to do when you opened the door and attacked me."

"How did you find me in the first place?"

"I promised not to tell." Owen got a constipated look on his face, as if that proved he was the soul of discretion.

"Janet told you, didn't she?" It had to be Janet, my best friend in Boston. She was the only one who knew where I'd gone, aside from my former employers. My parents knew, of course, but Owen would never approach them. Even when we were going together, he refused to meet them.

"Janet told me," he admitted.

So much for his vow of secrecy. No truth

163

serum or bamboo shoots under the finger-nails needed here.

"But don't blame her," Owen continued. "She actually put up quite a struggle. I had to use all my powers of persuasion."

Since Janet had a heavy crush on Owen, I didn't think she'd put up a heck of a lot of resistance. Maybe she even enjoyed being persuaded.

"That brings me to a new question," I said. "Why the hell are you here?"

Standing in the middle of the kitchen with his coat still on, Owen made me feel a bit ungracious. His expectant glance toward the living room sealed the matter. Somehow Owen always managed to guilt-trip me into being nicer to him than I intended. Probably it was the thick comma of hair falling down across his forehead.

"Oh, take your coat off and come into the other room," I said, stomping past him into the living room and flopping down on the sofa.

He followed me into the room. He removed his coat and carefully placed it on the other end of the sofa from me. Then he sat in the wing chair on the far side of the room, next to the fireplace. He glanced around slowly with the air of someone who was considering whether to make an offer on the house. Then he crossed his left ankle on top of his right knee and smiled at me. I'd always envied Owen's ability to quickly settle into a new environment. Throw him into a tribe of pygmies and within the hour they'd be sure he was one of them, although taller and a lot lighter.

"So why are you here?" I asked, tired of his contented smile.

"I wanted to see you."

"Six weeks after I left Boston you suddenly decided that you couldn't live without me and drove all the way out here?" The sarcasm in my tone would have etched glass, but underneath it all some part of me really wanted to hear him say yes. So I could tell him to get lost, maybe. Or maybe not.

He squirmed a little in the chair. It felt good to see something bother him.

"I came here to see you," he said, "but I'm in town for another purpose."

"Oh, so you were already in the neighborhood and thought you'd drop by." Now I really did feel bad. "Aren't you afraid exposure to rural life will make you stupid?"

"The country has its charms. I may even do some pastoral drawings while I'm out here. My agent says I should diversify my work. Hard-edged urban isn't chic anymore. People want more restful scenes and agricultural nostalgia is big."

"So you came all the way out here to sketch?"

"Actually, I'm here for a few days to conduct some master classes at the college. Show the budding art students how to paint the stuff that will really sell, instead of the Impressionist and Abstract rip-offs their teachers encourage them to grind out."

"I didn't know you did classes." I'd never known Owen to teach. He had frequently turned down requests from museums and art schools with the terse statement that those who can't do teach.

He looked at the top of his brown loafer for a long moment, as if deciding how much to tell me. He wore tan chinos and a knit polo shirt. For a painter, he had always dressed rather neatly. As a breed artists ran to worn jeans and paint-splattered T-shirts, but Owen had always considered that an affectation. One of the things I'd liked about him was his unwillingness to go along with the starving-artist stereotype. A painter paints, he would say, and anything else about his life is irrelevant.

"I usually don't," he said, "but a member of the faculty contacted me. He offered me so much money, I owed it to myself and my bank account to accept. However, it now appears he failed to notify the powers that be of his intention, and, unfortunately, my contact person isn't available anymore."

"Jack Proctor."

"You know him?"

I nodded. I didn't think it necessary to say I had been lying on top of Proctor when he gasped his last breath. Someone at the college would doubtless fill Owen in soon enough.

"Are you heading back to Boston, now that the golden goose has been killed?"

"Fortunately, the provost found a copy of Proctor's correspondence with me and agreed to the arrangement. That means I'll be here for a few days. I have a room at the Collins' Inn."

"Swell. I'm sure you'll enjoy your stay." He and Gran had never met, or else that might have led to an awkward moment in the lobby.

Owen's glacier blue eyes locked on mine. "I meant what I said before about wanting to see you."

I spread my arms wide. "Look, then."

"It's what attracted me to you from the first."

"My looks."

He laughed. "Your looks were part of it, but I meant your irreverent sense of humor."

"Yeah, that's me, a barrel of laughs."

He leaned forward in the chair, his expression suddenly solemn. "I know the business with Philippa upset you, and maybe I didn't handle it as sensitively as I should have, but I thought what we had together was special and could survive a little bump in the road."

"I guess you were wrong, or maybe Philippa was too big a hump . . . I mean bump."

A pained expression came over his face at my coarseness. "Can't you see your way clear to forgive me?"

I studied the design in the worn carpet. This was a new angle. Owen had never asked me to forgive him before. In fact, he'd never even admitted he'd done anything wrong before, so the question kind of threw me. The sagging sofa cushion moved. Owen had gracefully slid across the room and was sitting next to me. Those intense, observant artist's eyes studied my face as if he were trying to memorize it so he could paint it later.

"You haven't answered me," he said.

"I don't know the answer."

His face moved closer until my vision blurred. I felt his lips on mine, pressing hard with a desperate urgency.

"Are you sure you don't know the answer, Laura?"

It would be so easy. We were alone and Gran wouldn't be back for hours. Owen and I could go upstairs. I could make my mind a total blank for a while, and enjoy the closeness of the moment. Maybe forgiveness would come in time. So what if it didn't? It would certainly be fun finding out.

I was about to leap up, grab his hand, and pull him toward the staircase. I could already see the expression that would appear on his face. Anticipation mixed with something else. The something else would be absolute confidence. He would have known all along I would cave. I think that's what stopped me. That and my sudden recollection of a quote Gran had laid on me the other day.

"To be a complete person, your higher interests must dominate your lower interests," she had said in reference to some question of mine about when we were going to eat.

I pulled back from Owen and jumped up from the sofa.

"It was nice seeing you," I said. "I hope you have a pleasant visit in Ravensford."

The momentarily stunned expression on Owen's face almost made it all worthwhile. Except my body felt like it had been jerked from a sauna and plunged into ice water. *Well, get used to it, body,* I thought. *This is what being a complete person is all about.*

Owen stood and looked down on me sternly, as if I were a patient who had foolishly chosen to ignore the doctor's orders and was doomed to face tragic consequences.

"Are you sure this is the decision you want to make?" he asked, the tone of reproach obvious in his voice.

If he had seemed hurt rather than miffed, I might have caved and let the old lower interests come charging back to take control. But his patronizing tone revived too many painful memories of the things I didn't like about him. Old wounds opened and the blood began to flow again.

"You made the decision when you decided to do the down and dirty with your ex," I said. "Don't try to put it all on me."

I guess Owen figured he wouldn't even dignify that with a response. He picked up his coat and walked into the kitchen. A few seconds later I heard the door close. I followed him and made sure it was locked. Funny, I hadn't felt as anxious to lock it after the intruder hit me on the head the other night as I did right now. Talking to Owen made me feel more defenseless.

Sticks and stones may break my bones but words tear the hell out of me.

CHAPTER 12

Chief Farantello sat across the desk from me. The glasses he'd put on to read the draft copy of my next story on Jack's murder gave him a studious look that seemed to be at cross purposes with the automatic he was wearing in a shoulder holster. He had draped his jacket over the back of his chair, so the arsenal was obvious. His blue shirt seemed clean and unwrinkled, yet he managed to give the impression of someone who had dressed hurriedly and without attention to details. I wondered if he had a woman in his life. An irrelevant thought, but who can control thoughts? That's why it's called stream of consciousness.

He picked up a pencil and crossed out one word. I tensed. I know professional writers have to take editing well, but my initial reaction has always been to reach across the table and snatch my copy away from a disrespectful reader. A habit I'd have to learn to break as a journalist.

Farantello must have sensed my reaction because without looking up he said, "You typed 'and' twice."

When he had finished, he handed the sheet of paper back to me. His large brown eyes had their standard sad, solemn look, as if he'd been reading the obituary of his best friend.

"It's okay," he said.

I nodded. I'd given a short bio of Proctor, leaving out any mention of his peeping proclivities. I'd said Jack Proctor had been stabbed, but hadn't said it had been in his back because Keith had told me in confidence. I'd left out any reference to the suspects in the case or any speculation as to a possible motive. And I'd ended on a high note by informing folks that "police investigations were continuing," in case the public thought murders were routinely ignored by police in favor of traffic tickets and diverting cars at road repair sites.

"You're not afraid of the Boston papers getting wind of a murder in Ravensford?" I said.

Farantello shook his head. "There was a double murder and suicide in Cambridge last night to keep them occupied. They aren't going to be looking this far west for a story."

"Is there any information you can give me? Something I can add to my story?"

"Not at this time."

Although he managed to appear heartbroken at having to give me the bad news that there was no news, I remained undeterred. I didn't plan to back off just because the chief of detectives looked like he needed a friend.

"What about something off the record?"

"You already know about Proctor being stabbed in the back and the absence of fingerprints."

I kept my face blank.

"Keith felt guilty and told me he spilled the beans to you. He shouldn't have done that."

"I coerced him."

"How?"

"By using my feminine wiles."

I thought I saw the edges of Faranello's mouth lift slightly into the ghost of a smile, but it might have been my imagination.

"Are you going to use them on me?" he asked with genuine curiosity.

If his expression hadn't remained so funereal, I'd have thought he was flirting with me.

"It depends," I said.

"On what?"

"On whether you really have any more information. I don't throw my feminine wiles around with reckless abandon, you know."

Just ask Owen, I thought. Respecting yourself in the morning can sound like abstinence propaganda, but if I'd slept with Owen I would have felt like scrubbing my skin raw with a steel wool pad. Stepping into the shower this morning, I happily stuck with the loofah.

The chief nodded slowly, as if he was considering whether he had any information that would merit my turning on the charm.

"The only thing I can tell you, off the record, is that Proctor mentioned something to his department secretary the day he was killed about his having a bright future."

"How did that come up?"

Farantello frowned. "She's a new girl, young and cute, so I imagine Proctor was trying to impress her. That's why we can't be certain he was telling the truth. Maybe he used the same line on every attractive woman he met."

"Did he give any hint as to why he was going to suddenly be in the spotlight? I'm sure he never imagined it would be as a murder victim."

"He didn't give the secretary any details. She acted like talking to him was pretty distasteful to her, so I don't think she prolonged the conversation by asking him questions. A pity. We might have gotten some useful information."

"Is Heidi Lipton still on the top of your list of suspects?"

Farantello sighed and ran a hand across his face. Then his eyes focused on me, sad and soulful. I felt something lurch deep in my chest. *He isn't really my type,* I told myself. *I like tall types.* The mighty oaks of men one can cling to when heavy winds come up. Farantello was so thin, it looked like a good breeze would whisk him off to Kansas. I wondered exactly how old he was.

"She's still at the top of our list," he said. "She had means and motive."

"What about Keri?"

"She's number two."

"Why isn't she in a tie for first?"

"Two reasons. She came back to the dining room before Heidi did, so she had less time to commit the crime, although she still had enough. Secondly, as Keith no doubt told you, she's tall enough to have gotten her arm around Jack's neck, but she can't weigh more than one hundred and ten. I'm not sure she's strong enough to stab a guy who goes one eighty-five and throw him down the stairs. Hard to be sure, though. She could have gotten lucky or caught Proctor completely off guard. A guy like Jack Proctor never believes one of the women he's harassing will fight back."

"But Heidi's bigger and stronger."

Farantello nodded. "All that metal sculpting. Have you seen the muscles in her arms?"

I nodded, not mentioning I'd been worried about those muscles in a directly personal way.

"But you're still not satisfied," I said.

"There's certainly not enough evidence for me to feel comfortable making an arrest. Apparently, Proctor was the kind of guy who made enemies wherever he went, especially among women, and possibly among their husbands and boyfriends. My people are digging into his background to see if he had received any threats recently."

"Sounds painstaking."

He smiled. "Most police work is."

Maybe it was seeing him smile, an event that was probably about as frequent as a sunny day in Seattle, but I wanted to know him better. His smile was kind of nice, although that might have been by comparison with his usual woebegone expression.

"When we were talking the other night at my grandmother's house, you seemed to hint that your wife had left you because you were a cop. Is that true?"

He shifted in his chair. "Is this off the record, too?"

"Way off. I don't do human interest stories."

Another smile. I was batting a thousand today.

"Not much of human interest in the story," he said. "We met in college. We were both English majors. We both went on to become high school teachers. We got married. Then I decided my standing around in a classroom all day wasn't the right thing for me, so I joined the force . . . about ten years ago. She stuck with it for three years, then decided she wanted out."

I did the math and figured he must be around thirty-one or thirty-two.

"Was it because of the pressure of being a cop's wife? I wouldn't think the crime rate in Ravensford would make the job real risky."

"It has its moments. But Amanda had always thought of me as a sensitive soul, a poet. We'd read poetry together, especially when we first met. She said my being a cop had changed me and I wasn't the man she'd married."

I shrugged. "People change whether they become cops or not. That's part of the territory. If you love someone, you make adjustments."

Farantello nodded. "I guess I was an adjustment that she couldn't make."

"Do you have a first name other than chief?"

"Michael." He paused for an instant. "Not Mike."

"Okay, Michael. Why don't you call me Laura? If you're sure I'm not a suspect."

"You certainly screwed up our crime scene, coming into such close contact with the victim. But you're not a suspect . . . Laura."

"Where are you going with this? You're being downright flirtatious," Auntie Mabel grumbled.

"I'm trying to stay in good with the cops so I'll get some information," I told her, albeit silently.

She made a rude sound in my head.

"Is there anything else you can tell me about the case?" I asked Michael.

"No, not on or off the record. Maybe in a few days, after we've checked around some more."

"May I come back then?"

"Will it still be news by then, or has Jack Proctor already had his fifteen minutes of fame?"

"Even if it isn't, I've a personal interest in the outcome. It's not every day I land on top of a guy who's just been murdered."

Michael resumed his doleful expression, as if he thought I'd suffer from posttraumatic stress disorder for the rest of my days. I'd had a few disturbing dreams, but I figured it would run its course in about a month. In the most frequent dream, Proctor's eyes opened and he accused me of suffocating him by lying on his chest.

"Sure, you can come back," Michael finally said.

I could have been wrong, but it seemed he even *liked* the idea.

Back in the office, I tried to catch up on Auntie Mabel letters. A guy wanted to know whether he should return the underpants a woman had inadvertently left behind in his apartment one night. He had no plans to see her again, but he didn't want to do anything that would be considered ill mannered.

I was imagining the circumstances under which someone would "inadvertently" leave her underpants behind, when Roger St. Claire appeared in the newsroom doorway. He gestured for me to come with him. Dorie wasn't due in for another ten minutes, so I was the only one holding down the fort. But if the boss wanted me, I figured office coverage was his problem. I followed him down the hall, into his office, and took my usual chair.

"How did your grandmother enjoy our date last night?" he asked.

"I didn't see her this morning."

He frowned as if I'd somehow been remiss in my duties. Then he rallied with an optimistic expression on his face. "I think Jessica had a good time. We talked about the past, about the things we used to do when we first met."

Since Gran almost never talked to me about the past, I decided maybe it worked better, conversationally, if you discussed it with someone your own age.

"I told her about the newspaper," he continued, "and some of the things happening in town. She hasn't kept up much, you know."

I wasn't going to correct him, but Gran knew everything about what she wanted to know. Local politics didn't interest her, but she was on top of all the yoga studios, herbal healing salons, deep muscle massage parlors and aromatherapy shops within a twenty-mile radius. If St. Claire didn't watch out, she'd have him stretched, rubbed and smelling good before he knew it.

"One thing bothered me, though," he said.

"What's that?"

"I mentioned Victor to her a few times. After all, Victor and I saw each other around town for almost forty years. Whenever I went to something at the college, he was there."

"Uh-huh."

"Well, I thought Jessica might like to talk about Victor a little bit with someone who knew him. But whenever I brought him up, she immediately cut me off and changed the subject."

"I see."

"I was wondering if it was too soon."

"Too soon for what?"

He sighed as if I hadn't been paying attention. "Too soon for Jessica to be going out with anyone. It seems to me she's still so deeply in mourning, she can't even bear to talk about Victor. Maybe I should leave her in peace for a while longer."

I didn't have an answer. Gran went to all sorts of classes and other types of events. But, of course, a date with a man was different. It would certainly bring home to her that Grandfather was gone and she had to go on to a new stage in her life. Maybe it did upset her more than I could imagine. Granddad hadn't been in the grave two months yet, but she had seemed happy to be going out with Roger.

"The best thing here might be to let her decide for herself," I said. "After all, if my grandmother doesn't want to go out, she can always refuse. We shouldn't try to make the decision for her."

St. Claire brightened. "Do you really think so?"

I nodded. "As long as she doesn't feel pressured."

"I would never pressure her," he said quickly.

"Then go for it."

He smiled faintly at my enthusiastic encouragement. I wondered whether he had ever gone for anything with whole-hearted eagerness. He seemed more like a guy who had never quite gotten out of second gear, especially in the romance department. But who knows? Still waters run deep, they say.

"I have an assignment for you, Laura. It's come up quite suddenly, so I hope you're free tonight. It's something right up your alley, especially with your background in art."

I was tempted to lie and pretend I had at least three dates to cancel. To give the impression that men were flocking around me so thickly, I had to stack them up like flights at O'Hare. But then I figured it wasn't worth the effort, and he'd probably find out the truth about my pathetic love life from Gran.

"I'm free," I admitted.

"They're having a special reception tonight at the college. It's for a visiting artist from Boston, and it's being held in the rotunda of the art gallery. I thought it would be nice to cover a cultural event at the college. It might help offset the rather tragic event that happened there so recently. I'd like you to interview him for the paper."

He wanted me to interview Owen. The day after virtually tossing him out of my bed, I was supposed to approach him as a stranger and ask him questions about his career. The words would stick in my throat. The questions would never get past my teeth. I'd gag at the very sight of his pompous, condescending face.

"Sure, I'll do it," I said. After all, a girl has to make a living. And the thought of having a second chance to write an interview with Owen could be a gift. My first piece for *Picture This!* had been far too gushy, conceived in the first blush of new love. Now I had a second shot. This time my piece could be critical, conceived in the ashes of disillusionment.

"Fine. Be there by eight. Marty will meet you at the museum. He'll take some pictures. I'll probably stop by later, as well."

"See you there," I said, getting to my feet.

"And you're sure about how I should proceed with your grandmother?"

"Yes. Fortune favors the brave," I quoted. Something I'd gotten from Auntie Mabel.

I walked back into the newsroom at the same instant Dorie came through the door. She whipped off her Ravensford College jacket, revealing a midi-sweater. A pair of jeans struggled to stay on her hips with the help of a wide belt.

"You won't believe it," she announced.

"The way the last few days have gone, I'll believe almost anything. In fact, I'll even believe you'll graduate some day."

"Very funny. Do you want to hear my news or not?"

"Okay. What won't I believe?"

"My friend Tammy told me they had a guest speaker in her art class, an incredibly hunky artist from Boston. So I slipped into

Karla's painting class because I wanted to get a look at him."

Owen, I thought. Would my trials and tribulations never cease?

"He was a little old but really sexy. There was just something about him. And his hands. By the way he held the brush, I don't know, you could tell those were experienced hands and they could do almost anything."

I felt a congestive tightness in my chest. Owen did have incredibly long, spatula-like fingers. Each one seemed to have a mind of its own and work independently. Soft and yet so firm.

"Are you okay?" Dorie asked.

"Sure."

"You got a little red in the face there for a minute."

"Just my allergies. So what did he paint?"

"He painted his girlfriend."

"His *what?*"

"This really cute girl who was hanging onto him like kudzu. I guess she was a model or something. She sure looked like one. Couldn't have been much older than I am. Anyway, Owen — that's what he told us to call him — sat down at an easel and painted a portrait of her. Without doing a drawing or anything. And the picture looked just like her. It was absolutely amazing."

What was amazing was that he had been trying to get into my pants when he had his girlfriend waiting for him back at the inn. I said a short prayer to the gods of self-control. Whatever their mistakes in the past, they certainly hadn't let me down last night.

"They're having a party at the art museum tonight in his honor," Dorie said.

"I know. I'm covering it for the *Chronicle*."

Dorie beamed. "Great. Then you'll see this guy, Owen. You wouldn't want to miss him for the world."

"I'm sure."

The last thing I wanted was for anyone to know Owen was an old boyfriend because they'd never believe that *I'd* been the one who dumped *him,* instead of the other way around. I didn't think Owen was about to make our past public, especially with his new girlfriend in tow, and I'd never told anyone in town about him. Even if I might have mentioned his name in passing to Gran, what were the odds a woman in her seventies would remember the name of her granddaughter's former boyfriend?

So why did I have an apprehensive shiver running up my spine, telling me that the other shoe was about to drop?

"Great news," St. Claire said, standing in the doorway of the newsroom. When he saw

Dorie, he nodded to her and walked across to me, where he dropped his voice down to a barely audible whisper. "She's agreed to come with me tonight to the reception."

"Who?"

"Your grandmother."

I heard a loud *thunk* in the background. Dorie had knocked the ledger book off her desk, but to me, it was the sound of the other shoe falling.

CHAPTER 13

My grandmother glanced up from the pot of liquid boiling furiously on the stove. Rather strange-looking mushrooms covered the center of the table. I hoped they had been purchased and she hadn't picked them herself.

"I see your former boyfriend, Owen Reynolds, is in town," she commented, not taking her gaze from the pot.

If she had said she was cooking up a tasty pot of Deadly Nightshade soup, I couldn't have been more surprised.

"How did you know Owen was my former boyfriend?" I blurted.

"Your mother told me, of course, back when the two of you were still together."

"And you remembered?"

She gave me a gentle smile. "I am old but not senile, my dear. I've always paid attention to anything your mother told me about you."

"Sorry, Gran. It's just . . ."

I swallowed the rest of my words. I couldn't say "sometimes you seem so vague, I'm not sure you even know I'm here."

"And anyway," she continued, "your grandfather recognized Owen's name when I mentioned it to him. He went on and on at the time about the huge step backward these new realists, as he called them, were taking. 'Why be representational now that we've got photography?' he said. 'Sheer technical skill is taking the place of art.' And so on. Victor really could be quite tiresome on the subject. So there was no way I was likely to forget your boyfriend's name."

"I'd like you to forget it now, Gran."

She raised a quizzical eyebrow.

"I'm not his girlfriend anymore, and I'd rather not have people know about my past. I left Boston so I could put Owen behind me, I don't want to resurrect him."

Gran nodded. "I quite understand. A cheating man should be left in the dust, if possible."

I wondered if that was a Taoist saying. I also wondered how much my mother had told her. I'd never realized they'd had such extensive conversations about my love life. When I arrived in Ravensford, I told Gran I'd lost my job, broken up with my boyfriend, and wanted a change of scene. I had been embarrassed about the whole thing with Owen, and I wasn't sure how much of my personal life I wanted to share with a woman in her mid-seventies, who had stayed married to the same man for fifty years.

Sexual snobbery on my part? Ageism? Who knows? It certainly didn't matter now, because apparently that was one cat that had long since left the bag, thanks to my mom. Fortunately, even my mother didn't know Owen's cheating had been with Philippa, his ex-wife. It would have been too mortifying for words. Philippa was older than Owen. She had to be at least forty, which really bothers me. I had lost out to a woman old enough to be my mother . . . almost.

"Can you be sure that Owen won't mention your past relationship to anyone?" Gran asked

"He has his new girlfriend with him. I doubt he'll want to bring it up."

"You never know with men," she said, and began dumping mushrooms into the broth of death.

"Did you enjoy your date with Roger last night?" Since she was privy to my romantic life, I decided I could ask about hers.

She stared off into space in that unnerving way she has, then smiled sadly. "I remembered him as such fun as a young man, but I'm afraid that he's become rather stodgy. I blame it on Marie, his wife. All she cared about was being proper. She was the wrong woman for him and took all the joy out of Roger. They never really made a suitable couple."

"He is quite a bit older than when you dated last," I pointed out. "People change."

"The brightest day fades into night," Gran intoned.

"Right."

Gran peered at me through the steam rising from the mushroom stew, probably trying to detect whether I was making light of the wisdom of the East.

"But I did think that there was still a faint spark of the boy I remembered, buried under all his pomposity."

"Then maybe you can turn the spark into a blazing fire," I said.

Gran looked at me closely again, to see if I was making fun of her. I kept my face neutral and she smiled. "But one must handle men carefully, as if cooking small fish."

Amen to that, I thought.

■ ■ ■ ■

I left early so I'd arrive at the reception on the stroke of eight, when it began. My prime objective was getting the interview with Owen out of the way as quickly as possible, before the crowds arrived. I parked in a rear lot and walked around to the front of the building. From the back, the art gallery was a three-story brick structure with small slit-like windows; the kind you'd see in a castle. Maybe the architect figured art needed to be defended from barbarian hordes. I entered through double oak doors into a large atrium with glass walls that went up two floors. A balcony on the floor above overlooked the lobby. My gaze happened on a shiny new plaque next to the door, and I was surprised to see it was a dedication to the St. Claire Family for their generous gift of the monies needed to completely renovate the museum three years ago. I hadn't realized Roger was such a public benefactor.

The reception was in the huge lobby. Tables were arranged along either side, and the wait staff was putting the finishing touches on lavish piles of food. Obviously, a stand-up buffet had been planned. It was a good thing the floor was sturdy terrazzo.

A quick sweep and it would be clean. Eating off paper plates while trying to make conversation can be awfully messy.

As I did a quick scan of the crowd from where I stood in the doorway, I felt a momentary twitch of fear, a gut-level warning that it might be a good idea to turn around and run right out again. The last time I broke bread at the college, I ended up with a broken body lying under me. But lightning didn't strike twice, did it?

Keith walked across the lobby toward me, his face lit up with a welcoming smile.

"It's nice to see you here, Laura. They've got quite an event planned for the evening."

"Well, I'm here for business, not pleasure. I'm covering the occasion for the paper."

I looked up at him, admiring once again the chiseled jaw and rich head of hair. He seemed so strong and centered. Maybe a little too centered, like he was rooted to the spot. Still, I felt myself gravitate in his direction, wanting to lean on him. Once again I cursed my weakness for strong, stable men. Here I was swinging once again from the unreliable but exciting in the form of Owen to the stalwart — almost stodgy — Keith. But could I help myself? Of course not.

His gaze left me and I followed it across the room to where Heidi stood. She was dressed in a flowing arrangement of brightly colored robes that made her look like a large psychedelic shepherdess. The vacant expression on Keith's face told me he was entranced.

"You may not win this one," Auntie Mabel warned me. *"This guy's got it bad. If you fall for him, he'll just let you hit the ground."*

"The battle's not over yet," I replied in my head, with more confidence than I felt.

"Smile, you two!"

Keith and I dutifully turned in the direction of the voice and a camera went off.

Marty was already at work.

"Good shot, little darlin'," Marty said, sidling up to me. "The center of attention of this shindig is over there. He just started talking to the Amazon."

Marty drifted away to take more pictures, and I glanced at Keith to see if he had overheard Marty's description of his honey. By the expression on his face, he hadn't heard a thing. His focus was on Heidi's animated conversation with Owen. The jealous green devil had clearly taken residence on his shoulder, and I couldn't really blame him. Owen was at his best when he looked down at his shoes with his lovable "aw shucks" face and, at the same time, peeked up at you through the wave of hair falling over his forehead. Just an innocent, naive artist looking for a good woman to stroke his fevered brow and teach him the ways of the wicked world.

I shook myself. The guy was hypnotic. Heidi was touching his arm and devouring him with her eyes, completely under his spell. Keith mumbled something about seeing me later and made a beeline across the room. When he reached Heidi, he took her arm and whispered something in her ear. From the expression on her face and the way she pulled her arm out of his grasp, I could see she wasn't pleased. All the while, Owen stood slightly off to the side, watching and yet not watching, as though denying all responsibility for his part in creating any kind of conflict. There was something passive, almost feminine, in the way Owen liked to use his sex appeal to create awkward situations, then stand back and observe, as if what had happened wasn't his fault.

Again, Keith said something to Heidi. This time she turned to Owen with a dazzling smile, reached out and touched his arm, then allowed Keith to take her hand and lead her toward another group. But she stayed one step behind him, making it obvious she'd left Owen reluctantly.

I walked across the room to where Owen

stood, momentarily alone. I planted myself directly in front of him and took my notebook and pen out of my jacket pocket. I wore a red linen jacket over a white tailored blouse and black linen slacks. With my short, curly brown hair I looked highly efficient and professional, a regular Bob Woodward.

"I'm here to interview you for the *Ravensford Chronicle,* Mr. Reynolds."

His face froze, which told me he was really angry about last night. My heart sang. Then his complacent smile slipped back into place.

"Don't try to be funny, Laura."

"I'm not. This is my job."

"I don't usually give interviews. You know that."

"And I don't usually try to get them, at least not anymore. But you know what they say. Any publicity is good publicity. If you don't give me an interview, I'll write an article based on my extensive personal background information."

He hesitated, probably wondering if I was bluffing. "I can give you a few moments," he finally said.

I asked him about his concept of Superrealism, and sketched doodles of a stick-figure man with a dagger through his heart while he rattled on in his predictable way about the artist's true role as a mirror of nature. I pressed him on what he expected the students at Ravensford College to get out of his presence. The question seemed to please him, and he talked with animation about the value to the students of meeting someone who could serve as the role model of a commercially successful artist.

I was getting ready to ask him whether he also served as a role model of the artist as a lying, deceptive bastard who tries to bed one woman while another waits back at the inn, but before I could, a tall, thin woman who looked vaguely familiar intruded herself between us.

"Mr. Reynolds, I've missed you during your comings and goings," she said. "Are the accommodations proving to be comfortable?"

Owen seemed a bit confused for a moment, then the penny dropped as he recognized her.

"Certainly, Miss Collins. Everything is quite comfortable."

Ah, Millicent Ashcroft Collins of the Collins Inn, preserver of the colonial tradition.

"Hello, I'm Laura Magee with the *Ravensford Chronicle*," I said, smiling brightly.

She looked down her long, thin nose at me, as if newspaper reporters should have been expelled with the British.

"We pride ourselves on providing the most gracious accommodations in Ravensford," she said, turning toward Owen, giving me a choice view of her scrawny shoulder.

I wondered if all the recent openings of fancy bed and breakfasts in Ravensford had her worried. I decided to ask her if I got the chance.

"And we at the Collins Inn are very proud to be offering our hospitality to such a famous artist," she added.

Owen smiled faintly, appearing slightly uncomfortable. Maybe it was due to hearing such lavish praise, or maybe he was thinking that praise from a source like this could hurt his reputation.

A more perceptive woman would have recognized the mechanical politeness of Owen's response, but Millicent Collins was on a mission that precluded any sensitivity to the feelings of others. She was there to preserve, and if possible enhance, the memory of her distant, pseudo-heroic relative.

"You should really go up to the second floor of the museum if you have the time," she said with the tone of an order. "There's a wonderful bust of the Captain. The family commissioned it in the nineteenth century, but I believe it's based on a portrait by Trumbull that is unfortunately now lost."

I almost laughed out loud. Trumbull, the painter of the founding fathers, wouldn't have wasted any pigment on a portrait of the legend-in-his-own-mind captain.

"I will certainly try to find the opportunity," Owen said with a stiff smile. "Now, you'll have to excuse me. My companion is looking for me."

I watched him cross the room and put his arm around a slender woman a few inches taller than me, who had brown hair hanging halfway down her back. Young and beautiful, the long hair appeared seductive rather than silly. She rested her head against his shoulder as she listened to the conversation of the two couples standing across from her.

"Got all you need from him?" Marty said, appearing at my side like a genie.

Millicent Collins had disappeared from my vicinity as soon as Owen left. Maybe she was afraid I was going to ask some tough reporter-like questions about the precious captain.

"All I want," I replied. Suddenly, fighting with Owen over his new girlfriend seemed pointless. I'd just be buying into his image of himself as utterly irresistible.

"I'm going to ask His Holiness if I can take him off into one of the side rooms and get some more posed single shots. I'm working on my portrait skills. If they come out okay I'll send him some copies. Do you think he knows anyone in fashion photography?"

"Maybe a couple of models."

"You mean like the one he's with?"

"Exactly," I said, trying to keep all emotion out of my voice.

Marty shook his head. "He looks kinda spineless to me. What do women see in a guy like him?"

"Good looks, brains, fame," I murmured.

Marty stared at me. "Sounds like you've got it as bad as the rest of them."

"Not me," I said. "I'll take a plain, average guy any day."

"So there's still hope for me?"

He smiled in such a self-deprecating way, I could see why women might find him attractive. Although his face was rugged rather than handsome, he wore a tatty leather vest over a blue denim shirt, and he squinted across the room like he was checking out the north forty. He would appeal to women who always wanted to grow up to have a cowboy.

"Sorry, Marty. Office romances aren't my thing."

He smiled. "Not mine either, really."

Marty sauntered across the room with an exaggeratedly bowlegged stride. He spoke to Owen for a moment, and the two of them headed off into one of the side galleries. I figured they might be there a while. Owen was an avid photographer himself, often painting scenes from his own photos.

Suddenly alone, I surveyed the room. I felt oddly content, like the eddy of calm in the midst of a rushing stream. The woman I had seen with Owen detached herself from some people and headed in my direction. I expected her to walk past me and was surprised when she stopped and put out her hand.

"You must be Laura Magee. I'm Clarissa Revik."

I shook her long, thin hand and smiled politely. I wondered how she knew who I was, but played it cool. Like, hey, everyone in town knows Laura Magee.

"We have something in common," she said with a smile.

"What's that?"

"Owen."

Owen had told her about me! I was stunned. Stunned and hurt. Did he think that I was such a dog, his new girlfriend couldn't possibly be jealous?

"That hardly puts us in an exclusive club," I said, proud I'd regained my footing so quickly.

She laughed, a high musical sound. Apparently, everything about her was maddeningly attractive.

"Not in Boston," she said, "but in Ravensford, perhaps."

I granted her that. Even an unfaithful swine such as Owen probably hadn't been in town long enough to cut a wide swath through the female population.

"How did you know about me?" I asked. "Did Owen tell you?"

She shook her head. A curtain of hair swirled gracefully around her body. She looked like one of those slow-motion shampoo commercials.

"I did my research," she said.

"What kind of research?"

She took a step closer and lowered her voice. "I graduated from art school two years ago. After I mucked around for a while, thinking talent would be enough to make me successful, I realized it's who you know that counts, just like any other field. So I decided to find an established artist who would help promote my career."

"And striking up a personal relationship with Owen seemed promising?"

"Let's face it, artists are a selfish lot. No artist is going to promote another one unless there's something in it for him. I don't have money and I don't have connections. The only thing I have is me."

I studied her high cheekbones, full lips, gorgeous figure and perfect complexion.

"That's quite a bit," I said.

"Thank you."

"Has investing it in Owen paid off yet?"

"Definitely. Oh, don't misunderstand. Owen hasn't reformed and become human. He's made no effort at all to help my career. However, just by being around him, I've met gallery owners, museum curators and wealthy patrons. Whenever Owen is off preening, I make it a point to have my own little conversations with these people. I've already made a couple of sales, which, of course, I haven't mentioned to Owen. He'd think any sale by another artist would be bread stolen from his mouth."

"He'll find out, eventually. Especially if you're as honest with everyone you meet as you're being with me."

She shrugged. "Doesn't matter."

"So you aren't planning to stay with Owen for the long term?"

"I'm already seeing someone else. He's an older man and owns a large New York gallery. I see him when Owen is too busy painting to notice whether I'm alive or dead. I'm sure you can remember how often that happens."

I did and half-wished I'd made as good a use of those times as she obviously had.

"That's why I'm telling you all this. If I still wanted Owen, I wouldn't be so frank. But if you want him back, you can have him. This is our last trip together, although he doesn't know it. In fact, this may be our last night."

"Why did you even come out here with him if you've got a new . . ." I paused for the right word. "Sugar daddy" was dated and "lover" didn't quite fit someone who had such an overtly mercenary approach to her love life. "A new admirer lined up?" I finished.

Clarissa frowned. "I feel sorry for Owen. His sales have been fading. Super-realists are a dime a dozen these days, and urban scenes are harder to sell since all this terrorist stuff. That's why Owen came out here. He's thinking of doing country and landscape scenes, the whole nostalgia bit, which is not his thing at all."

Great. Now that Owen was down and out,

speeding into the long, dark tunnel of failure, Clarissa was willing to turn him over to me. Visions of long days spent walking on the beach, maybe up in Maine, while I helped him repair his tattered self-respect and begin a new career as a scenic painter, filled my mind. He'd be vulnerable and appreciative. His normal arrogance would dissolve and be replaced by genuine gratitude and love. When he became more famous than ever before, he would conscientiously give me all the credit and —

"Clarissa, when did you and Owen first become involved?"

"Four months ago."

I didn't have to whip out a calendar. That was two months before I'd seen Philippa prancing in the all together across Owen's living room. Which meant he'd started cheating on me with Clarissa six weeks after he and I met.

She must have read my mind because she reached out and put a hand on my arm. "I'm sorry, Laura. I thought you knew, although I did wonder why you made such a big deal over his one-off with Philippa."

"You knew about me?"

"Of course. Like I told you, I did my research. But I didn't steal him away from you, please don't think that. There were plenty of other women all along."

The room spun for one sickening moment, before it slowly settled back into place.

"You didn't know?" Clarissa's tone mixed sympathy and surprise.

I realized I had forgiven Owen for his tryst with Philippa. After all, she had once been his wife. Maybe I'd swallowed the "for old times' sake" line more than I thought I had. Clarissa on the side was harder to handle, even though she *was* a charmer. But to discover Owen had been so busy in bed he required a social secretary to keep his sexual appointments in order was the final blow. I hadn't even made the short list. I was just a foot soldier in Owen's battalion of concubines.

"Thank you for telling me, Clarissa."

My face must have been grim. I wasn't sure whether I wanted to cry, howl, or kick Owen in the crotch. Actually, all three seemed like a good idea.

"Will you be all right?" Clarissa seemed concerned.

I took consolation in the fact that by dropping Owen she'd be doing more damage to his manhood than I ever could, so I managed a smile. "I'll be fine. And thanks again for telling me."

She nodded and walked back toward Owen, who had returned to the lobby with Marty. The two men were talking earnestly, probably something about f-stops. A loud squawk sounded from the microphone, set up at one end of the lobby, and Winnie asked for everyone's attention. He motioned for Owen to join him. Owen sauntered over, looking down at his shoes in that phony, humble way he has.

"I'd like to say a few words about our celebrated guest," Winnie began, his jowls shaking vigorously as if this were going to be a particularly stirring call to arms. He then began to grind his way slowly through Owen's resumé, emphasizing each of his awards as if they were citations for artistic heroism.

After several minutes of boredom, I glanced behind me. My grandmother and Roger St. Claire stood at the end of the lobby, farthest from the speaker. I hadn't noticed them arrive. Gran saw me and I gave her a weak wave. My face must have betrayed my unhappy feelings, because she took a couple of steps toward me. St. Claire shifted over slightly, as if about to follow. I shook my head, hoping she'd stay where she was. The last thing I wanted was to chatter on about my personal problems in front of my boss.

A blurry object came down, making a line through my field of vision. Before I could register what it was, a crash echoed throughout the lobby. People jumped, some screamed, even Winnie paused mid-sentence as Roger St. Claire crumbled to the floor.

CHAPTER 14

It may be a cliché, but I did stand frozen to the spot as my brain took a few seconds to process what had happened. When I saw my grandmother turn and drop to her knees, I raced across the room, shoving aside a couple of immobile gawkers, and bent down next to her. Shards of what looked to be white plaster were spread out on the floor around us, like snowflakes.

"Are you okay?" I asked.

She nodded. "It's Roger."

His eyes were open and he appeared to be conscious, but his lips were tightly pressed together in shock or pain or both. He made a move to get to his feet by leaning on one elbow. But after a sharp cry, he fell backward.

Keith forced his way through the circle of onlookers, who were keeping a respectable distance away. Maybe they were scared of a second falling object.

"I've called the EMTs," Keith said. "Don't let him move. Something might be broken."

"Roger, are you all right?" Winnie bellowed next to my ear.

I glanced up at his quivering jowls and wondered if he was about to launch into a morale-boosting speech about the need for the injured to return to the front to stop the Hun.

"I should think it's obvious that he's not all right," Gran said, giving the college president a thoroughly repressive look. He nodded and shrank back a step.

"Oh, my God!" a woman's voice shrieked.

Millicent Collins staggered forward and looked at the figure on the floor as if her best friend was about to expire. The thought flitted through my mind that perhaps Roger and Millicent had been, or still were, an item. I hoped not, for Gran's sake. I didn't want her to go through the same sense of betrayal I felt.

I needn't have worried. Millicent bent forward and picked up the base of the statue that had fallen on Roger. It was made of some solid material because it hadn't shattered.

"It's the Captain," she screamed, showing surprising strength by holding the base out in front of her at arm's length. She gazed at it as if it were a skull and she'd launch into Hamlet's soliloquy any moment.

But Millicent was right. There, for all to see, was carved the Captain's rank and name.

"What's the matter with her?" Heidi asked, coming up to join Keith.

"Her great, great, great, great grandfather's head just broke," I said.

Heidi glanced around her for signs of brain matter, then stared at me as if I were demented.

"I mean the plaster cast of his head," I clarified.

Roger suddenly let out a piteous moan and reached up with his right hand. Since Gran was already busy holding the left one, I seized it. His eyes opened and he smiled at me.

"Auntie Mabel," he said like a little boy. "I hurt myself, Auntie Mabel."

His eyes closed again.

"Why did he call you Auntie Mabel?" Heidi asked, her eyes narrowing. I glanced over my shoulder and saw Keith standing right behind her, also listening with rapt attention.

"He's delirious," I said. Roger was squeezing my hand so hard that four of my fingers were threatening to merge into one. A little longer and I'd have a hand like a mitten.

"Why did you call her Auntie Mabel?" Heidi bellowed. If Roger had been dead, he would have heard her. His eyes popped open, wide with fear.

"Because she writes the *Ask Auntie Mabel* column for the paper," my grandmother said. "Now will you all please leave the man alone."

The one time I wished my grandmother could have come out with an obscure Taoist remark — something like "Who knows all the names in nature?" — and she clearly and concisely spills the beans.

What saved me from more interrogation and possible physical harm from Heidi was the simultaneous arrival of the EMTs and the police. In the ensuing confusion, I slipped through the crowd like an Indian scout and made my way upstairs to the shadowy second floor. Only the security lights were on, so I sat on the floor behind a large statue and rested for a moment in the semi-darkness as I tried to recover from what had just happened and hoped Heidi hadn't followed me.

After a few minutes I felt composed enough to look around. The art gallery was designed like a small theatre with the second floor mezzanine running around three sides of the lobby below. A waist-high glass wall, topped by a wooden railing, defined the boundary. Rows of busts on pedestals were placed at regular intervals along the wall. They reminded me of an ancient Roman bath, or maybe it was an Italian restaurant I'd been to once in New Jersey.

Staying well back from the edge so I couldn't be seen from below, I followed the heads. I didn't pause to read the inscriptions on the bases until I came upon a pedestal missing its occupant. Sure enough, it was the Captain's, as all the erroneous information on the plaque made clear. I peeked through the glass wall and estimated I was directly over the spot where Gran and Roger had been standing.

The pedestal was at least two feet from the wall, so the bust couldn't have accidentally toppled into the lobby due to an unnoticed seismic event. Someone had lifted the plaster head and carefully dropped it to the lobby. Even though the head itself was hollow and quite light, the base was probably heavy enough to do some injury to anyone it might hit.

I edged closer and saw Heidi, who stood out from the crowd in all her magnificent, muscular blondness. She surveyed the lobby, probably on the lookout for my head of short, curly hair. If she saw it, I had a bad feeling it wouldn't be on my shoulders for very long. She'd be sure to suspect some dark conspiracy in which I had told her to dump Keith in order to get him for myself.

I took another peek and saw Owen standing below me and off to the right. He was in line with the bust of Louisa May Alcott on the next pedestal. The evil thought crossed my mind that there would be a sort of poetic justice in having him done in by the bust of the author of *Little Women.* The idea was tempting, but I pushed it from my mind. Scorned, angry and injured I might be, but I wasn't going to resort to murder. At least, not yet.

"See anything interesting?" a soft voice asked from the shadows behind me.

I spun around, relieved that in the dim glow of the security lights my guilty blush wouldn't show. Michael Farantello emerged from the darkness.

"Hi, Chief," I said in a shaky voice. In these circumstances, I felt more comfortable using his title. "You gave me quite a start."

He nodded as if scaring me had been his plan all along.

"How did you get here so fast?" I asked.

"I was already here. I walked in just before all hell broke loose."

"I didn't know you were interested in art."

"I've been making a point of attending campus events since Proctor's death." He glanced around, as if noticing where we were for the first time. "You shouldn't be up here, Laura. This could be a crime scene."

"I was trying to get away from the crowd."

"Why?"

I debated whether to tell him the truth or not. If it had been daylight and I felt okay, I would have lied. But we were in the dark and my head whirled.

"Because Heidi found out I'm Auntie Mabel and now she's out to get me. It's a long story."

He showed no surprise.

"You already knew I'm Auntie Mabel, didn't you?"

He nodded.

"How did you find out?"

I thought he'd give me an inscrutable look and say something like "it's my job to know." But he said, "I knew who the original Auntie Mabel was, so I knew she'd died. We worked together once in a while."

"Worked together?"

"Sometimes one of her letters would

216

include evidence of a crime that had been committed or was about to be committed. She'd pass the letter along to me and I'd investigate. When she died, I asked Roger to tell me who took over the job. I would have contacted you in a few more weeks if it looked like you were going to hang in there."

"So I'd be your informant the way Auntie was?"

"Would you have a problem with that?"

A person writing to an advice columnist couldn't expect confidentiality. Heck, that's why most of them gave phony names. I wasn't a priest or lawyer. If I really thought I could prevent a serious crime, I guess I'd be a police snitch. I told Farantello the snitch part.

"We prefer 'informant' or 'concerned citizen,' " he said.

It was my turn to shrug.

"So this is where the head was," he said, walking up to the pedestal.

"Yeah. Unless it took a hop, skip and a jump and cleared the railing, it had help."

"Did you see anyone up here right before it fell?"

"I wasn't looking. I had things on my mind."

Farantello walked to the railing and looked down. He turned back to me with a frown.

"I don't like coincidences," he said. "Two serious crimes at the college in one week makes me uncomfortable. I want to see a connection."

"Heidi Lipton is one connection; she's here tonight," I said. I figured if they took Heidi away in cuffs, I could get out of the museum alive.

"When the statue fell, she was standing next to Keith, on the side of the room, by the college president. A number of people saw her, including me." Farantello smiled. "She's hard to miss."

"What about Keri Tinsdale?"

"Keith has been keeping tabs on her. She isn't working here tonight. It's possible she slipped in unnoticed, but why would she try to drop a bust on Roger St. Claire?"

"How is Roger?" I'd been so busy worrying about myself, I'd forgotten to ask.

"I spoke to the medics briefly before I came up here. They say Roger most likely has a broken collarbone. The base of the bust slightly grazed his head. That's why he was a bit loopy for a few minutes. But he should be okay in the long run."

I breathed a sigh of relief for both my grandmother and my future employment. I couldn't be sure a new owner would choose to keep me on board as Auntie Mabel, dispensing pearls of wisdom.

"So, any theories?" Farantello asked, looking at me expectantly.

"I don't know why anyone would want to bean Roger St. Claire, but I'm sure it isn't because of our hard-hitting investigative reporting. the *Chronicle* is corruption and dishonesty's best friend with its hear-no-evil-see-no-evil approach."

"What about your grandmother?"

"What about her? She wouldn't want to kill a guy she was going out with. Anyway, she was standing right next to him."

"That's my point. Maybe someone was trying to kill her and aimed wrong."

I remembered Gran moving just before the bust fell, and I told Farantello.

"Any connection between your grandmother and Jack Proctor? I mean one you didn't tell me about?"

"Nope. Proctor was an old friend of my grandfather's. He'd been around lately, trying to get her to donate Granddad's pictures to the college gallery. That's all there is."

"Are you sure the pictures aren't valuable?"

"Granddad never was able to sell any, except a few portraits he did of local people. He tried to get an agent a few times but finally gave up. I could take a look at his stuff and tell you what I think, but I really doubt they have anything more than historical value."

"Why did Proctor want them?"

I thought back to my conversation with him on the night he died. "He said he wanted to have them in the gallery to show the history of art at the college and as a memorial to my grandfather. I think he was also trying to encourage current art majors by showing them that Ravensford College had an artistic tradition."

"And that's why he invited Owen Reynolds to be here? He wanted to boost the art program?"

"I guess so."

Farantello nodded in the special way they must teach them at the police academy, where a nod means they think you're lying through your teeth.

"Why don't you come downstairs with me now, Laura?" he said, putting a gentle hand on my elbow.

Maybe it was hearing about Owen's trysts, maybe it was seeing Roger St. Claire almost killed, or maybe it was someone showing a little kindness, but as I started to walk, my knees buckled and Farantello caught me in his arms before I fell. For a little guy, he was strong. He righted me easily and held me against his chest.

"Are you all okay?" he whispered with real concern.

"Hmm," I said, enjoying the moment. "It's been a tough night."

He didn't say anything and I drew back to see his face. It had the same sad, tired but kind expression it always had. But the face moved toward me and soft lips gently pressed against mine. I pressed back — hard. Losing myself in a moment of mindless emptiness.

"We'd better go downstairs now," Farantello said, his voice husky.

I nodded and let him escort me down the stairs, still feeling a bit giddy after the kiss. I also felt like an elegant lady as I looked out on the crowd in the glittering lobby.

"Your grandmother went with St. Claire to the hospital," Farantello said. "They shared an ambulance with Millicent Collins."

"Was she hurt?"

"No, hysterical. But she kept making so much noise about the captain having died twice, I decided it would be best if we got her away from the scene."

"She'll get over it," I said. "It's probably worth a human interest story in the *Chronicle,* which *will* be good publicity for the inn. I'll make sure Joy Pleasant, our feature writer, hears about it."

"Do you have a way to get home?"

"My car is here."

Heidi saw me walk down the stairs and began making her way across the lobby. A woman on a mission, she straight-armed people out of the way like a running back in sight of the goal line. Her hands were clenched as if ready to bend a pipe, but I had a feeling the only "pipe" she wanted to bend was the one I breathed through.

"You have to save me from the Avenging Aryan," I whispered to Farantello.

"What has she got against you? Why does she care so much that you're Auntie Mabel?"

I gave him a quick, abbreviated version of the Keith story. He had the nerve to laugh.

"I can see how she might wonder, Laura, since Keith was your escort at the dinner right after she dropped him. To the suspicious mind it might all seem rather convenient."

"Yeah, but can we have a good laugh over this some other time?" I watched with apprehension as Heidi strode to within twenty feet of us. The expression on her face didn't seem to invite a congenial sharing of viewpoints.

I started to pull free to make a bolt for the door. If I could get around the heavy woman in the blue floral print, I'd have a shot at getting away while Heidi was rolling over her. But Farantello held tightly to my arm. He made an almost imperceptible gesture and a strapping young giant in uniform broke through the crowd at a trot.

"Escort Ms. Magee to her car," Farantello said, "and make sure she gets off all right."

The officer stayed close beside me as we left the museum. I felt like a dignitary, although some of the people watching seemed to be thinking that I might be under arrest. I glanced back as the glass door closed behind me, and saw Heidi staring after me with a vindictive look. I wondered if she was putting some kind of ancient Teutonic curse on me, but decided she probably wasn't.

She was the type who'd want to do the job herself.

CHAPTER 15

I had a rough night and woke up in the morning feeling lousy. At first I thought it was guilt. When it comes to guilt, I hate being a woman because we're so quick to take it on. I knew I wasn't technically guilty of deceiving Heidi. I had answered her letter in full compliance with whatever ethics code covers those who give unprofessional advice. I hadn't known Keith, so my opinion was completely unbiased. There was absolutely no reason for me to feel guilty.

Oh, sure, there was the little matter of going out with Keith later on, but I didn't tell Heidi to dump him. Oops, I guess I was the one who did. But she didn't have to listen. Who would listen to someone called Auntie Mabel, anyway?

I rolled over on my side. Even though Heidi could be waiting outside in helmet and breastplate, with sword in hand, ready to sever my head from my body, what really bothered me wasn't guilt. It was the other deadly twin of the female psyche — shame. The more I thought about what Clarissa had told me last night, the more I realized I should have seen it coming. Given the number of times Owen said we couldn't get together because he was working, he'd have had time to slap three coats of paint on the ceiling of the Sistine Chapel.

If I hadn't been so blinded by the idea that a semi-famous painter wanted me as his girlfriend, I would have detected the three warning signs of a cheating male: the vague excuses when he had to cancel a date, the accidental then quickly glossed-over references to recent movies or plays we hadn't seen together, and the slight hesitation at critical moments before saying my name, as if he were rapidly running through a mental Rolodex to make sure he didn't mix me up with someone else.

I had been a fool, and I was ashamed, but I wasn't sure what to do. A part of me wanted to confront Owen, really have it out with him. Then I'd walk away, having salvaged some shred of self-respect. Another part of me wanted to snatch him up as Clarissa let him fall and offer to start all over again, if he'd change his ways.

"You can't expect a tiger to change its spots,"

Auntie Mabel warned.

"Stripes," I corrected.

"Whatever, as you young people say. The point is the same. Owen is unfaithful, that's part of his nature. And although, like all attractive young women, you believe that you have supernatural powers, you are not going to be able to change him. If you go back to him, you will simply be having this same conversation with yourself six months or a year from now."

I hated to admit it, but the old girl had a point. And when you hear the truth you'd better listen up, even if it comes from a figment of your imagination. Another person on my mind was Chief Farantello. I had to stop calling him Chief. His name was Michael. If by any stroke of fate we ever ended up in bed together, I couldn't very well turn to him and say, "Wow! The earth really moved for me that time, Chief."

Owen and Keith and Chief . . . Michael. My mind was filled with men. It's really unusual for me to have more than one man in my fantasies at the same time. I have always been serially monogamous. The line may be semi-long but it has always been single file. I can also say that I have never been involved with a man when I didn't at least toy with the idea of marrying him in this or some roughly parallel universe. If I ever gave up completely on the thought of marriage, I would probably become celibate. Of course, I doubted that I ever would give up. Even if I was single at the age of eighty, I'd harbor hopes.

Footsteps sounded down the hall outside my room, and I heard the creak of old wood as someone descended the stairs. Gran must be up. I leapt out of bed and pulled on my sweatshirt and jeans, which I've heard is the way every star reporter begins her day.

By the time I got down to the kitchen, Gran had the coffee pot going and was filling a bowl with some kind of Asian grain she kept moldering in a refrigerator container. I'd tried it once at her insistence, but it had tasted so . . . well . . . healthy is the only word I can use to describe it. Since then, I'd given it a pass.

I said good morning and retrieved a box of corn flakes from the closet. Gran mumbled her reply. She stood staring out the window as the coffee dripped into the pot. Gran wasn't very good in the morning until she'd had her shot of caffeine. It might seem odd that someone so dedicated to Asian ways hadn't converted to green tea or a nice cup of miso soup to start things rolling. I'd asked her why, shortly after I moved into the house. She had stared into space for a long moment with such an intense look on her face, I was afraid I had insulted her by suggesting she was less than fully dedicated to her lifestyle of choice. But when she answered me, all she said was, "She who desires little is easily satisfied. And this," she said, holding up her cup of java, "is the little I desire."

A good cup of coffee to start the day wouldn't be enough to make me die satisfied, and I wasn't quite sure it was enough for Gran, at least not anymore. The haggard, worried look on her face this morning suggested that Roger St. Claire had perhaps joined the list of things she desired, and possibly was even edging out coffee for the number one slot.

Gran poured each of us a cup. I began to spoon up corn flakes while she picked at her bowl of grain. I waited until the coffee fix had enough time to take effect, then asked how Roger was.

"He has a broken collarbone. They've placed him in a rather peculiar-looking cast to keep his shoulder immobilized."

"What about the blow to his head?"

"A bad bump, but he doesn't have a concussion."

"Good." I returned to eating but could

228

tell that by Gran's expression that there was more to come.

"I'm going to stay with him until he's recovered," she said.

"You mean at the hospital?"

"At his home. The doctor said he could leave the hospital today."

Two dates and she's going to move in with the guy, I thought. That seemed a little fast, even by today's standards.

"Doesn't he have anyone else who can take care of him?"

I knew St. Claire lived in a big, old house. In Ravensford it would qualify as a mansion. He must have help. Surely, if Gran wasn't there with him, he wouldn't end up lying helpless on the floor, wishing he had a medical alert buzzer.

"A woman comes in four times a week to clean, but he cooks for himself or eats out," Gran said. "There's no live-in help."

"What about family?"

"He has a son in town, but Roger has never said very much about him. I don't think they're close."

I stood up and popped a piece of bread in the toaster. Not immediately acclaiming her plan as a good idea was the same as criticizing it, but what was really wrong with it? Here were two consenting adults, so where was the harm?

"You won't mind living alone, will you?" my Grandmother asked.

I realized with a jolt of surprise that I wasn't really thrilled with the idea. In fact, it bothered me a lot. Funny, I'd lived by myself in Boston and never felt nervous or afraid, but the thought of rattling around in this old house all by myself definitely lacked appeal. Maybe I'd done better in the city because I'd always lived in an apartment building where other people were only a piece of cheap wallboard away. The fact that those people could be indifferent, crazy or murderous didn't matter. They were people, and human closeness meant you never felt truly alone. Anything above the normal speaking tone could easily be overheard by any but the stone deaf. While in a neighborhood like this one, where the houses were far apart and concealed by trees, even high-decibel screams would go unnoticed unless you managed to stagger out into the middle of the street.

In the last few days I'd been on the scene of one murder and one attempted murder. And that was without counting the attack on me, which I definitely did count. Those statistics would make anyone a bit jumpy. I took a deep breath and tried to find my place of inner peace. Unfortunately, the door to inner peace was locked.

"I'll be fine here by myself," I said. Brave words muttered in a petulant tone.

Gran nodded but gave me a long, dubious look.

"And if you are concerned about what people will think, Roger has five bedrooms in his house. So there will be no cause for gossip."

I refrained from pointing out that most people would assume four of those bedrooms were going unused.

"So you'll cook for him," I said, trying to diffuse the situation by focusing on details.

"And he may need some help bathing."

I let that slide, although somehow it seemed to undermine the multiple bedroom argument.

"How long will you be staying there?"

"At least a month. That's when the cast is due to come off. After that, it will depend on how Roger feels." Gran smiled. "But I'll visit you several times a week, and you can always come to Roger's house to see me."

I stared at my empty cereal bowl as I summoned my courage to ask the real question.

"Are you sure, after only two dates, you want to make that kind of a commitment, Gran? I mean, Roger could always hire a nurse. He certainly has the money. You'll be taking care of him when he's almost a semi-invalid. That won't be much fun."

"Exactly the point. I'll be seeing him while he's at his worst. It's a way to find out if we have a future together or not. I wish I'd had the opportunity to live with your grandfather before we were engaged. I never would have married him."

"You wouldn't?" I asked in surprise.

"Of course not."

"What was wrong with him?" I could hear a trace of anger in my voice. My grandfather, after all, had taught me to paint. I didn't want to hear him maligned without a good reason.

Gran sighed. It was a sigh I recognized; the same one I used when I was about to embark on a task I didn't really want to do.

"He was an opinionated, self-centered man who never cared what he did to anyone else as long as it benefited him."

Gran must have seen I wasn't convinced, because she hurried to add, "Plus, he was a hound."

The image of a dog with long ears and a vague facial resemblance to my grandfather, loping along with its nose to the ground, flashed through my mind. It took a moment before the import of her words sank in.

"You mean he chased other women?"

My grandmother's laugh was bitter. "Chased and caught. When we were first married and he was still in his late twenties, it was undergraduates. Later, it was graduate students, then junior faculty."

I found it hard to reconcile my picture of the rather kindly if somewhat eccentric man, who had charmed me as a child, with the unregenerate lothario my grandmother portrayed.

"Why didn't you leave him?" I asked.

"I didn't know about his philandering until we'd been married five years, and by then your mother was born. I only found out when some twenty-year-old showed up on my doorstep to inform me that my husband would soon be divorcing me to marry her. When I told Victor, he said she was deluded, a girl who had confused his attempts to guide her artistic creativity with a personal interest, a young woman given to romantic obsessions."

"It could have been true."

"The girl knew about the butterfly tattoo on your grandfather's rear end. He got it in France. Do you think she would have discovered that while he was guiding her creativity?"

A tattoo on Grandfather's butt! I'd been

thinking about getting one there myself. Now I was glad I hadn't.

"But you said there were others. How did you find out about them?"

"I cultivated a few women friends at the college. They kept me informed. They were women who'd had similar problems with their husbands. The college is a small community and things don't stay secret for long. I never said anything to him after the first time. I knew it wouldn't make any difference. But I kept a record of names. I never told your mother. But once she was happily married and seemed settled, I threatened your grandfather with the messiest, most public divorce the town of Ravensford had ever seen. I also said I'd present the college with enough detailed evidence of his moral turpitude to get him fired."

I stared at the farm-style sink and the knotty pine cabinets, trying to cling to something unchanging. My gentle, Taoist-quoting Gran had turned into a fury. A Medea seeking revenge on her unfaithful husband. If an earthquake had suddenly swept through western Massachusetts, causing the streets to break open and the buildings to fall, I would hardly have been more surprised.

I also realized that maybe Gran and I had

a lot in common when it came to men. On some level I had always felt that we were more alike than my mother and I. Mom and Dad had the kind of stable, happy relationship that had gone out of style after the 1950s. I envied them, but at the same time I wasn't sure their kind of life was in the cards for me. I wasn't certain I could rub off the rough edges of my personality enough to make a happy, stable relationship work. Or maybe I just tended to make bad choices when it came to men, picking the exciting losers over the nice guys. Maybe man problems skipped a generation.

"What did Granddad say when you gave him your ultimatum?" I asked, hoping to learn from her mistakes.

"He fell apart. He started crying about how he'd lose his job and his position in the town. He even went on about how he'd rather kill himself. Of course, I didn't believe him for a minute. Your grandfather never would have left the world before he'd given it the full benefit of his company. But as he talked, I began to realize it wouldn't help me much to be known as the wife of a philanderer. This is a small town and twenty-five years ago people's minds were even narrower than they are today. No matter how innocent, the woman always shouldered part of the blame."

"So you forgave him?"

A glint of something hard flashed behind Gran's eyes. "I don't think a woman ever does that, not completely. But I got over it, after a fashion. We never shared a bed again, and I made sure he'd think twice before he returned to his philandering ways. I made him change his will."

"Change it how?"

"When he died, he wanted all of his paintings to go directly to the college. I think he took great satisfaction in the idea they wouldn't disappear. He clung to the hope that someday they would be rediscovered by an eager young scholar who would see they received the attention they deserved. I demanded he leave them to me. If I outlived him, I'd decide whether the college got them or they ended up in the Ravensford dump. He was like a dog on a short leash after that . . ." Gran paused. "An intelligent man knows his own worth and does not require others to recognize it. Your grandfather was not an intelligent man."

There was one bit of Asian wisdom I could follow.

"I also made him destroy all his portraits of women. He slept with most of the women he used as models."

I thought of Jack Proctor and Heidi. Maybe my granddad and Jack had more in common than their professions. "Did that stop his cheating?"

"As far as I know. At least, none of my informants at the college ever reported any new women."

I slumped back in my chair.

My grandmother's expression softened and she reached over and took my hand. "I don't want to upset you, Laura, but you have to understand why I'm going to stay with Roger. I have a few more good years left, and I want to find out if I should spend them with him. But I have to be sure. I'd rather be alone than live with a man I don't love."

I gave her hand a squeeze and smiled. "Makes sense to me, Gran. Give Roger my best." I walked to the kitchen door. "Did Roger happen to notice anything unusual right before the bust fell?"

She shook her head. "Neither one of us saw a thing. One minute we were standing there feeling safe and warm, and the next minute that stupid statue almost killed him. After listening to Millicent Ashcroft yap about it in the ambulance last night, you'd have thought the least Roger could have done was try to cushion the statue's fall. I felt like telling her that smashing the bust was the act of an aesthetically just God."

"It wasn't an act of God or an accident. Someone threw that bust over the railing."

Gran's jaw dropped and for once a handy Taoist saying didn't spring to her lips. "Are you certain?"

I nodded. "And so is Chief Farantello. So maybe you and Roger should sort of stay on the alert."

"Why would anyone want to hurt either one of us?"

"I have no idea, if you don't."

She shook her head. "It must have been an act of mindless vandalism, or a student prank gone awry. No one would intentionally want to hurt us."

"You could be right. But be careful. After all, you are responsible for Roger's well-being."

She nodded, and her face took on a firmness of purpose I had never seen before. If she stayed by his side, it would be all to the good. If they were together, they could look after one another.

While they looked after one another, I'd try to find out what was going on.

CHAPTER 16

I left for the newspaper right after breakfast. I threw my bag on the desk, then walked down the hall to Stan Aaronson's office. I figured I'd better check in with the general editor to see if he wanted me to write the story about last night's events. Inside his tiny office, Stan bent over his desk, his green eyeshade in place. He stared at his computer screen. He always seemed to be sitting right there, working. I wondered if he ever went to the bathroom. I wondered if his eyeshade helped him see the computer screen.

For a general editor, Stan's duties were remarkably circumscribed. He edited. In all the months I'd been there, he'd never made a general policy decision. All decisions were handled by Roger St. Claire. But Roger called Stan the "wordmeister" and language was his job. He shaped the story. When I gave a perfunctory knock on the door of his cell, and then stepped inside, he glanced up with a trace of annoyance, as if I were keeping him from his job.

"Stan, I need to know if I've been authorized to write the story about the incident at the college art museum last night."

"Mr. St. Claire called me first thing this morning," Stan replied in a raspy voice that sounded like it didn't get used very much. "He said for you to go ahead on it."

"Any other instructions?"

"Write well," he said, and I thought I saw the hint of a smile.

When I returned to the newsroom, Bill and Joy were chatting at their desks. It was unusual for them to hang around in the morning. When I asked, they said they had just wanted to check on Roger's condition and decided to stay and do some work.

By some sort of mental osmosis, they seemed to know I once again encroached on their news reporters' domain. Both had mumbled their hellos with accusing glances. They managed to make me feel like I was stealing the food from their children's mouths. Although, now that I thought about it, St. Claire hadn't promised me any extra compensation. He'd merely hinted at some future promotion. I'd have to get a firmer commitment from Roger while Gran had him at her mercy. He might be more approachable if he thought that I was in the position to cut off his daily sponge bath.

A half hour later, I put the finishing touches on my story, which true to *Chronicle* form, gave just the facts and even limited those. The whole thing had been a horrible accident, I suggested. I didn't even remotely imply that this must have been, at best, an act of dangerous vandalism and, at worst, attempted murder. I dropped the copy off in Stan's office. As I was returning to my desk, ready to pull another letter out of the Aunt Mabel shopping bag, the front door opened and Keith Campbell walked up to the counter.

He still looked good. Seeing him stand at the counter, a rush of emotions washed over me: a feeling of security mixed in with a healthy dose of lust — the same way I felt the first time we'd met. Keith smiled at me and made a small gesture indicating he'd like me to join him outside. I glanced over at Bill and Joy, who were carefully pretending not to pay attention. Then I lifted the gate and slipped over to Keith's side of the counter. I grabbed my coat and almost skipped out the front door.

It was one of those days in late September when it starts out cold enough to warn you that bad things are coming in a couple of months, but then warms up enough by afternoon to remind you of the summer regretfully left behind. At mid-morning there was still a chill in the air, and I was glad to have my light coat.

"Sorry to bother you at work," Keith began. "I tried to catch you at home but you'd already left. Your grandmother told me you'd be here. I'm not angry at you for the Auntie Mabel thing, Laura. I was so bent out of shape when I barged into your office, I don't blame you for not telling me who you were. And based on the letter Heidi wrote to you, distorting the facts, I don't think your reply was unreasonable."

"I'm glad that you feel that way, Keith." Hearing that the man you wanted to have fall in love with you didn't hate you was a beginning. A small beginning, but as Gran would say, every journey begins with the first step.

"And you did try to help me get Heidi back by going to the dinner with me."

I struggled not to blush with guilt. For an ex-cop, he could certainly be naive about women. Of course, his profound innocence was probably what had attracted Heidi to him in the first place. Only a man who automatically put women on a pedestal would feel he had to remain loyal to the

242

Hubcap Queen.

"I've convinced Heidi that she shouldn't blame you either," Keith continued. "She realizes you didn't know me when you answered her letter, and later you were only trying to make her jealous so she'd take me back."

I stared hard at Keith to see if this was some kind of a joke. There was no way Heidi would swallow that story. Maybe he'd bend over slapping his thighs any second, shouting that he'd "got me!" But his beautiful eyes retained their childlike solemnity, and I knew he was serious. Serious but wrong. I was sure Heidi's feelings were still borderline homicidal when it came to me. Maybe they had moderated somewhat from last night, but I didn't think we were about to have a girls' night out together. I wasn't quite ready to meet her anywhere but in a crowded room where there were armed guards.

He cleared his throat in a way that told me important news was coming. I glanced around at the surrounding rooftops, wondering if the news involved Heidi getting a bead on me through a sniper scope.

"I just wanted you to be the first to know that Heidi and I are back together again."

"How nice," I replied automatically. Then

common sense took over. "But isn't she still a murder suspect?"

"Farantello seems to believe that whoever dropped that bust on Roger last night is probably the same person who knifed Jack Proctor. And Heidi was standing right next to me when that happened, so she's off the hook for both."

"Why does the Chief (I had to stop calling him that!) think it had to be the same person?"

Keith shook his head. "He didn't say. Maybe he can't believe there would be two killers wandering around the campus, given the very low murder rate in town."

"What about Keri Tinsdale?"

"She was in her dorm room during last night's reception. At least four students saw her at the time of the attack." Keith smiled. "And you were right in the middle of the lobby, so you're off the hook."

"So the suspect list has gone from three to zero. Farantello can't be happy about that." I paused. "And, of course, no one saw a person up there dropping the bust."

"It's not easy to see up to the second floor unless you crane your neck. No one was spotted going up the front stairway, either, but there are back stairs behind the main gallery. No guards were on duty there, so he or she could easily have slipped upstairs unseen."

"Well," I said, putting on my happy face, "I'm glad you and Heidi are back together again. When is the wedding?"

Keith frowned. "We're back to dating again. I'm not sure about a wedding."

I tried to look innocent. "Oh, I thought Heidi was anxious for the two of you to get married."

"She's changed her mind. She thinks we should wait a while."

I nodded. Clever Heidi. She had made her move too soon, so she'd changed her tactics. Of course, it was also possible that after meeting Owen last night, she'd come to believe she could do better and was keeping her options open. At any rate, since she had Keith back, perhaps she really would forgive me. After all, she'd won and I'd lost. She could afford to be gracious. And poor Keith didn't know there had ever been a fight.

Keith proved this by leaning forward and giving me a brotherly hug. "Thanks for all your help, Laura."

I wasn't sure what help I had been. I certainly hadn't planned to bring the love-birds back together. Sometimes our worst intentions can end up bringing about good, damn it. If you could call Keith and Heidi together good.

He walked across to the parking lot, looking as desirable as ever.

I walked back into the newsroom and flopped down behind my desk, still feeling a little raw about losing Keith.

"You never had him," Auntie Mabel objected.

"I had something better. I had the dream of having him."

"And now you have to face the facts."

"Which are?" I figured it was about time to get someone else's opinion on the real facts of the situation.

"As far as potential relationships are concerned, you currently have two. You have a former boyfriend who constantly cheated on you and now has a mistress who is about to abandon him, and a man who is an officer of the law and has not, as of yet, even invited you out on a date."

"Sounds like more than I had two days ago. Now get lost."

I went through my files. To my surprise, I had already written enough Auntie Mabel replies to cover me for tomorrow. Since I had worked last night and come in early today, I figured I could take the rest of the day off. I was badly in need of some exercise to get my head back on straight, so I checked it out with Stan to see if I could leave early.

"As soon as Dorie comes in," he said, not glancing away from his computer screen. "She's supposed to be in early today."

Dorie charged through the door five minutes later, her blouse barely covering her midriff, and the ring in her eyebrow virtually aquiver.

"Wow! Where you go, people die," she announced.

I was glad to see that Joy had left and Bill was in the men's room. He spent an inordinate amount of time in there. I wondered why, but couldn't think of a tactful way to ask.

"First of all, no one died last night. Secondly, there is no cause-and-effect connection between my presence and either of the two incidents to which you are referring," I replied primly.

"Huh?"

"It's not my fault."

"Oh, right. Whose fault was it?"

"It was an accident."

Dorie's eyes narrowed. "The word's already out. No way the Captain's bust got from its pedestal over the wall without help."

I shrugged. "Probably some vandal. Vandalism happens all the time at colleges."

"A vandal might have smashed that statue on the floor, but throwing it over the balcony into a crowd of people is something else. Somebody could have been killed."

"Roger St. Claire almost was."

"I wonder if someone was purposely trying to do him in." Dorie leaned in closer, but she was still talking far too loud.

I motioned for her to lower her voice as I saw Bill make his way back from the men's room. "Who would want to 'do him in'?"

"What about his creepy son, Mark?"

"Who?"

"His son. Mark teaches at the college. He's in the computer science department. Word is, a robot acts more humanly than he does."

"He's not a people person?"

"Not even close. Connie, a friend of mine majoring in math, says that even the other faculty members think he's a weird genius of some kind."

"Okay, but why would he want to kill his father?"

"The first thing that crossed my mind when I heard the boss was hurt was to wonder whether his son would be in here today, running things."

"He inherits?"

Dorie shrugged. "Who else? He's

St. Claire's only kid. It stands to reason."

"Why would Mark want to kill his father now?"

Before she could answer, a man walked into the office. As Dorie sauntered over to the counter, she gave the potential customer an annoyed look for disturbing her conversation.

"Think about it," Auntie Mabel whispered. *"Nothing would worry St. Claire's son more than the possibility of his father remarrying."*

"You think?"

"I used to get letters about that kind of thing all the time. A child expects to inherit, then the parent decides to remarry. The child sees his future being pulled out from under him and feels badly wronged. Roger's son was probably counting on that inheritance, and all of a sudden he sees it being snatched away by your grandmother."

"Gran is no gold digger," I objected.

"Do you think the boy is willing to take that chance? He throws the bust. Whichever one gets killed, he's still ahead. If his father dies, he inherits immediately before his father has the opportunity to remarry. If he hits your grandmother, he eliminates a threat to his future fortune."

I thought about Auntie Mabel's theory. It made so much sense, I called the college to find out when Mark St. Claire had office hours. The woman who answered the phone said he didn't have any official office hours this semester. When I said I was a reporter from the *Ravensford Chronicle* who wanted to interview him for an article, she said he was usually in his office from one to two o'clock. Good. I had enough time for a workout at the gym and a quick lunch. I wanted to feel strong when I faced Roger St. Claire's son.

Big Billy's Gym occupies the top floor of what used to be Sandorval's Furniture warehouse. People used to buy furniture right out of the warehouse. Sergei Sandorval, from what people have told me, was a marketing genius of sorts. He believed that even if you charged normal retail prices, people would happily pay them and think they were getting a bargain, especially if they were in a large unfinished space with twenty-foot ceilings and industrial lighting. Sergei stayed in business for twenty years, only selling out after the cold war ended, when he could return to Russia and live like a czar.

The warehouse was then divided up into four commercial rentals, and Big Billy, a man of great girth, opened a gym. According to those who remembered him, Big Billy never hefted anything other than food and beer. Although he himself was no model of physical fitness, he purchased good second-hand equipment cheap from a chain that had gone out of business. He also knew that the essence of running a successful gym was simple: keep the prices down and have lots of heavy things to lift. The gym had no pool. Its locker rooms were infrequently cleaned by a surly, underpaid staff member who appeared to be in a prison pre-release program. Billy paid minimal rent, and he prospered. The more he prospered, the more he ate. One morning the opening staff discovered him sprawled across a weight bench, dead of a coronary. It was the first time anyone had ever seen Billy using his own equipment.

Although the next owner kept Big Billy's name on the door, he was called York. No one knew whether York was his first, last, or even his real name. Some people speculated that he was a displaced New Yorker. I figured he had been looking for a good alias and glanced at one of the weight plates in the gym and taken the York name.

It was a tough name, but York was the kind of guy who lived up to it. The lazy staff was replaced with eager go-getters, and now you could eat off the locker room floors — assuming you should ever want to. I'd seen York grab a beefy guy who was shouting obscenities over some imagined insult and toss him out the door. York hadn't even broken a sweat. Thin and wiry, anywhere between thirty-five and fifty, he boasted a ponytail and a closed-mouth approach to things.

Stories spread around the gym that he was a former mercenary who had run guns in Asia until his partners were permanently put out of business by the Red Chinese. Others said that he was ex-CIA and had done bad things to people to ascertain information vital to national security. Some even said he was a DEA plant, placed in the gym to get information for a future large-scale raid on steroid abusers.

In the mere four weeks I'd been a member, I'd heard all these stories because I was one of the few women the guys talked to. A handful of women around my age who had the hard, small-breasted look of fanatically serious body builders came on a regular basis, but aside from cautious "hellos," the guys left them alone. Several older women who might have been competitive athletes thirty years ago stopped by some mornings, but they pretty much kept to themselves. I was the only youngish woman in the gym who didn't frighten the big boys into keeping their distance. Not all the men there were body builders. The regulars were a mix of professional guys, members of the local fire department, law enforcement officers, and a few who looked as though they had, at one time, been clients of the penal system. Most were more than happy to talk to me. Hence my detailed knowledge of the history of the building, Billy's untimely departure and the various conflicting theories regarding York's past.

Within a week, I was having a hard time getting through my routine in two hours with all the interruptions. Being by nature a polite person and, truth be told, a shade flattered by all the male attention, I couldn't come up with a gentle way of avoiding all the charm directed my way. York rarely appeared on the gym floor. He stayed in a tiny office up by the front door. But one day I saw him speak quietly to several of the more gregarious members, and the next day he motioned for me to step into his office.

"This is the way it works," he said without preamble. "The guys can say hello to you, Magee, but after that you have to initiate the conversation if you want to have one."

"Are *they* all right with that?"

"They know the rules. It's my gym. They don't have a choice." He gave me an appraising glance. "You're here to work out, not socialize, right?"

I nodded.

"Good. Otherwise, I'd give you your money back and tell you to go somewhere with a juice bar and a hot tub."

"Don't worry about it!"

He smiled. "I've seen you leg press one-seventy-five. Not bad. But you should work on your chest."

In most contexts I'd have taken that as an insult, especially since I've always thought my breasts looked pretty good. But I knew what he meant.

"What are you bench pressing?" York asked.

"Forty. Fifty on a really good day."

"Try pushing it up to sixty. If you need a spotter, let me know."

I had nodded, wondering whether in the world of weights that was a come-on.

After my conversation with York, the guys kept to the rules with a rigidity that could only have been inspired by a fear based on the mythic stories of his past. And I pretty much kept the conversations to a minimum, with only one exception. About three weeks ago, I started talking with Jason Needham, a handsome, seemingly charming guy who sold real estate. Normally I avoid men who are in sales because I have enough trouble figuring out when men are lying to me without seeking out paid professionals. But Jason seemed to be a nice guy. So I went out with him once, for dinner at the Collins Inn.

The first person that I saw as I entered the gym this morning was Jason Needham, sweating away on the treadmill. His hello sounded rather grudging. The only other available piece of aerobic equipment was the treadmill right next to his, so I hopped on and started it up.

"How have you been?" I asked.

He shrugged.

"I did mean to call you back, Jason."

"But you didn't," he said, a hurt look around his cute but weak mouth.

"I was angry and hurt."

"But it wasn't my fault, Laura. You didn't have to take it out on me. I left four messages on your grandmother's machine and you never called me back."

He got that choked-up look of disappointment that only a million-dollar seller who had failed to close on a deal can muster.

"Well, you have to admit, it wasn't much of a date," I said.

"I didn't know Holly was going to be so prickly."

I stifled a laugh as he pulled another hurt look from his arsenal. I knew we'd never have made it in the long run because he hadn't been blessed with a sense of humor. Oh, he could tell jokes, probably ones he'd memorized from a book titled *Salesman's Humor,* but spontaneous humor was a dimension beyond his ken.

The abbreviated version of what made me *persona non grata* at the Collins Inn goes like this.

Jason and I were having the more or less standard first date conversation where you tactfully ask trivial questions and hope they will lead to the revelation of vital information that will determine whether there will be any physical contact. We were still on cocktails and things hadn't been going well. The goodnight kiss had already been downgraded to a polite handshake. Jason was in the midst of a long, offensive story about how he had managed to sucker some poor buyer into purchasing a home with a huge crack in the foundation and marginal wiring, when I looked up and saw a woman standing by our table.

"I don't think I'll have another drink right now," I said, thinking it was the waitress. I wanted to have my wits about me when I made my escape.

"You bitch," she said.

I was about to say I realized she worked for tips and the more we drank the larger her tip would be but this was not the diplomatic way to go about increasing it, when she stuck her hand in my hair and jerked me to my feet. With her other hand she gave me a resounding slap across the face. I staggered a bit and sat down hard in my chair, more stunned than injured. To my dismay, Jason neither stood up nor made any effort to defend me.

"And you, you louse," she said, picking up the basket of rolls and throwing it at Jason. The rolls bounced off him like so many fluffy snowballs, and the wicker basket lightly clipped him on the forehead.

Still in shock, my cheek smarting from her slap, I tried to figure out what we could have done to offend her. Then I heard Jason say, "Holly honey, why don't we talk about this like civilized adults?"

That line and the tone in which it was given told me I was auditioning for the role as the other woman.

Holly's hand came back toward my head, and I had a bad feeling it wasn't to give me a friendly pat. Although in principle I was sympathetic to her plight, I had no intention of turning the other cheek. I grabbed her wrist and desperately tried to remember what I had once learned about throwing the aggressor in the Judo class I had taken when I lived in Boston.

Holding Holly's wrist, I used my other hand to push her body away from me while I rose up from my chair, driving forward with my quads and twisting. It worked amazingly well. With a startled yelp, Holly was propelled several yards away and might have gone further if she hadn't ended up lying across the table of a couple of senior citizens dining nearby.

"I'll be waiting outside when you've taken care of things," I announced to an ashen Jason. Marching past Millicent Collins, I left the dining room. I walked through the lobby and into the parking lot, where I would have thrown up if I'd been fortunate enough to have had any dinner.

To be fair to Jason, he did offer to take me somewhere else to eat, but I refused. Who knew what girlfriend might be lurking there? The next one might be armed. I told Jason I was tired and to please take me home. Along the way he explained that Holly was someone he'd gone out with a few times and she had exaggerated the seriousness of their relationship, even though he had made it quite clear that they were both free to date other people. A story I'd heard so many times, my mind shut down in self-defense. When he dropped me at my door, he asked if he could call me and I said something vague like "fine," never expecting he actually would. For the next couple of weeks he called on a daily basis. I never returned his calls, hence his expression of injured pride.

"So you didn't return my calls because of that business with Holly?" He leaned so far over from his treadmill toward mine, he almost fell off.

The note of incredulity in his voice made me pause to consider how different people can be. What I considered a humiliating experience, Jason ranked as a minor faux pas, like a discreet belch at the table.

"I'm looking for a man who's ready to make a commitment," I said. "A man who wants to settle down and raise a family. If you're ready for that, we can certainly go out again."

I watched his eyes as he considered the possibility of lying to me. Could he get what he wanted and then avoid me with more success than he'd had with Holly?

York walked by.

"Don't you think York is a great guy?" I said. "He treats me like a younger sister."

"Laura, I'm going to be really honest with you here. I don't believe I'm ready for the kind of commitment you're looking for," Jason said in a voice made cautious by his fear of York — and possible extermination. "I think we should just be friends."

I returned his polished smile with one of my own, and nodded.

A more cunning expression came over his face. "Say, has your grandmother thought any more about selling her house?"

That had been the topic Jason and I discussed when we first met. He had asked me my name and wanted to know where I lived, a natural question for a realtor. He knew my grandfather had died. He wanted to know if Gran was going to sell. I think he was hotter to get the listing than he was for me.

"Nope. I don't think she has any immediate plans to move."

I didn't think Jason would already know about Gran's new living arrangements, although it would probably be the talk of the town before long.

"Too bad. As soon as I get a house, I sell it. I just wish I had more. I thought I had a new listing in a good part of town about a month ago, but the guy backed out. In the long run, it was just as well. He got killed and now the place will be tied up in probate for months."

"Are you talking about Jack Proctor?"

"Yeah. Did you know him?"

"He was a friend of my grandfather's. Did he say why he changed his mind about putting his house on the market?"

"He planned to build a new place up on the bluffs, but then he told me he'd decided to stay where he was. He said money wasn't everything."

"What did that mean?"

Jason shook his head, as if the sentiment had no place in his philosophy of life.

What could be more important than money to a man like Jack Proctor? That was an easy one: sex. For the Ravensford Peeper, notable harasser of women, sex was more enticing than money. But how did that fit in with his murder? Frustrated, I sighed.

"You sound tired, Laura," Jason said. "We could go somewhere and have a cup of coffee."

I glanced meaningfully in the direction of York.

Jason cleared his throat quickly, as if trying to swallow his offer. Then he said, "Maybe some other time."

CHAPTER 17

I parked in one of the handful of visitor's spaces on the Ravensford campus. A helpful security guard had directed me there when I stopped by the gate to ask how to get to the Bliss Building. Just asking made me want to giggle. I was tempted to ask whether that was where the testing of hallucinogenic drugs took place, but the earnest expression on his face made me doubt he'd see the humor.

When I stepped inside the building I half expected to see people in caftans strolling around with expressions of unspeakable serenity and happiness. But in reality, it looked like any other school building from the 1920s, vaguely like a mill. Education was no laughing matter, the building seemed to say, and its purpose was to fit you into your proper role in life. Wide, dark wood moldings and stained plaster walls created a dreary atmosphere, even on this bright, sunny day. I made my way up the iron staircase to the third floor and walked down the wide hallway, checking the names until I came to a door with a small brass plaque on it that read "Professor St. Claire." Although all the other doors had office hours prominently posted on them, this one didn't. I hoped the secretary had given me accurate information and hadn't informed Mark St. Claire of my pending visit. I had a suspicion that the very thought of a reporter coming to call would inspire him to disappear.

I knocked, and detected the faintest of sounds from inside, as if someone had cautiously adjusted his or her position in a squeaky swivel chair. I knocked again. No one came to the door. I knocked a third time and loudly called out St. Claire's name. If he was in there, he wouldn't want the entire floor to know he had refused to see a guest.

The door opened about a foot and two eyes peered out at me from the shadows.

"What do you want? I don't see students in my office."

"My name is Laura Magee. I'm a reporter for the *Chronicle* and I'd like to talk to you about the attack on your father last night."

"I have nothing to say." He began to close

the door.

"Okay, I'll directly quote you in my story. When asked about his father's injury, Mark St. Claire, Professor at Ravensford College, replied, 'I have nothing to say.' Have I got that right?"

the *Chronicle* would never print anything that insulting, but —

The door opened wider, and Mark St. Claire jerked his head, a less than gracious invitation for me to enter. The pen was clearly mightier than the sword when it came to its potential to cause embarrassment.

The only light in the office came from a desk lamp. The window shades were down and covered by a heavy drape. A computer screen glowed eerily on the desk, making me feel like I had just entered a cave where the god of computing was worshipped. I managed to find an empty chair in the darkness and sat down without being invited. That way I'd be harder to budge. Mark settled back into his squeaky chair in front of the computer screen, and turned so that he could see both the screen and me at the same time. Maybe he planned to use the Internet to help him answer my questions.

I smiled in a friendly manner, then took a moment to study him. A tall man in his mid to late forties, his features were more pinched than his father's, and he had a remarkably pale complexion. He also had a rather prissy expression, as if my being here created a slightly off aroma. He stirred restlessly in his chair, obviously anxious for me to finish and leave him alone.

"Why don't you have any office hours this semester?" I asked.

"I teach all my classes over the Internet."

"Oh, are your classes in different parts of the country?"

He shook his head. "The majority of them are right here on campus."

"So your students sit in their dorm rooms rather than meet together in class?"

"If they have questions or problems, they write to me and I write back. They can also discuss matters with each other through a classroom chat group. It's much more efficient."

"Ravensford College, where every student counts," I said, repeating Winnie's slogan.

"Don't criticize what you don't understand! Anyway, we aren't here to discuss pedagogy. You wanted to talk about my father."

"The police think the bust that fell on your father was intentionally dropped. Do you have any idea who might have wanted to hurt him?"

Mark turned back to the screen as if seeking inspiration. "I've already been over all of this with the police," he finally said. "I have very little contact with my father, so I have no idea how many people might bear him a grudge. And in case you think, as the police seemed to imply, that I might have attempted to kill my own father in order to gain my inheritance, you are wrong."

"Why is that?" I asked, disappointed. I thought I was so clever, but Farantello had been here ahead of me.

"My mother saw to it that I received the bulk of what was coming to me before she died."

"Why did she do that?"

"Mother was afraid my father might squander it all on some floozy after she was gone."

Floozy? "Why would she think that? Was your father unfaithful to her?"

It was a none-of-your-business question and Mark rightfully ignored it. Instead, he said, "My father and I were never close."

"If you received the bulk of your inheritance, will you receive more when your father dies?"

I thought maybe he'd ignore my second rude question, but he said, "I'll inherit the newspaper. Whatever else is left will go to several designated charities."

"Still," I said, chewing on my pen thoughtfully, "the *Chronicle* must be worth quite a bit."

He gave a derisive snort that sounded odd coming from such a self-controlled man. "I have more money than I'll ever need, especially since I am single and lead a very simple, scholarly life."

Maybe you'll find a floozy some day and need more, I was tempted to say, but kept my mouth shut. "Why are you and your father not close?" I asked. "Off the record," I added when he hesitated.

"My mother met my father when he was on a business trip to Boston. She came from a socially prominent family, and would never have agreed to move here if she hadn't expected Father to sell the paper as soon as my grandfather died, then move the family back to Boston. But when my grandfather passed away, my father said the newspaper was the most important thing in the world to him. That left my mother stranded in this backwater."

"Why didn't your mother return to Boston?"

"Without my father? And admit her marriage was a failure?"

"When you had to choose sides, you chose your mother's?"

His lips formed a tight line. "There was no other side as far as I was concerned. There still isn't."

"Why haven't *you* left Ravensford?"

"I did. I worked at a college in the New York City area, but then my mother needed me."

"When she got sick?"

"Before she became ill. She was miserable for the last fifteen years of her life. I believe she regretted not having left my father earlier, but it was too late for her to start over."

"Why did you stay in town after your mother died?"

He smiled for the first time, a grudging smile, but it brightened his face remarkably, suggesting that the vestiges of a normal human being lurked.

"I like teaching here. To tell the truth, I like Ravensford. After all, for better or worse, I grew up here."

I nodded and rose to my feet.

"The police said a woman stood with my father when he was attacked," Mark said.

"So I heard." Somehow, I managed to maintain a neutral expression.

"Do you know who it was?"

"Sorry, but I can't reveal that information."

He turned back to the computer screen as if I had already left the room, but he continued speaking. "Maybe the falling bust had nothing to do with my father. Maybe the woman he was with fleeced some other man and *he* was trying to get revenge. Maybe he *accidentally* hit my father."

Steaming, I walked down the hall. I wanted to tear a strip off Mark St. Claire for suggesting that my grandmother was a gold digger. But a bit of Gran's Eastern wisdom kept running through my head. "The wise man knows when to be silent." I had found out what I wanted to know. Satisfying my anger would be a self-indulgence. I smiled. A lesson in self-discipline never hurt anyone.

I was walking across the campus when a voice called out my name, and Ben Mather, the college provost, hurried across the main plaza toward me.

"This is a fortunate meeting," he said. "I planned to call you about your grandfather's paintings. The college is interested in purchasing them."

I almost said that Jack Proctor had never used the word "purchase," but I decided to keep my mouth shut and see what developed. If Gran could make a few bucks on Granddad's art, she might find some poetic justice.

"Why the interest, Ben?" I tried to look sophisticated, yet canny, like every art dealer I've ever met. A used car dealer in an Armani suit.

"Owen Reynolds suggested they might be worth owning . . . because of your grandfather's reputation. . . ."

His reputation as what? But the word "purchase" had a pleasant ring to it, enough of a ring to keep an interested smile on my face. "What about my Grandfather's reputation in particular impressed Owen?"

Mather frowned as if trying to recall. "I believe Mr. Reynolds said something about your grandfather's time in Paris . . . in the early 1950s. A period that's becoming hot, I think he said."

I nodded sagely, as if all that meant something to me.

"Of course, we can't pay very much," Ben continued. "But given your grandfather's long and close association with the college, I'm sure your grandmother would give our offer serious consideration."

"I don't know. She turned down Jack Proctor when he tried to get the paintings for the college. I'm not sure whether she'll feel any differently about it now."

Mather stared at me. "Jack Proctor made an offer in the name of the college for those pictures?"

"No money was discussed," I said carefully, not admitting Jack wanted them for free. "The whole thing was in the preliminary stages because my grandmother wasn't sure she wanted to part with the pictures."

"Jack came to me with the idea, but he hadn't been authorized to make any approach in the name of the college."

"Maybe he didn't think he had to get approval until it was time to actually make an offer." *Or maybe he figured he could get them for free and then sell them to the college.*

"Still, he shouldn't have done it."

Well, chastise him at the morgue, I felt like saying. Instead, I shook my head, as if bemused by the vagaries of human behavior.

"Anyway," Mather said, putting Jack Proctor behind him, "if your grandmother is interested in selling those works, I hope she decides in the next few days. I'd like to have Owen look them over before he leaves. He can estimate their value."

I told Ben I'd be in touch. As I walked across the campus, I wondered what Jack had been up to with his claim that the college wanted to possess my grandfather's

271

paintings. And did it have anything to do with his optimistic view of his future prospects? I couldn't see how obtaining the collected works of my grandfather, Victor Hallowell, would put much of a feather in Jack's cap. But maybe I shouldn't make a judgment until I'd had a look at them for myself.

CHAPTER 18

I should have called first. How often in life have people said that, I wonder? It even sounds like an ad for the phone company. I would have called, but Roger St. Claire's house was on the way from the college back to the paper, where I figured I'd spend some time on my Auntie Mabel answers. I thought it would be easier to stop by and present Gran with Ben Mather's proposal.

I parked in the driveway of the Tudor mansion and walked up to a massive oak door that looked like it had been designed to withstand a siege. I pushed the doorbell, set in the middle of a decorative lion's head. I wondered if the house had been in the St. Claire family for several generations. Maybe Mrs. St. Claire would have taken better to life here if she had been allowed to live in a house of her own choosing. I rang the bell twice. No answer. A second lion, the clone of the first, stared at me from a large brass knocker so I gave that a try. Still, no answer.

I walked up the driveway and saw my grandmother's car pulled up near the rear entrance to the house. I didn't like the look of that. If they had gone out, my grandmother would have driven. So they were home and either unable or unwilling to answer the door. I went to the back door and rang the bell and knocked with no success. I tried the handle, and it turned. I opened the door and walked inside.

"What are you so afraid of, girl?" Auntie Mabel said.

"Excuse me, but I'm not too keen on finding the mutilated bodies of my grandmother and employer."

"Pish, tosh. You'll see worse before your life is over."

I stood in the kitchen, a huge room with cupboards reaching up to the top of nine-foot ceilings. There was no light on, and the shadowy afternoon sun, filtered through the window over the sink, revealed a table off to one side and a doorway that seemed to lead down a hall. I walked around the table, noting that it was clean. I had taken only a couple of steps into the even darker hallway when a figure began coming toward me from the opposite direction.

274

I may have made a little squeak of surprise, or it might have been a full-blooded shriek of sheer terror. I heard a startled series of squawks like a duck being strangled. A light came on, and I saw Roger St. Claire wearing a pair of paisley boxer shorts and house slippers. Before I demurely lowered my eyes to his rather gnarly toes, I had a full view of his thin white chest, one side of which was hidden by a cast.

"What are you doing here?" he said in what struggled to be an imperious tone. But his outfit, or lack thereof, made his question merely querulous.

"I'm sorry," I said, trying to keep my focus on the floor. "I rang the bell and knocked, but no one answered."

"How did you get in?"

"The kitchen door was open."

St. Claire suddenly realized that perhaps this wasn't the best setting for an interrogation. He quickly switched off the light, leaving me almost blinded.

"Wait here. I'll get your grandmother." He turned and, disoriented by the sudden loss of illumination, bumped his cast into the door frame and went away muttering angrily under his breath.

I didn't see much point in standing in the hallway like some lady-in-waiting, so I went back to the kitchen and took a seat at the table.

My mind began to wander to thoughts of Roger St. Claire making love to my grandmother with only one usable arm. Maybe there was a Taoist quote covering such a situation. Unwanted images began to flood my imagination. Fortunately, Gran, fully dressed, thank God, walked into the kitchen. I had been afraid that she'd be angry, but even in the dimly lit kitchen I detected a small smile as she sat down across from me.

"You gave Roger quite a shock," she said. "No woman has seen him in his underwear in twenty years, aside from his late wife Marie, and even that's doubtful. Now there have been two in one day, which might not be good for his heart."

"I didn't mean it to happen, Gran."

"Of course not, and I'm sure no real harm has been done. Roger could use a little loosening up. But why are you here, Laura?"

I told her about my meeting with Ben Mather and the offer for my grandfather's paintings. I also told her that Ben knew nothing of Jack Proctor's approach.

"How very odd. I distinctly remember Jack saying it was the college that wanted the paintings as part of its collection. He also told me the powers that be had said they would be pleased to have the works but couldn't afford to purchase them. Jack said having a few of them on display would be a wonderful way of honoring Victor. I told him the money didn't matter. I simply wasn't certain I wanted Victor's paintings to be viewed by the public."

"Jack must have been doing it on his own. If he planned to store them in the museum and pull out one or two to show on occasion, maybe he didn't think it was any big deal."

Gran nodded. "Why does Owen Reynolds believe the college should buy Victor's paintings? Could they possibly have any value?"

"Not much beyond what value they'd have as part of the history of the college, I'd think, but I don't know for sure. According to Ben Mather, Owen thinks the works of someone who studied in France during the 1950s would be worthwhile."

"Worthwhile perhaps, but worth buying?"

"I'll know better once Owen has a chance to see the paintings, if you're interested in the deal at all, that is."

She surprised me by running her hand through her hair in a youthful, almost sensuous way.

"Oh, why should I care anymore?" she

finally said. "Victor is gone. Let him have his little bit of posthumous fame. I don't want to keep the paintings in the house for old times' sake."

"So I can go ahead and have Owen come over to make an appraisal?"

She nodded. "Would you like me to be there?"

"Want to keep an eye on him in case he tries to snatch a picture?" I asked with a smile.

"I was thinking more along the lines of what he might want to snatch from you."

"He's harmless," I said with forced casualness but felt myself blushing.

"Is he?"

I stared at her.

"What I mean to say is, are you still interested in him?"

"And if I am, you think I might want you along to supply a little self-control?"

My grandmother shrugged. "We can all use a bit of self-control sometimes."

I shook my head. "Owen is a horny little weasel who repeatedly cheated on me."

"I always figured he was."

"Why?"

"I had enough experience to know. A man who deceives you once will often do it again, especially if he has an inflated view of his own importance to the world. I saw Owen briefly the other night, but he reminded me a bit of Victor."

"I've got his number now."

"If he offers some money for the paintings, and I don't really care how much, unload the stuff. You take care of it, okay? It brings up painful memories for me."

I reached across the table and squeezed her hand.

"Sure, Gran." I pretended to glance around the kitchen for a moment. "Is everything all right with you and Roger?"

She smiled. "You mean aside from his running around in his shorts and scaring my granddaughter?"

I returned her smile. "Aside from that."

"He's coming along, but it's going to take a while. His wife did a real number on him."

"I talked to his son. He teaches at the college. I thought he could tell me who would have dropped the bust on his father. He didn't seem to have anything new to contribute, but he takes his mother's side. He says Roger refused to move to Boston like he'd promised when they got married."

"I suppose there are two sides to every argument, Laura. But it seems like a poor reason to withhold affection for almost twenty years."

I stood up. "No new ideas on who tried to injure Roger? Or you?"

She shook her head.

"Try to keep the kitchen door locked from now on, huh?"

Gran smiled. "I'll try, but small-town habits die hard."

I almost said more, then remembered the Taoist phrase that the worst try to improve others by condemning their conduct. The best try to improve themselves. I decided to keep my mouth shut and focus on self-improvement.

CHAPTER 19

"I didn't expect to see you back here again today," Dorie said as I entered the office.

It was five o'clock and she was heading out the door. Since the office was empty, she made me promise on my honor as a journalist that I would remember to lock up when I left. Once she was gone, I called Ben Mather to give him the good news. Despite my suspicion that administrators in all walks of life came in late and left early, he was still at his desk. He expressed moderately polite pleasure at the thought of getting my grandfather's paintings, and asked if I would call Owen myself at the Collins Inn to work out a time for him to stop by my house and make his appraisal. I agreed.

"Hi, Owen, it's Laura," I said when the person working the desk at the Captain Collins put my call through to his room. I tried to infuse my tone with just the right combination of pleasantness and casual indifference.

"How are you, Laura? How are your grandmother and her friend after last night's disaster?"

Everything was fine, I said, except for Roger's clipped wing. Then I explained why I was calling.

"I don't have any wheels," he said. "My girlfriend had to go back to Boston today for some kind of emergency meeting, so I'm stranded here. She's not due back until tomorrow."

You're stranded for longer than that, buddy, I thought, figuring she had left him for her sugar daddy. "I can pick you up, Owen."

"Yes, but if I decide to purchase your grandfather's paintings, I'll need a vehicle to deliver them to the school. Probably a van. I was going to rent one tomorrow morning."

"You're going to pick them up yourself? I thought you'd submit an estimate and the college would send a mover."

Owen laughed. "I think they figured they could save some money by having me do both jobs."

Great! Was I supposed to disrupt my entire work schedule tomorrow because Owen hadn't had the foresight to rent a van? My annoyance was only slightly diminished at the thought that, unknown to Owen, Clarissa probably wouldn't be coming back.

"The rental place is probably still open," I said. "Why don't you give them a call, and I'll come by and get you? We can pick up the van and go right over to my house. I'd like to get this done tonight."

There was a long pause as if I'd just laid out the plans for the landing at Normandy, and he was trying to absorb it all. I'd never known Owen to be slow. Maybe Clarissa was right and his life was on a downhill slide.

"Sounds fine," he finally said.

"I'll see you in fifteen minutes," I said quickly, before he could change his mind. "Meet me out in front of the inn."

I turned out the lights and carefully locked the door behind me. Bill and Joy had their own keys in case some hot, late-breaking news required them to come in and write up their stories.

When I pulled up to the inn, Owen wasn't outside. Cursing him for the lousy, self-centered ingrate I knew him to be, I parked, then charged up the steps and into the lobby. He stood by the front desk, being held onto, literally, by Millicent Collins, who was going on in full voice about some pictures of the Captain that were in the inn's attic. Owen gave me an apologetic smile and told her he had to leave.

"How are you enjoying your stay?" I asked as we walked out the front door.

He rolled his eyes.

"Breathe deeply when you're inside the inn. Remember, the dust you're choking on once passed through George Washington's lungs."

Owen snorted. "Washington would never have stayed in that place."

"He might if he came by to court martial the Captain for cowardice in the face of the enemy."

"Is that true?"

"It was a close thing."

I wasn't lying. According to my historian friend, the Continental Army was moving the cannon from Fort Ticonderoga across Massachusetts to force the British out of Boston. Captain Collins was ordered to join them around Worcester for the assault on Boston. He never showed, claiming later that he hadn't received the order. Washington, furious, threatened to shoot the coward on the spot if he ever encountered the Captain again. No problem there, because the Captain had the good sense to stay far away from any action.

I drove up Elm Street to the rental agency.

After filling out the necessary paperwork, Owen followed me back to Grandmother's house. We went in together through the kitchen. Although I wasn't all that comfortable being alone with Owen, I was happy to have someone with me when I entered the empty house. How much protection he would be if we happened upon a burglar, I wasn't sure, but he might say something offensive to the man and distract him long enough for me to escape.

"Where are the paintings?" Owen looked around, as if they might magically appear. "I noticed the other night that they weren't in the living room."

"My grandmother moved them up to the attic."

Owen made a face, as if picturing layers of dust and fist-sized spiders. For an artist, he was an unusually fastidious man.

"Why did your grandmother do that?"

Ignoring his question, I walked down the hall and opened the door to the attic. As I switched on the light, Owen stood at the foot of the stairs and looked up into the attic with a dubious expression.

"Is there enough light up there for me to know what I'm looking at, Laura?"

"I've never been up there."

I'd suggested several times to Gran that it

might be interesting to go upstairs and look over Granddad's work, but she'd always shot down the idea. Although I'd thought it odd at the time, I now understood why the attic had been off limits.

I went into the kitchen and got a flashlight. "There are probably some lights," I told Owen, "but if we need more, this will do. We can always bring the paintings down into the living room if you need to examine them more closely."

Did he think he'd be authenticating a Rembrandt for the Met?

I led the way up the stairs. I've been in a few attics in older houses. Most of them overflowed with stuff, requiring an archaeological dig through the junk to reveal the family's history. Gran's attic was an exception. There were a couple of chests and an old dresser. An easel leaned crookedly against one wall with a coffee can hanging on the front of it, like a homeless person looking for a handout. Otherwise, it was a large, empty space. Maybe happy marriages generated more junk than unhappy ones. At any rate, this made it easy to see the two stacks of paintings leaning against the far wall with an old pink chenille bedspread thrown over them. Strings attached to a couple of bare-bulb ceiling fixtures dangled down, and I pulled the lights on like a peripatetic bell-ringer as we headed toward the paintings.

Owen eagerly threw off the dust covering. He started with the top canvas, a rather muddied country scene. He examined each of the pictures as I drifted across the room. I enjoyed looking at pictures myself, but one of the things I had learned during my time with Owen is that artists look at works of art in a completely different way from non-artists. Civilians want to know the story behind the painting. They wonder why the artist painted this house on this day.

In my opinion, an artist couldn't care less what the painting is about because he is usually focused on some small point of technique. The whole history of art is a sort of tool kit for the working artist, a grab bag of ideas to be used to improve his or her own work. By the speed with which Owen was going through my grandfather's work, he wasn't finding much that would be of benefit to him.

"Anything interesting?" I asked.

He shook his head. "You'd think someone who studied in Paris in the early fifties would have had a more modern style. Most of these are third-rate impressionist imitations, outdated at the time they were done."

I refrained from pointing out that most Super-realists probably didn't have much of an appreciation for the Impressionists, even for a real genius like Van Gogh. However, as I glanced at the pictures Owen had put to one side, they didn't strike me as anything special. A few were landscapes, some with a barn or farmhouse. Many were stereotypical scenes of Paris, proficient but uninspired. Granddad's paintings were the work of a good art student, not a true artist. There wasn't any real passion in them. The word "passion" made me wonder if the paintings of his various girlfriends had been more inspired — the paintings Gran insisted he destroy. No one would ever know.

"Are these all there are?" Owen asked.

"As far as I know."

"Odd." Owen walked around the attic, poking behind the dressers, opening drawers and lifting up the lids on the chests.

"What are you looking for?"

"I thought your grandfather would have painted some portraits."

I wasn't about to tell him about Granddad's seraglio collection. "You don't paint portraits," I said.

That earned me a grudging smile. "True. But most of these impressionist types do nudes or, if they're more sentimental, young mothers with children or flowers on their laps."

"What you see is what you get."

"Give me a hand and we'll haul these downstairs."

I suddenly remembered how much of our conversation in the past had been in the form of Owen issuing commands to me, as if I were an employee. I'd been happy to be of service then. Now I resented it. "Do you really have to look at them in a better light?" I snapped.

"No."

"Then why are we bringing them down-stairs?"

"So we can haul them out to the van," he said, as if I were simple minded.

"You want these?"

"*I* don't, but Ravensford College does."

He picked up a couple of paintings and headed for the stairs.

I blocked his way. "Wait a minute, buster! What is the college offering?"

I was all set to refuse an offer of a thousand or two. Even if Gran didn't want the paintings, I felt it was a matter of family pride not to let them go too cheaply.

"Ten thousand."

I stared in disbelief. Owen must have taken my expression as one of refusal because he quickly said, "Okay. Fifteen, but that's the limit. I'm not authorized to go any higher."

I stepped to one side, allowing Owen to head down the stairs. When I came to my senses, I began to help him. The sooner the paintings were out of the house and Gran had her money, the happier everyone would be.

It took us about twenty minutes to carry all the pictures outside and stack them in the van. There were exactly forty. Feeling generous, I threw in the old bedspread to cover them.

When everything was loaded, Owen stopped by the kitchen counter and took out his checkbook.

"What are you doing?" I asked, as he began filling out a check.

"I'll give you a personal check for five thousand as a deposit. The college will pay you the rest when all the paperwork clears. I'll get my money back from them."

"Are you sure? Gran can wait until the college processes the voucher."

"This way will be easier," Owen said, then smiled. "Hey, you know better than to turn down my offer of money."

True enough, for he had never been a generous date. For a guy whose pictures sometimes sold in the six figures, more often than not he let me pay for dinner and drinks out of my meager salary. I snatched the check out of his hand.

"Maybe I'll see you some time if you come to Boston," he said. "Good luck here in Ravensford."

He gave me a quick kiss on the cheek, and before I could even ask when he was heading back to the city, he was out the door.

My feelings were hurt. He hadn't put any moves on me. When you can't get a compulsive womanizer to look at you, what does that say about what you've got to offer?

Since nobody seemed to be interested in my body tonight, I made myself a cup of cocoa. As I sipped and reflected, I realized that I was feeling lonely for human company of either gender. Gran wasn't exactly garrulous, and she spent most of her evenings out with her buddies, but the house felt empty in a different way, now that I knew she wouldn't be coming back to sleep.

If she was going to be staying with Roger St. Claire for a while, I had better come up with some friends. Aside from Dorie, whose lifestyle, if not her chronological age, made her too young for me to hang out with, I didn't have any girlfriends. I'd confined my life to the newspaper, the gym, and reading or watching television.

Time to expand my horizons. I thought about calling Michael Farantello. He probably wouldn't be at his office. However, his home number was listed — I had already checked. But what would I talk to him about? I could ask him how the case was going but that was police business. On the other hand, after that kiss the other night at the art museum, he might suggest he come over so we could get to know each other better and — no! Calling Michael would just reveal the true depths of my lonely desperation.

Eventually, I decided to go to my maidenly bed. I was pretty tired from all the trips up and down the attic stairs. I grabbed a volume on Impressionism from a bookcase in Gran's room. I got into bed, opened the heavy book on my lap, and leafed through the color prints. It must have been frustrating for my grandfather to see how far short of the late nineteenth century masters his work fell. Not for the first time, I was happy that I'd never fancied myself an artist. I stared at the cool geometric spaces of the Mondrian knock-off by Torvic, hanging on the wall across from me, until I felt drowsy. The book was still on my lap as I drifted off to sleep.

CHAPTER 20

Dear Auntie Mabel,

My boyfriend Wally was at my house playing with my pit bull terrier, Pumpkin. Now, Pumpkin is the sweetest dog you'd ever want to meet and I don't know what Wally did to antagonize her, but she took a small nip out of Wally's upper lip that took twenty stitches to close. Wally is suing me, and since this is not exactly the first time Pumpkin has been involved in a biting incident, my insurance company is threatening to cancel my homeowner's insurance. I am finding it difficult to continue my relationship with Wally and at the same time keep Pumpkin happy. What should I do? I have a hard time keeping my hands off of Wally. But I love Pumpkin. Which one should I keep? Sad Samantha

Dear SS,

Neither one. Pumpkin is clearly a vi-

cious, out-of-control animal that should be made into a pie, but a boyfriend who would sue his girl is no keeper either. On second thought, you might want to let Pumpkin stay around because she's obviously a better judge of men than you are. You should enroll Pumpkin in an obedience class. Both of you would benefit from learning a little self-discipline.

I had pushed the key to send another piece of Auntie Mabel's wisdom into cyberspace when the phone rang. It was Michael Farantello. In his official chief-voice, he said, "Am I correct in believing that you have some kind of relationship with Owen Reynolds?"

"Where did you hear that?"

"Millicent Collins says you picked him up at the inn last night."

"Yes, I picked him up. We have a *business* relationship. He's representing Ravensford College in the purchase of my grandfather's paintings."

"Where did you go after you left the inn?"

I gave Michael a quick recap of my evening with Owen, barely resisting the urge to ask what this was all about.

"So the last time you saw him, he was leaving your grandmother's house in a van filled with your grandfather's paintings?"

"You got it. Why? Is he missing?" I gave a thin, nervous giggle. What if those paintings were worth millions and Owen had run off with my grandmother's fortune? I shook my head. That would be too fantastic for words.

"No, he isn't missing," the chief said. "I'm looking at him right now. He's lying in a hospital bed."

"What's wrong with him?"

"A possible concussion, and the doc thinks there could be some internal bleeding."

"Did he have an auto accident?" I knew from experience that, like many Bostonians, Owen was a terrible driver. He either went too fast or too slow and rarely signaled.

Farantello hesitated and I had a feeling he was staring at Owen when he said, "No, someone did it to him."

"Someone did it," I repeated in disbelief. "Why?"

"He says he was mugged."

"You sound like you don't believe him."

"Laura, could you come down and talk to him? Maybe he'll open up to someone he knows. We can't reach his girlfriend. She was supposed to come back from Boston today, but she isn't here and there's no answer at their Boston apartment."

I resisted telling him that Clarissa was probably in New York, making nice with her elderly gallery owner.

Instead, I said, "I'm not sure what I can do."

"Please give it a try."

I agreed to come right over.

The Ditmore Howorth Memorial Hospital wasn't very large, but it was still quite impressive for a town the size of Ravensford. The Howorths had lived in Ravensford from the time the first Puritans left Massachusetts Bay colony with the vague goal of heading west. The Howorths only traveled ninety miles, but that was enough to gain them bragging rights as a first family of Ravensford, which has stood them in good stead for over three hundred years. According to my historian friend, one of the first Howorths owned a blacksmith shop and gained something of a reputation for treating sick animals. His son continued the veterinary tradition. Somewhere in the middle of the eighteenth century, the first Ditmore Howorth made the leap upward or not, depending on your point of view, and began treating sick people.

A number of Ditmore Howorths followed, and in the second half of the nineteenth century, one of them decided to build a hospital. Several moves and expansions later, Ravensford had a reasonably modern-looking building. As I entered through the front door, I was immediately greeted by a bad oil painting of the current chairperson of the hospital board, Dotty Howorth. In my opinion, a woman chairperson was a nice change of pace.

Chief Farantello met me by the nurse's station, right outside the elevator on the third floor. He led me into a small waiting room with tile floors and plastic furniture. His face looked even longer than usual, his eyes more soulful. I almost expected him to tell me that Owen had died from his injuries.

"How's Owen?" I asked apprehensively.

"About the same."

"You said that he had a possible concussion."

"Yes. We know how that happened. He staggered into the lobby of the inn and tripped over a reproduction of the Revolutionary War drum Millicent Collins had placed on display. When he fell, he struck his head on the reproduction eighteenth-century cherry wood table next to the drum."

"I see."

"Millicent heard the commotion. It was quite late, around eleven-thirty, but fortunately she was waiting up for Reynolds's return to show him some paintings of the Captain."

"I'm surprised she didn't prop him up and show him the paintings anyway."

Farantello gave me the ghost of a smile. "She might have, but he was bleeding all over her reproduction eighteenth-century carpet, so she called an ambulance."

"You said something about a mugging."

"The doctor who examined him said he'd been given quite a beating. The damage was all to his abdomen and back. It looked like a professional job."

"What did he say when you asked him about it?"

Farantello shrugged. "At first he said it happened when he fell in the lobby. Of course, that was absurd unless Millicent attacked him. Then he said he had taken a nighttime stroll downtown. He claims he was mugged, fought back and was injured in the struggle."

"Why didn't he tell you that in the first place?"

"He said he was embarrassed to admit it."

"Isn't the mugging story believable?"

"He still has his wallet."

"Maybe it was a nutcase out to beat up on someone."

"We don't have many of those around here, Laura. Oh, two guys might get drunk and get into it. That's common enough. But this has a more deliberate look to it. Especially since there's no damage to his face."

"But he's an artist, not a professional criminal. Who would want to harm him?"

Farantello pushed his hair back and frowned. His hair immediately flopped back onto his forehead. He needed a haircut, maybe even a good woman to look after him. I forced myself to focus on his words.

"I have the feeling he's holding out on us, Laura. If you talk to him, we might be able to find out more about what actually happened."

I nodded.

"By the way, about the other night," Farantello said, as we walked down the hall, "I don't want you to think I do that all the time."

"You mean kiss women you're interrogating at the scene of a crime? I figured it was just part of your investigatory technique, and wondered what you did to more viable suspects."

He may have blushed under his olive skin, I couldn't be sure. And the little quirk at the corners of his mouth could have been a smile. "I enjoyed it," he said.

When I walked into Owen's room, his eyes opened and looked at me expressionlessly. A tube came out of his arm and another tube snaked under the blanket, leading to a bag partly filled with urine. The bag hung by the side of the bed.

"So what happened to you, sport? Get caught with some guy's girlfriend, or his sister, or maybe his mother?"

There was no response to my attempt at jollification. Not even a change in expression.

"C'mon, Owen, you have to talk about this. If you give the police a lead, maybe they can find the guy. After all, we're not in Boston now. Muggers really get caught around here."

He turned his head away from me. I toyed with the idea of giving his catheter a good pull to get his attention, but decided that might be going a shade too far.

"Why won't you tell me, Owen?"

"Because it's none of your business."

There was the old Owen arrogance again. I felt anger wash over me like high tide at the beach.

"You'd better talk to me about this, Owen, because no one else in this town is going to look after you. Clarissa is gone and she's not coming back."

That got his attention. His eyes focused on mine with a sudden intensity. "What are you talking about? She'll be here today. Then we'll go back to Boston."

"She's not coming back. She told me she's got a new guy, some elderly gallery owner in New York."

Owen tried to sit up straighter in bed as if, with a little more altitude, he would see Clarissa hiding in the room somewhere, having a good laugh at his expense. Then he gave a loud moan and sank back down again. He looked even paler than before.

"You're lying, Laura."

"No, I'm not. Clarissa told me about all the women you slept with while we were supposedly together. Do you think she would have told me if she planned to stay with you? It was her good-bye gift to me. She said if I wanted the lying, cheating bastard back, I could have him."

Owen lay in silence.

"Now, why don't you tell me what this so-called mugging is all about?"

He shook his head with all the petulance of a small boy turning down a plate of brussels sprouts. But the emotion that came over his face told me that he wasn't playing. I'd seen passion, anger, envy, happiness and triumph pass over his features in the time we'd been together. He had a mobile face and showed his emotions clearly. What I had never before seen was fear.

"I can't tell you," he mumbled.

"The police will protect you. This guy has already beaten you half to death. What else can he do to you?"

Owen whispered, "He said he'd crush my hands."

"Oh, my God! Why?" When he didn't reply, I said, "You've got to tell the police!"

He turned his face away and stared out the window.

"Owen!"

He refused to look at me. I needed to tell Farantello. I had almost reached the door when Owen said, "I'm sorry for the way I treated you."

"Sure you are."

"I owe you something for what I did to you, so listen to what I'm saying. Be very careful."

"What do you mean?"

"Just be careful, okay?"

"Okay." I walked outside the room, closed the door, leaned against it, and began to hyperventilate. Was Owen's hand-crusher coming after me next? And, more importantly, why?

An average person would have rushed up

to the first cop she saw, especially if he was a reasonably handsome guy whom she had recently kissed, and blurted out the whole story. She would beg for around-the-clock police protection. But I stood there, my breath sounding like I'd just finished a triathlon in record time, and tried to figure out why anyone would want to harm me. And, for that matter, why would anyone want to hurt Owen?

I didn't have any answers to either question. When I saw Farantello coming down the hall toward me, I had another rush of desire to tell him everything. But then I spotted Heidi and Ben Mather right behind him, and I decided on the spot to be quiet — for now. After all, what could Farantello do? He wouldn't know any better than I did why anyone would want to hurt me. If Owen didn't find the courage to explain what happened, I'd have to try to figure it out for myself.

"Any luck?" Farantello asked.

I shook my head and whispered, "He's too frightened to talk. Whoever beat him up threatened to crush his fingers."

The chief frowned.

"How did they hear about Owen?" I asked softly, nodding in the direction of Heidi and Ben, who were still a few steps behind.

"Millicent Collins called the college. She thought they'd want to know."

"She probably hoped that the college would pay to have the rug Owen bled on cleaned."

"How is he?" Heidi asked, her face filled with so much concern, I wondered whether she and Owen had already hopped into bed together.

Maybe Keith, enraged with jealousy, had beaten Owen up. I put the idea out of my mind. Keith might beat Owen to a pulp in anger, but not in the premeditated way Owen had been beaten. And Keith didn't seem cruel enough to threaten to damage Owen's hands.

"Naturally he's shaken up and in some pain," I replied.

"The poor boy." Heidi turned to Farantello. "Is it all right if I go in to see if there's anything I can do for him?"

Dressed in a tight black sweater, leather pants, and knee-length boots, topping out at well over six feet, Heidi made an impressive dominatrix. I almost said that Owen had already had his beating for the day but decided the comment would be in bad taste under the circumstances. Farantello nodded and followed Heidi into the room. Maybe he was afraid she was the mugger come back to finish the job.

Ben Mather cleared his throat.

"I realize that this may seem inappropriate, but did you have a chance to discuss your grandfather's paintings with Owen before the . . . incident?"

"Sure. Owen came to my house last night. He examined the paintings and we closed the deal. He had the paintings in the back of his rental van."

"Where are they now?"

"I guess they're at the Collins Inn. He drove there last night after the . . . incident."

Mather nodded. "I'm pleased to hear you didn't find our offer of ten thousand too insulting. I'm sure you felt the paintings were worth far more, but the college really couldn't afford to go higher at this time."

I was about to say that Owen had offered fifteen thousand, when I heard Auntie Mabel clear her throat loudly in the back of my mind. I nodded to her; maybe this was one of those times to keep silent.

"Since Owen is certainly in no condition to do so, perhaps you could deliver the paintings to the college museum. The acting director, Sally Norcross, can log them in and begin processing the payment."

I would be happy to have my voucher go through the college bureaucracy. If Owen later tried to say he'd only promised me ten thousand and paid half out of his own pocket, his claim for reimbursement might be denied. It was worth a shot. After all, our personal deal was for fifteen thousand.

"Okay. But I'll have to get the keys to the van from Owen."

"I'll go with you." Ben gave a tight smile, as if he wasn't looking forward to the experience, or maybe he was concerned with how the mugging of a college visitor might reflect on the institution. "I should check in on how our celebrity is doing."

"Of course I'll drive you back to Boston," Heidi was saying, as I walked into the room. "It would be my pleasure." She was sprawled halfway across his bed. If she took up any more space Owen would end up on the floor.

Owen glanced over at me with a spiteful look of triumph. "That's very kind of you, Heidi," he said. "It's nice to know that somebody cares."

I resisted saying that perhaps Keith should accompany them.

"When will you be getting out of here?" Mather asked.

"Probably by the day after tomorrow," Owen replied. "I was scheduled to teach for the rest of the week, but under the circumstances, I think I should go home to recuperate."

"Of course," Mather's eyes narrowed, and I could already see him calculating how much he was going to reduce his payment to Owen.

"If you'll give me the keys to the van, I'll see that it gets returned to the rental agency," I said. I purposely didn't mention the paintings. Why open that discussion now?

"Here they are." Farantello handed the keys to me. "We didn't want them to get lost, so I held onto them."

"I can take care of that once I'm up," Owen said.

He looked worried when I pocketed the keys. I gave his knee a cheerful pat. "Don't concern yourself about it. Anyway, you aren't in any condition to drive, so just rest and get better. Let Heidi do anything for you that needs doing," I said sweetly.

Giving his knee a final squeeze, I left the room. As the door closed behind me, I heard Heidi say, "You know, I'm a Reiki master. I'll bet I could make you feel a whole lot better."

I bet she could.

CHAPTER 21

I pulled into the parking lot of the Collins Inn and immediately spotted the van. It was parked almost diagonally across two spaces. Owen never drove very well, but perhaps the beating made him sloppy. I was tempted to hop in it and drive away, but knew that it would be just my luck to have Millicent Collins spot me and call the police, so I went into the lobby to inform someone in authority of my intentions.

No one was around. It was that quiet time between breakfast and lunch when all the staff is upstairs straightening the rooms. I rang the bell at the desk, thinking I could easily have gotten away with grand-theft-van and avoided a conversation with Mrs. Collins.

"Hello, Laura," she said, coming out from some secret room behind the counter. Her voice was so cool, I expected to see the words hanging frozen in the air between us.

"I'm here to take Mr. Reynolds's van." I waved the keys at her.

Her face instantly became the picture of solicitude. "How is the poor man?"

I gave vague assurances that he would soon be all right.

"I don't see how he could have tripped over that drum," she said, shaking her head with a mixture of wonderment and concern.

I turned and looked at the somewhat juvenile drum reproduction to one side of the door. Next to it stood a solid cherry wood table.

"Is that what he struck his head on?" I asked.

"Well, yes." She paused for a moment. "Did Mr. Reynolds say anything about suing?"

I gave her a conspiratorial look. "Now that I've seen the arrangement of things, I'll strongly discourage him from suing," I said, skirting the truth because Owen hadn't mentioned a lawsuit. "I'm certain he'll listen to me," I added for good measure.

Millicent smiled her gratitude. To my surprise, she even reached out and lightly touched my arm. "Thank you," she said. "A public accommodation has to rely on its reputation. If people thought that it was dangerous to walk in the front door, how would we survive?"

I nodded sympathetically. "It's possible Owen fell because he had a few too many last night."

Her eyes opened wide in disbelief.

"You know how artists are," I said with a wink.

A knowing look came into her eyes as she dredged up all of her stereotypes of drunken, dissipated artist types.

I gave her another sly wink and got one in return. Millicent Collins and I were now the best of friends. I might even come back there to eat some time. After giving her a fond farewell, I walked out into the parking lot. I was about to climb behind the van's wheel and deliver the paintings to the college, then get a taxi back to pick up my car, when I decided to make certain the paintings were still on board. Owen could have removed them and stored them somewhere before his unfortunate night on the town.

"If he had, wouldn't he have said something at the hospital?"

"He wasn't saying much of anything," I told Auntie Mabel, unable to think of an appropriate Taoist retort.

I unlocked the van's back door and pulled it open. The van had one row of seats up in the front so the rest of the space could be used for cargo. But instead of the neatly stacked rows of paintings Owen and I had loaded last night, the back of the van was a complete mess of pictures and frames separated from each other and tossed about at random. It was as if a frenzied family of chimpanzees had been let loose in an art gallery. I stood there gaping.

Finally, I came to my senses. If I stood here much longer, Millicent Collins would be by my side, wanting to know what was wrong. I slammed the back doors shut. Trying to appear casual, I sauntered around to the driver's side. I slid behind the wheel. As I pulled out onto Captain Collins Avenue, I decided — relying more on instinct than careful deliberation — that I'd drive to Grandmother's house and sort the whole thing out there.

A half-hour later, I had unloaded the van and carried everything into the living room. There was no time to speculate on the cause of this disaster; what needed to be done were repairs. None of the paintings seemed to be damaged, but each had been taken out of its frame, sometimes roughly, so several of the frames were split along the back edge. I went downstairs and got a hammer and the small clips that I needed to reframe the canvases. Fortunately, Granddad had mounted all his own work, so the necessary items were on his workbench. Then I systematically sorted through the mess, pairing pictures with likely frames. I used the kitchen table as a work surface, as I put each of the pictures back in a frame. When I finished, they looked almost as good as new. A few of the frames were a bit the worse for wear, but I didn't think that would matter to the museum. It might even add historical interest.

By now it was almost two o'clock and I was starving, so I sat down at the table and had a bowl of cereal. While I chomped my way through the corn flakes, my mind raced. There was no obvious reason for Owen to have done this kind of damage. Even if he were envious of my grandfather's work, which I seriously doubted, I couldn't see Owen spending five thousand dollars of his own money to destroy forty paintings, especially when the college expected to get them.

"But they weren't destroyed," Auntie Mabel broke into my thoughts to remind me, *"They were simply removed from their frames."*

"Well, none were stolen. I counted the pictures when I reframed them. And although I can't be absolutely certain, they seem to be the same paintings. No switches or substitutions."

"Then perhaps they were removed for another reason," she prompted, as if I were a slow student.

"Like somebody was looking for something?"

"Precisely."

"And the person who did that could have been Owen."

"Or," Auntie Mabel nudged.

"Or the person who beat him up."

"Very good. Now, the question is, what were they looking for?"

I sat there speculating. A letter? A will? A real estate deed?

"What would fit well behind a painting?" Auntie Mabel prodded.

"Another painting," I said.

"Another painting," Auntie Mabel said at the same time.

Another thought hit me. "So they must have found it," I said.

"I don't think so," Auntie Mabel said. *"If Owen's attacker had discovered what he was looking for, he wouldn't have beaten Owen in such a systematic fashion. I suspect he didn't find it, and believed Owen might have taken it for himself."*

"Wasn't the attacker running a risk that

the police would find out what Owen was up to?"

"Think about it, my dear. If all had gone as intended, Owen would have staggered up to his room and felt miserable for a day or two. Then he would have returned to Boston, too frightened by the threat to his livelihood to tell the police anything. It was only because he stumbled over the drum in the lobby and hit his head that the police got involved."

"Okay. So that means there should be another picture around here that Owen didn't take, a picture his attacker wants. But Gran took all Granddad's paintings up into the attic. And Owen and I both checked, and there weren't any left up there."

"Are there any others in the house?"

My mind flashed to the Mondrian knock-off across from my bed.

"Yeah, there's one left in the house, but it's not by my granddad."

"Are you sure?"

"Yes. No." I made a beeline into my bedroom and examined the Mondrian wannabe. In the lower right-hand corner printed in black paint was the name "Torvic."

"You see, I told you. It was probably done by some student of my grandfather's."

"And he hung onto this one painting from all the thousands created by his students, done

in a style that he didn't particularly approve of, because . . . ?"

I shrugged.

"Can you say anagram?"

The light dawned. Torvic equaled Victor.

I snatched the picture from the wall. I'd never noticed before how much it projected out from the wall. Sure enough, there was a second painting carefully taped to the back of the first. I raced into the kitchen and found a peeling knife. With shaky hands, I cut the tape away, being careful not to damage the picture underneath. By now I was convinced it was a Renoir, van Gogh or Monet. Granddad could have picked it up when he was in Paris. Visions of a seven-figure auction price danced before my eyes, making it hard to see as I gently pried the canvases apart.

"Hell!" I shouted to the empty room as I saw that the name carefully painted in the bottom right-hand corner was my grandfather's. What I had was another genuine — and completely valueless — Victor Hallowell.

Then I really looked at the painting, a picture of a woman. A naked woman sitting on a bed. She had her right shoulder turned toward the viewer, but you could clearly see her breast. Granddad had also shown a generous portion of her thighs and hips, which were partially covered by the folds of a bed sheet rendered with such sensuousness, you could almost feel the fabric.

But it was the luminescent intensity of the woman's face that caught the viewer's attention. If the term "naked desire" has any meaning at all, this painting captured it. The overall effect was of a woman who clearly had one thing on her mind. At any moment she might spring toward the artist with a complete loss of self-control. She wasn't a young woman, clearly well into late middle age, but that just served to make her sexuality more powerful.

The picture was captivating, and for a moment I was sorry Gran had made Granddad destroy the paintings of his various girlfriends. If only he had kept his hands off his models, he might have become as famous as he always wanted to be.

"It's still just another painting by my grandfather," I told Auntie Mabel. "He probably liked it or the model, so he wanted to hide it from my grandmother during the great purge, when she threatened divorce. But it isn't worth anything. Why would someone beat up Owen because he didn't have this painting?" I glanced at the picture. "This is a wild goose chase."

"I'm feeling a bit tired right now. We can talk about it another time," Auntie Mabel said, disappearing from my mind.

"Great. Disappear after you've gotten my hopes up and then led me down a blind alley."

Once I calmed down, I slipped the frame and the two paintings under my bed. I'd let Gran take a look at it when she was home next. She could decide what she wanted to do. It would be a shame to have it destroyed, but it should be her decision. She might even be able to tell me who modeled.

I returned to the kitchen and carried all the now nicely framed pictures out to the van. I stacked them neatly in the back, then drove to Ravensford College. I knew I'd feel better having those pictures out of the house, and I wanted to get my car back before Millicent Collins had it impounded.

I found a parking space around the back of the museum. When I walked inside and asked directions, a security guard pointed me toward a wing off to the right. The administrative offices were there, and I found one with S. Norcross on the door.

"Hey, how're you doing?" said the woman behind the desk when I knocked. She had red hair that was even more tightly curled than mine, and when she got to her feet to come over to shake my hand, after I had introduced myself, I saw that she was a couple of inches shorter than me. I liked her right away.

"Since Owen Reynolds is in the hospital," I said, "Ben Mather asked me to bring in my grandfather's paintings."

"Reynolds? Oh, yeah, he's the guy they've had on campus for a few days, talking to the students. I met him the other night at the reception. A Super-realist, isn't he?"

I nodded.

"I can't get into that stuff much myself. To me, it's a combination of commercial art and illustration. Showing the sun glinting off the bumper of a '57 Chevy isn't my idea of artistic creativity."

A sudden look of horror passed over her face. "Please don't tell me you think that it's the best thing since Velasquez?"

"Not to worry," I assured her. "But I'd like to be around to hear you present your views to Reynolds."

Susan Norcross blushed. "I probably wouldn't have the nerve to say it to a real artist."

"Aren't you an artist?"

"Nah. I'm an art historian and curator. Although I play around with oils once in a while."

I smiled. "Then you're pretty much like me."

I told her where the van was parked, and we went downstairs through the basement level. Susan opened a large garage door in the back of the building and said, "Pull the van in here. How many pictures are there?"

"Forty."

She rolled her eyes. "Okay. I'll unload here and carry them next door to the storage room."

"All by yourself?"

"Usually I have some work study students to help me with this sort of thing, but it's kind of late in the day to take a delivery."

"Why don't I give you a hand?"

She smiled and agreed with a look of relief.

I pulled the van into the bay, and we began carrying the paintings, one at a time, up a short flight of stairs, then next door to the storage area. After twenty trips, the van was finally empty.

Susan placed the last two of the paintings side-by-side in the storage room and eyed them critically. The look of surprise on her face told it all. I could see she was debating whether to say anything.

"I know they're not very good," I said. "Actually, I think he did his best work on female nudes."

"Are there any here?"

I shook my head and lied a little. "They were all destroyed."

She glanced at me quizzically, but merely said, "Thanks for your help. I'll let the treasurer's office know to start processing your check." She probably noticed I was a little the worse for wear. "I don't know about you, Laura, but I've worked up a thirst. I've got a couple of sodas in my office. Care to join me?"

I nodded and followed her back upstairs. She pulled two colas from an office fridge, then settled into her black mesh desk chair. I sat in a plastic office chair. She curled one leg under the other, swiveled toward me, and smiled.

"I didn't mean to bad-mouth your grandfather's paintings," she said. "I never knew him personally, but he was almost an institution around here. I'm sure he inspired some students who went on to become good artists."

"One of his students came back here as a teacher. Jack Proctor."

The pleasant expression disappeared from her face. "I know you shouldn't speak ill of the dead and all that," she said. "But Jack wasn't my favorite guy."

"Most women seemed to feel the same way. Did you have trouble with him, too?"

She shook her head. "I told him to get lost when he started bothering me, and the director of the museum, Simon Ross, backed me up. He liked Jack even less than I did. Called him Proctor the Poseur because Simon said Jack was only a pretend artist."

"And now you're the acting director. What happened to Ross?"

"He had to retire for health reasons at the end of July — cancer." Susan took a long sip of her soda. "An emergency search committee was set up at the beginning of August to pick his successor. Jack Proctor applied for the job."

"Surely a jerk like Jack wouldn't have a prayer of getting it," I said.

"I thought he didn't have much of a chance. No credentials and the female faculty unanimously hated his guts. But the day before he was killed, he came around here acting like he was a shoe-in for the job. He was going on in his usual smarmy way about how much fun we were going to have working together. I was ready to quit. In fact, that afternoon I began updating my resumé. No way I'd work with that sleaze. We have a large female staff here, and they all felt the same."

I must have given Susan my tough private eye look because she reddened.

"I know I had more reason to kill him than most, but I wasn't at the dinner that night. I intended to go, but I came down with some kind of stomach virus at the last minute. Guess for once it was good luck to be sick."

"The police wouldn't have put you on their suspect list anyway," I said with authority.

"Why not?"

"You're not tall enough. Don't ask me how I know, but it saved my bacon too."

"Anyway, Jack is dead, and while the committee is still deliberating, I'm holding down the fort."

"Couldn't you apply for the job?"

"I don't have enough experience. Also, the college is looking to develop more of a reputation as an art school. They've remodeled the museum in the last few years, and they want the director to be a good front person. A fundraiser with the alums and local businesses. So they're looking for someone who's a bit older and has broader experience, combined with a managerial background."

"But that last part doesn't seem to fit Jack,

either. Why would he think that he had a good chance at the job?"

"Some of the old timers on the committee might have wanted to reward one of their own. Plus, even some of the folks who didn't like him much probably figured it would only be temporary. Jack was in his mid-fifties, and he'd be giving up tenure to take the director's job. So he'd only have the job for about five years and then could be forced to take early retirement."

"It's not that easy to force someone into retirement," I said.

"Maybe they figured there would be other grounds to get rid of Jack, other than his age. Incompetence or malfeasance were the two most frequently mentioned."

"You seem to know as much about these deliberations as the people who actually sat around the table."

Susan smiled. "They made the mistake of putting a woman under forty on the committee. We stick together."

"Who else is on the committee?"

"A mix of faculty and administrators. I think the faculty reps were a guy from history and someone from science and a computer science person."

"Mark St. Claire, by any chance?"

"I think so. Why? Do you know him?"

"Only slightly."

"Well, he may have had more influence than the others because his father put up so much money for the museum renovation."

"But I've heard that they hardly talk."

"All the same, some on the committee, especially the administrators, might be afraid to offend the relative of a big donor."

"Was Mark a fan of Jack's?"

"One of the biggest, or so I've heard."

I struggled to see a connection. "All the same, I find it hard to believe that Jack would have been their first choice."

"He wasn't." Susan hesitated. "I probably shouldn't be telling you this because it's committee business, but Jack's name was on the list of three finalists the committee came up with last week. On paper, the other two guys looked a lot stronger. They were already running museums at other colleges."

"So once again, why was Jack so confident he'd get the job?"

She shrugged. "Guys like Jack are always confident because they're completely lacking in self-awareness."

I nodded and we sipped our sodas in silence for a few moments, until another thought occurred to me. "I know enough about art to know bad art when I see it, and my grandfather's work isn't very good.

The question is, why did Jack Proctor want the college to acquire it for the museum? He was after my grandmother about it constantly."

Susan set her soda can down on top of the desk. "I don't know why, Laura, but I know exactly when it started. Jack came rushing in here right around the middle of August. He wanted to know if I could approve paperwork for the museum to acquire Victor Hallowell's paintings. I explained that, if there was money involved, he would need Ben Mather's authorization because, as acting director, I could only use the budget for normal expenses, not new acquisitions."

"Then he asked you whether you'd accept the paintings if he got them for free," I said.

"How did you know?"

"He never offered my grandmother any money. He kept going on about what it would mean for my grandfather's legacy."

"Cheap jerk. Anyway, I told him I couldn't offer to store any new paintings without approval. Even warehousing them is a responsibility because everything has to be catalogued and archival storage is expensive. Plus, a few of them would have to be hung in the main gallery since the artist was a faculty member and the pictures a gift from his family. I couldn't commit the museum to that on my own."

"And this conversation happened when?"

"August fifteenth. I remember Jack saying that he had been to the hospital that morning. Your grandfather had asked to see him, so Jack visited him in intensive care."

"Jack talked to my grandfather?" Granddad's heart attack had occurred on August twelfth, but I hadn't known he regained consciousness. Gran and I never discussed the days leading up to his death.

Susan nodded. "It was just the two of them. Jack said it was the most valuable conversation he'd ever had with your grandfather."

"Did he say why?"

"When I asked him, Jack gave me one of his little winks. Like he had important information but wasn't going to share it with someone as insignificant as me."

I tossed my empty soda can in the trash. "Thanks for telling me, Susan. I'm not sure what it all means, but it's fascinating."

"A college campus is an ongoing soap opera."

"I'm sorry to be saddling you with my grandfather's paintings."

She shrugged. "It's the next director's problem. Anyway, it's not your fault. Owen

Reynolds is the one who talked Mather into pushing for the purchase." She paused. "Maybe it will turn out to be a good thing. Every art museum needs its own identity, and we certainly can't afford a lot of expensive works. Our permanent collection is made up mostly of colonial period portraits, given to the college by the founding families of Ravensford. It might not be a bad idea to supplement those with works by lesser known artists of the fifties and sixties."

"I guess lesser known would define my grandfather."

"Who can tell?" Susan smiled. "Maybe we'll make him famous."

CHAPTER 22

I woke up the next morning, relieved I had slept well. If I hadn't spent much of yesterday lugging around my grandfather's paintings, I might have had difficulty going to sleep in the empty house. But by the time I had returned the van to the rental agency, then picked up my car and returned home, I was exhausted. However, as I ate a humble supper of tuna and chick peas on a lettuce leaf, the thought kept crossing my mind that Owen's attacker might look for . . . whatever . . . in Gran's house.

He was probably the same guy who had hit me on the head once already, and since I wasn't looking forward to an encore, I carefully locked all the windows and doors. I even blocked the door to my bedroom with a dresser. The physical effort on top of my busy day made me so tired, after a few nervous moments I drifted off into an oblivious sleep. The entire house could have been stripped bare and I wouldn't have known.

After pushing aside the dresser and making certain my security precautions had paid off, I went back to my bedroom and hauled out the pictures from under the bed.

After I studied the painting again, I once again regretted that Granddad's less lubricious works hadn't achieved the same level of artistry. Then I sat on the bed and stared into space. What was I going to do about all this? If I delivered Granddad's painting to the museum, I eliminated the danger to myself. The paintings wrenched from their frames had to be related to the attack on Owen, and might even have something to do with Jack's death, maybe even with the attack on Roger St. Claire. If I had been able to draw all these connections at the hospital yesterday, and told Farantello, would Owen have revealed the name of his attacker? It was hard to know whether catching the criminal would have overridden his fear of having his hands broken.

One thing was certain, I wasn't going to get over my own fear until I knew who had attacked Owen and what the attacker was looking for.

When I got to work, I'd call Michael Farantello and tell him the whole story.

Maybe he could put some pressure on Owen.

The newsroom was empty when I walked in. I could hear Marty Gould — in Stan Aaronson's office — discussing a photo shoot, and a few minutes later he sauntered into the newsroom.

"Something wrong?" I asked, noting his expression.

"Bill is late, li'l darlin'. We're supposed to slog around in that swamp they're planning to drain to put up those half-million-dollar houses. I figure every spring they'll float off their foundations, but the town planner doesn't think so. 'Course he's not paid to think. He's paid to smooth the way for development and a better tax base."

"Is that the angle you and Bill are going to take on the story? Sounds pretty hard hitting for the *Chronicle.*"

Marty gave me a slow Texas smile. "Yeah, I thought so too. But Sam said he got a call from the boss at home last night. The boss said it's about time the paper started doing some real journalism and we should do the story without pulling any punches."

My grandmother's influence? Maybe living with a newspaper man had replaced her passion for the wisdom of the East with a concern for local events. If so, the town had better watch out.

"Aha," I said. "So what was going to be a puff piece on how the town is growing and attracting all the right kinds of people is now an exposé on corruption and unbridled land development."

"You got it. Sam called Bill last night to tell him how the boss wanted the story handled, and I guess Bill just about fainted. He started mumbling something about not feeling well, maybe not coming in to work today. I guess Sam made it pretty clear to Bill that not showing up wasn't an option." Marty waved in the direction of Bill's empty desk. "But I don't see him."

"Bill hates controversy."

"He hates to say hello."

I had to admit that was true.

Marty cast a calculating eye in my direction. "You know, if Bill blows me off, maybe you could do this story. You've been doing a good job on the Proctor case."

"I don't know. I haven't had any real training as a reporter."

"The best training is just doing it. Or are you afraid of riling people up, too?"

"That's never been my particular weakness. If Bill doesn't show, then I'm your reporter, assuming Stan goes along with it."

Marty gave me a slow nod of approval,

walked over to his worktable and began fiddling with his camera. I was about to pick up the phone and give Farantello a call when the door opened and Keith Campbell stormed into the vestibule. He rushed up to the counter so fast, I thought he'd vault over it.

"Where is she?" he shouted.

"Who?"

"You know who. Heidi."

"Has she disappeared?"

I knew my questions were making him angrier, but sometimes you have to ask dumb questions to get the facts.

"She's not at her apartment and her car is gone. You know who else has disappeared?"

Owen Reynolds, I thought.

"Your ex-boyfriend, Owen Reynolds," Keith said.

"He's in the hospital, and how do you know he was my boyfriend?"

"Reynolds told Heidi. He gave her a big line about how the girl he came here with had deserted him, and how you were so angry at being dumped, you wouldn't help him get back home. You know how sympathetic Heidi can be. He played on her emotions."

I stifled a snort. "So I take it that Owen isn't in the hospital?"

"Not anymore. He checked himself out after breakfast, and the nurse said a tall, blonde woman was helping him."

Given the expression of pain, anger and betrayal on Keith's face, I figured any anti-Heidi remark would be cruel. So I said, "I heard Heidi offer to drive Owen back to Boston when he was discharged, but I never thought it would be this soon."

"Where does he live in Boston? His phone number is unlisted."

Maybe it was a sign of my calling as a journalist, but a banner headline immediately splashed across my imagination: SCORNED BOYFRIEND KILLS CHEATING GIRL AND HER LOVER, which was probably a little too long, even for a tabloid.

"I won't tell you where he lives," I said as calmly as I could manage, although my mouth was a little dry and I'd lost most of the feeling in my legs.

I sensed Keith, a generally gentle guy, was thinking about leaping across the counter and choking the information out of me.

Just then Marty, who was sitting just outside of Keith's field of vision, cleared his throat. "Yep, women sure can be fickle creatures," he said with a thick western drawl. "If you want a friend, you're better off with a dog."

That bit of philosophy sounded dimly familiar, like I may have heard it in a country western song, but Keith shook his head and seemed to suddenly be back in control. "Sorry I got so excited," he said, then turned and left the office.

I watched him go, thinking how narrow the line is between loyalty and possessiveness. Because Keith was faithful to Heidi through thick and thin, he thought she owed him the same loyalty. Too bad life isn't fair and sometimes one person does all the giving and the other all the taking. Too bad Keith hadn't been smart enough to know it.

"Thanks," I said to Marty as I got up and walked down the hall to St. Claire's office.

"Don't mention it. I just felt that it was time for me to say my piece."

I went into St. Claire's office to call Farantello privately, in case Keith came charging back into the newsroom. I didn't bother to close the door. Sam was slightly hard of hearing and, anyway, his computer rattled like it needed a lube job.

I got through to Farantello and told him everything — about the paintings, about Jack's wanting to be director of the museum, and about Owen's speedy exit from town. I had expected at least some gasps of excitement, but when I finished talking, there was a long pause.

"I'll have a talk with Keith," Farantello said. "We can't have him killing an important witness in a murder investigation. I'll also have the Boston PD pick up Owen at his apartment. Maybe he'll feel more like talking once he's back home."

"Is that all?"

"What do you mean?"

"I guess I was expecting at least some comment about how this puts a whole new angle on the case."

Farantello laughed. "If you're right, this puts a whole new angle on the case."

"If I come up with anything else that solves the case for you, I'll let you know," I said, somewhat mollified.

"Laura," he said, and I could visualize his sad expression, "I'd be happier if you stopped pursuing this and stayed with your grandmother and Roger until it's over. Being alone in that house isn't safe. Someone obviously thinks the hidden painting you found is valuable. Even if it isn't true, you don't want to be there if he stops by for another visit."

This is the point in most television mysteries where the plucky heroine declares she doesn't know the meaning of the word fear and she has no intention of accepting any advice that might save her life. I've always thought that was stupid.

"Yeah, I guess you're right," I said. "When I come back from covering this story, I'll give Gran a call."

After I'd hung up, I thought through my plans for the day. As I glanced up, I saw a photograph on Roger's desk. There was something familiar about the woman, as if I had known her years before. A burst of light caught me unaware and I jumped. Marty's head was in the doorway with the camera in front of his face. He lowered his hands and gave me a sheepish smile.

"Sorry, I couldn't resist."

"Who is this?" I asked, turning the picture so he could see it.

"Marie St. Claire, the late wife of the boss."

She was also the nude in my grandfather's painting.

Marty drove west, toward the foothills of the Berkshires that formed the western boundary of Ravensford. I studied the hills, which already showed early signs of changing into their fall colors, while Marty briefed me on the questions I should ask the contractor. I was supposed to appear the slightest bit bubbleheaded in order to get as many hard facts as possible concerning the size of the lots, their elevation, the gradient and drainage plans. I tried to concentrate on his advice, but I still wondered about my grandfather and Marie St. Claire. Somehow, I felt that I had the final piece of the puzzle in my hand and just had to figure out how to turn it the right way to complete the picture.

The barrel-shaped man who met us in front of the one fully constructed model home seemed thrilled to have the chance to speak with the media about his project. He was especially gracious while conducting me around, Marty having quickly drifted away to take photos of the surrounding slopes and gullies. By sounding properly impressed by his plans and asking about things with my winsome female charm, I soon had all the answers I needed. We parted forty minutes later with a friendly handshake, and his promise to look for my article in the *Chronicle.*

"We're going to ruin that guy, aren't we?" I said to Marty as we drove back to the paper.

"You liked him, huh?"

"He seemed nice."

"Just think how the folks who buy those

houses are going to feel when that slope washes down on them and the street turns into a pond. I'll bet he won't seem like such a nice guy to them."

"Okay, I see your point," I admitted grudgingly, not sure that this reporter business was all it was cracked up to be. "How did the paper find out about this in the first place?"

Marty shrugged. "The boss heard some rumors. People in authority tell him things because he's connected."

"In the past he hasn't done anything about it."

"Just like Bill, he didn't want to make enemies."

I glanced over at Marty who for the first time had spoken without his casual drawl.

"And you like that?"

He shrugged and gave me another of his lazy smiles. "I don't like the rich folks gettin' away with stealin' everything, lil' darlin.' "

Marty asked me if I wanted to go for some lunch. I told him I'd better check in with Stan, and that I'd already brought my lunch. Then he took a shot at inviting me to dinner, but when I turned him down with a grin and the comment that I *still* didn't date colleagues, he shrugged his acceptance and grinned back.

"Must get lonely being all by yourself in that big house, though," he said.

"My grandmother lives there."

"Stan told me she's staying with the boss."

"Well, I won't be in the house by myself tonight. I'm going to stay with her."

Marty gave me a quizzical look, but I wasn't about to go explain my need for safety. Next thing he'd be inviting me to stay with him.

After Marty dropped me off at the paper, I organized my notes and had a chat with Stan. He sent me off to the city hall to check the town's environmental regulations. Before I left, I called Gran and told her Farantello had suggested I stay with her. She immediately agreed and seemed confident Roger would, as well.

After two hours of going from office to office to get the material Stan had listed, I was done for the day and headed home. I hadn't answered one Auntie Mabel letter, but fortunately I had a couple of days' worth stored up. Still, I'd have to get back to the column soon. After all, that's what they were primarily paying me to do. And speaking of pay, since I was bound to see Roger St. Claire this evening, I wanted to pin him down on what my raise would be for all my investigative journalism.

I wasn't going to bring up my grand-father's relationship with Marie St. Claire. There had been a date in the corner of the photograph on Roger's desk. The photo had been taken shortly before she died, two years ago. I tried to recall the face in grand-father's painting. Marie had definitely been younger then. Perhaps the painting had been done during the difficult period Mark St. Claire mentioned his mother having. Right before he decided to move back to Ravensford.

A simple story was emerging. A wealthy older woman in a loveless marriage gets involved with an attractive older artist who makes her feel the way she's always wanted to feel. I had a suspicion my grandfather had a special talent for bringing out the sensual side of women. I wished I'd seen him when I was older so I could judge for myself whether he had that kind of charm, but all my recollections were limited to the adoring ones of a young girl.

His affair with Marie had to have taken place after my grandmother's ultimatum. Maybe he'd felt safe because Marie had no involvement with the college, so there was little chance of their relationship being discovered. She was Granddad's last fling, so he had hung onto the picture. Or maybe he realized that it was the last good painting of his in existence. I almost felt sorry for him. When the wild side of his life faded, so had his art.

The big question was whether to tell Gran. She didn't need to hear about yet another of Granddad's indiscretions, especially one with her current boyfriend's dead wife. Nor would Roger be happy to hear that his sainted wife had discovered her inner woman in bed with Victor Hallowell. It would be a double blow to Roger. First, he lost my grandmother to Victor. Then, thirty years later, Victor seduced his wife. If my grandfather hadn't died already, I'm sure that Roger would have been happy to send him on his way.

I pulled up the driveway and walked in through the kitchen entrance. I stood inside the doorway for a long moment, listening to the arthritic creakings of the old house, making sure that no one had broken in during my absence. Aside from its usual moans, the house sounded normal. Just to be on the safe side, I took my Grandmother's rolling pin out of a drawer and carried it at my side as I walked into the living room and up the stairs to my bedroom.

I packed some things in an overnight bag.

If I had to stay with Gran longer, I'd return for more.

Before I left the bedroom, I hauled the picture out from under the bed. I stared at Marie's face, trying to imagine her as the same woman who appeared in the stern, pinch-mouthed photo on Roger's desk. The difference was amazing, even disturbing. What a shock it would have been if this picture had ever been made public. After all, Marie St. Claire was a highly regarded and very conservative local figure.

"Would your Grandfather have put the painting on display?" Auntie Mabel asked.

I hesitated.

"It is the last piece of really good work he did. Wouldn't he have wanted people to see it?" she asked.

"What are you saying?"

It was her turn to hesitate. Then she said, *"Let's put together what we know. Jack Proctor goes to see your grandfather shortly before his death. Your grandfather mentions the painting of Marie St. Claire and asks that Jack somehow get it from your grandmother and put it on exhibit in the college museum. Jack goes to the museum and broaches the possibility of acquiring your grandfather's works, with Susan Norcross, and when that doesn't seem promising, he actively pursues it with your grandmother, even lies by claiming he represents the college."*

"So?"

"Did Jack Proctor strike you as an altruistic man? Was he doing all this out of love and respect for his mentor, Victor Hallowell?"

I considered the point and had to admit it didn't seem likely.

"Fine. Then we have to ask ourselves, what was in it for him?"

"If he had the painting, he could blackmail Roger St. Claire or his son, Mark. They're both wealthy and neither would want Marie's secret life revealed."

"And remember, Jack talked to your realtor friend about building a new house."

"Then he changed his mind," I pointed out.

"Exactly. And shortly before his death, he hinted to his secretary that he'd be getting a more prestigious position soon."

I snapped my fingers. "Because he decided to apply to become director of the art museum once he heard that Mark St. Claire was on the committee. Instead of using my grandfather's picture to extort money from Mark, he'd use it to get the director's job."

"There's nothing Jack Proctor would have liked better than a job where he would have a whole staff of women to harass. And Mark

St. Claire became his strongest supporter on that committee."

"You think he was blackmailing Mark St. Claire and Mark killed him?"

"What would you have done if someone like Jack Proctor had that kind of a hold on you?"

"I wouldn't have killed him." I paused and did a self-check to see if that was really the truth. "At least I hope I wouldn't."

"But you aren't Mark," Auntie Mabel said. *"Mark is almost unbalanced when it comes to his mother, and how could he trust Jack to keep quiet even if he was given the director's position? Suppose Mark got the picture in exchange for the job? Jack might still threaten to gossip about the affair. He could make Mark pay forever for his silence. It would never end."*

I shivered.

"Why are you shivering?" asked Auntie Mabel.

"What if Mark told his father and Roger killed Jack?"

"You're not thinking. Roger wasn't at the dinner that night. You would have noticed him."

"But was Mark there? I don't remember seeing him."

"That's what you have to find out. Check with Chief Farantello. He has the guest list. But I'll bet Mark was there."

As usual, Auntie Mabel was spot-on. I

called Farantello but he wasn't available. I thought about talking to somebody else, but didn't want to waste time on long explanations. And anyway, somebody else might not check the guest list — might even tell me it was none of my business.

I shoved the painting back under the bed. I wasn't about to carry it into Roger St. Claire's house, or leave it in my car where he or my Grandmother might spot it. Once I got in touch with Farantello, he'd haul Mark in and the whole thing would be over.

Then I could go back to worrying about the important things in life, like whether I wanted to date Chief . . . Michael.

CHAPTER 23

I arrived at Roger St. Claire's, and my grandmother opened the door. She told me I could have the bedroom to the right at the top of the stairs. Gran said she was busy helping Roger and as soon as she was finished, we could have a chat. Then she disappeared upstairs. I put my stuff down on one of the sofas in the large, dark living room, and hurried into the kitchen. I figured there would be a phone there, and I wanted some privacy to call Farantello again. I had trouble picturing Mark St. Claire as the thug who beat up Owen and threatened to crush his hands, but it was possible that Mark's obsessive love for his mother could turn him into a monster.

This time the officer who picked up the phone at the station said Chief Farantello was in Boston and wasn't expected back until later today. Again, I didn't want to tell a stranger about my suspicions, and he refused to put my call through to Farantello's cell phone. The best I could get was a promise to have him call me as soon as he returned. Probably they'd caught up with Owen, I thought. I hoped they wouldn't have to hit him with a rubber hose too many times to get him to reveal what he knew. Once he spilled the beans, the Ravensford police would pick up Mark St. Claire and the case would be solved. If they didn't get anything out of Owen, I'd fill Farantello in on what I had discovered. Either way, Mark St. Claire was going to end up being charged with murder.

I went up to my designated bedroom and put my stuff away. Then I sat in the living room for a while, reading old magazines. Twenty minutes later Gran appeared with Roger. They both looked as fit as fiddles that had been playing a duet. Roger seemed to have gotten over our mutual embarrassment of yesterday, and he asked me questions about the story I was researching on the development going up in the wetlands. He and Gran both seemed hot to see this particular scam exposed. It was hard to tell who was more excited. Gran talked like she had more printer's ink in her veins than miso soup. All the oblique wise sayings of the East had been replaced with short, pithy statements of fact. The *Tao Te Ching* was out; the *New York Times* was in.

The conversation stayed on that topic until dinner. After we had finished eating the roast beef, in my opinion a welcomed departure from Asian cuisine, Gran turned to me and said, "You never explained precisely why Chief Farantello suggested you stay with Roger and me."

I couldn't give the real reason for my move without telling her about the painting of Marie and all that it entailed, including the accusation that my host's son was a murderer. None of which, in my opinion or Auntie Mabel's, was polite dinner table conversation.

I smiled. "The chief was concerned because he hasn't caught the intruder yet. He didn't want me to be there alone."

There was a twinkle in my grandmother's eye. "That's a lot of concern for a busy chief of detectives to show for one young woman. Perhaps Michael Farantello has a more personal interest in you."

I blushed and said, "I think he's just being a conscientious law enforcement officer."

"Maybe so," Gran said, still twinkling.

"He's a good man," Roger added heavily, as if he weren't sure.

I wondered if Roger was going to check into Farantello's background. Maybe I had just added a surrogate grandfather to my list of relatives. This evening I'd definitely approach him for a raise.

I helped Gran clean up. As I was filling the dishwasher, I saw her standing at the sink, clutching her hand.

"What's wrong?"

"My arthritis. I took all my arthritis medicine with me when I moved, but the new prescription I'd ordered hadn't arrived yet. I ran out this morning."

"It hadn't come yesterday or I would have brought it over. But it may have been delivered today. Do you want me to go back and check?"

I could tell she wanted to say no, but the pain in her fingers must have been severe because she said, "Would you?"

I smiled. "Sure. After all, I don't even have to go into the house to empty the mailbox."

The drive back to Grandmother's house took me all of ten minutes. Since the mailbox is right next to the front door, I marched up the front walk to the porch. Sure enough, the large box for packages contained the plastic bag with Gran's prescription. As I pulled the mail out of the box something — it may have been the shape of Gran's bottle of pills — reminded me that I had forgotten to pack my shampoo. My grandmother used medicinal herbs that smelled like it had been developed to repel insects, so I wasn't going to share her shampoo. Since everything seemed quiet, I decided to slip upstairs to the bathroom.

I was at the top of the hall stairs when I heard footsteps coming from the attic. Now, before you blame me for being foolish, consider what you might have done. If I'd been outside and seen lights in the attic window, I would have asked a neighbor to call the police. If I'd been right inside the front door, I'd have done the same. Even if I had only been halfway up the stairs, I'd have run back down. But I was at the top of the stairs. I could almost see inside my bedroom where the painting was hidden. A few quiet-as-a-mouse steps and I'd have the evidence and be out of there home free.

I slid forward, doing a little mental imaging like Gran had taught me. I imagined my feet were rose petals silently drifting to the ground on a calm day. My fragrant feet eased down the hall and into my bedroom. I switched on the bedside lamp, then reached under the bed and pulled out the painting. Wrong one — the Torvic/ Mondrian. I threw it face down on the bed.

Not even daring to curse silently, I reached under the bed and pulled out the other one and placed it face down next to the first.

"What have you got there?" a man's voice asked from the hallway.

I spun around as my heart quickly worked its way up into my throat. I couldn't make out who was standing in the shadows.

"Is that you, Mark?"

As the man walked into the room, there was a moment when my brain fooled my eyes into believing it actually was Mark St. Claire. Until everything came into focus.

"I think you've got something there that I want, li'l darlin.' "

"Marty? Oh, my God! What have you got to do with all this?"

"Everything, I'm afraid," he said. In his right hand he held a large, heavy-duty flashlight. He walked closer and nodded toward the bed. "One of those paintings is part of the deal Jack and I had."

"But you didn't even know Jack Proctor."

He smiled. "Jack and I go back a long way. When I first came to town, I'd do a little soft porn photography on the side. Lonely women trying to spice up their marriages or advertise for new ones. I'd make copies and sell them. The Ravensford Peeper was one of my best customers. I had a good little business going, until one of the women wrote to Auntie Mabel about it. Auntie Mabel threatened to go to the police if I didn't stop. She even made me destroy all the pictures I'd taken of her at the office in exchange for her silence. She was real sensitive about her weight."

"But how did you find out about these in the first place?" I asked, glancing at the paintings lying side-by-side on the bed.

"When Jack couldn't convince your grandmother to turn over Victor's paintings to the college, he made a deal with me to try to steal the one he wanted. The night of the dinner we arranged to meet, so he could give me the go-ahead. I figured we were going to split the blackmail money we'd get from that mama's boy, Mark St. Claire. Instead, Jack changed the deal. He said he'd pay me five thousand dollars to pinch the painting, but instead of asking for money from St. Claire, he was going to use it to blackmail Mark into making him director of the museum. So five thousand was all the money I'd get."

"That's why you killed him? Over money?"

"What else? He should never have told me about the painting if he was going to cut me out of such a sweet deal. I could get a thousand times more than he was offering by blackmailing both Mark and Roger St. Claire."

"And nobody saw you meet with Jack?"

"Who notices the guy with the camera?"

"But you still had to get the painting?"

He nodded. "You surprised me real good the first time. Sorry about that bump on the head, by the way." His expression softened in an almost convincing way. "I never wanted to hurt you."

"How did you get Owen to work for you?"

"When I took those photos of him at the museum the other night, I told him I'd pay him five thousand, plus whatever he had to pay for the paintings."

"And he didn't ask why you wanted them?"

"Sure. I told him it was none of his business, and once I showed him the money, he didn't seem to care."

This was a new low for Owen, being willing to make a deal for my grandfather's paintings with a guy he must have suspected of being a crook.

" 'Course the only reason Owen Reynolds was in town at all is because Jack had the same idea. He'd heard about you and Owen from your grandfather and figured Owen could sweet talk you out of the paintings if I couldn't steal them. Jack told me that on the night I killed him. That's when I realized how expendable I was." Marty shook his head. "Jack was really a stupid guy."

Only supremely overconfident, I thought.

"Did Owen know why Jack asked him out here?"

"Nope. Jack let him think it was for his artistic talent."

"And when he came back without the painting you wanted, you beat him up."

"I had to make sure he wasn't trying to cheat me. By the time I was done, I was convinced he told the truth. I had to get back in the house again, so when I found out your grandmother was living with St. Claire and you were staying with them tonight, I figured this was my best chance."

"But why did you drop the bust on Roger St. Claire?"

"I saw your grandmother standing under the balcony and scooted up the back stairs. I didn't think the bust would kill her. I just wanted to put her in the hospital for a day or two. I figured you'd stay with her at night, and I could break into the house. It was Roger St. Claire's bad luck that she moved at the last minute and he stood in her place."

I was about to open my mouth again

because I figured that the more he kept talking the less chance he'd start hitting. But as I opened my mouth, he raised a hand to silence me.

"That's enough, li'l darlin.' Too bad I didn't start on this floor. Then I'd have had the picture before you showed up. Just hand it over now and I'll be out of here."

I looked into his eyes and knew he wasn't telling the truth. Why hadn't I noticed those eyes sooner? SHE WAS A LOUSY JUDGE OF MEN they'd write on my tombstone, assuming it would fit. I picked up the painting and handed it to Marty. He turned it over and stared for a second, puzzled by the geometrical lines of the Mondrian, trying to figure out how that could possibly be Marie St. Claire. In the same instant, I picked up the painting of Marie and brought it down hard on top of Marty's head, shoving it as far as I could over his arms.

I darted around him and out the door. He probably would have caught me, but the painting was wider than the doorway and I heard him curse as he momentarily got stuck. When I sprinted to the front door and pulled it open, I plowed directly into Chief Farantello and his large sergeant, who looked surprised at the sight of a man wearing a picture around his shoulders chasing after me down the stairs. Obviously, the sergeant was new to law enforcement.

Farantello simply took the cuffs from his belt, looked at Marty, and said, "Please don't tell me you've been framed."

CHAPTER 24

This is for those of you who need your loose ends all tied up and put in a box with a ribbon around it. You already know how Jack and Marty knew each other and why Marty killed Jack. One of the things that still bothered me, after they led Marty away in cuffs, was why Mark St. Claire would support Jack's bid to become museum director before Jack got his hands on the picture and could begin blackmailing him.

When questioned by police, Mark said he knew nothing about the picture and he favored Proctor because he would be the worst possible director. Mark wanted the museum that his father had so proudly renovated to do badly. Ironically, Jack might well have gotten the job without resorting to blackmail.

As far as Mark is concerned, the existence of my grandfather's Marie St. Claire painting has brought father and son somewhat closer together. Roger has realized there was another side to Marie that he neglected to touch, so to speak, and Mark has had to grapple with the idea that his mother was a bit of a plaster saint. So far, he's adamantly refused to look at the now-ruined painting. However, he has gone into therapy, which will hopefully enable him to come to grips with his mother's sexuality.

The reason why Farantello turned up on my doorstep at the opportune moment was also the result of what I consider to be misplaced love. Owen and Heidi were on their way back to Boston when they decided to stop at a motel along the way to consummate their relationship. It took them four hours until they were fully consummated. That a man who had a concussion and possible internal bleeding could show such stamina was indicative of one of the few things I appreciated about Owen.

At any rate, they didn't get back to his apartment until the middle of the afternoon, at which time the Boston police brought him in for questioning. By the time Farantello arrived on the scene and wormed Marty Gould's name out of him, it was early evening. Farantello then rushed back to Ravensford. When he found Marty's apartment empty, he quickly decided that my grandmother's house was the next likely spot to find him. You know the rest.

Aside from being a murderer, there was one other thing about Marty that really disappointed me. He wasn't from the west at all. In fact, he'd never been west of the Delaware River, having been born and raised in New Jersey, where he had gone to school, worked on a local newspaper, and dabbled in pornography. Just goes to show that snakeskin boots and a slow drawl don't make a cowboy.

During my more idle moments I sometimes wonder whether I missed a real opportunity by not going out with him. There was something exciting about the guy, and I think he really did like me. Of course, he would have killed me to ensure my silence. But, hey, there are downsides to every relationship.

Speaking of upsides, my exclusive story on the murder of Jack Proctor really put the *Chronicle* on the map. The news services and Boston papers picked it up, although we had to doctor it quite a bit to keep Marie's name out of it. In the end, it sounding like a pornography ring turned homicidal. Roger St. Claire was so thrilled with my work, he offered me a raise and a new job. I still have to be Auntie Mabel, but now I get to handle the investigative reporting as well. Bill Lamb has been relegated to the softer stuff and a column on "men's issues." How hard hitting I'll get to be remains to be seen, but my grandmother's influence seems to be moving Roger in the direction of becoming the conscience of Ravensford.

My grandmother and Roger St. Claire have moved on to a new stage in their relationship. After a few weeks spent getting accustomed to the idea that their former spouses had been lovers, they both seem to have decided in some convoluted way that this has freed them up to get engaged and continue living together. I don't really understand it. Maybe it's some great circle of life thing, but I'll be living alone in Gran's house for the indefinite future — unless I can find a housemate. I still have hopes.

I should note in passing that Heidi and Owen are now living together in Boston. She gave up her job at the college, apparently thinking that attaching herself to a famous artist would be better for both her career and her personal life. Given the congenital unfaithfulness of both parties concerned, I wouldn't give long odds on the relationship's success. But maybe two philandering artists really are made for each other. What I find more doubtful is whether Super-realism and hubcap art can ever reside together in peace.

Ever since Heidi left town, Keith has been coming into the newspaper office to list classified ads for various pieces of household goods. He's already sold his microwave, treadmill, two lamps, an upholstered chair, and three bird cages. Pretty soon the poor guy will have nothing left, and I know he's just doing it to see me. He says hello in a sheepish way, hardly appropriate, especially for such a handsome stud. I'm polite, even gentle really, but I know that it's never going to happen.

I'm like Goldilocks. I started out with a man who considered sex nothing more than a handshake, and he shook hands with a lot of women. Then I met Keith, who thought of romance as a wrestling grip where you had to stay locked together in a perpetual grapple because any distance bred insecurity. Owen's bed was too soft from overuse while Keith's was too hard, because of his needy possessiveness. It was the whole pendulum thing all over again as I went from the irresponsibly exciting to drearily steadfast.

Where does that leave me? Farantello and I have been seeing more of each other lately.

Some of it is related to the Proctor case, but there have been a couple of lunches where the conversation has strayed to more personal things. Is Michael Farantello's bed just right? I don't know. Not yet anyway. But a cop who knows poetry has potential.

Some folks say that today's woman wants a man who freely shows his feelings. Give me a break. No woman wants a man who wears his heart on his sleeve. But what we do want is a man who has some feelings worth discovering. One of the pleasures of being a woman is slowly prying open a man like a barnacle-encrusted clam, to find the real meat of emotion inside.

For now, Farantello is my clam.

ABOUT THE AUTHOR

Glen Ebisch has had over a dozen mysteries published for both young people and adults. He lives with his wife in western Massachusetts. His interests include philosophy, yoga and reading.

The employees of Thorndike Press hope you have enjoyed this Large Print book. All our Thorndike, Wheeler, and Kennebec Large Print titles are designed for easy reading, and all our books are made to last. Other Thorndike Press Large Print books are available at your library, through selected bookstores, or directly from us.

For information about titles, please call:
(800) 223-1244

or visit our Web site at:
http://gale.cengage.com/thorndike

To share your comments, please write:
Publisher
Thorndike Press
295 Kennedy Memorial Drive
Waterville, ME 04901